The Last Bear

Mandy Haggith

TWO RAVENS
PRESS

s Ltd

Rhiroy
Lochbroom
Ullapool
Ross-shire IV23 2SF

www.tworavenspress.com

The right of Mandy Haggith to be identified as author of this work has been asserted by her in accordance with the Copyright, Designs and Patent Act, 1988. © Mandy Haggith, 2008.

ISBN: 978-1-906120-16-0

British Library Cataloguing in Publication Data: a CIP record for this book can be obtained from the British Library.

All rights reserved. No part of this publication may be reproduced, stored in a retrieval system, or transmitted in any other form or by any means, electronic, mechanical, photocopying, recording or otherwise without the prior written permission of the publishers. This book may not be lent, hired out, resold or otherwise disposed of by way of trade in any form of binding or cover other than that in which it is published, without the prior consent of the publishers.

Designed and typeset in Sabon by Two Ravens Press.
Cover design by David Knowles and Sharon Blackie based on an original photograph by Keith Price (*www.thinart.com*)

Printed on Forest Stewardship Council-accredited paper by Biddles Ltd., King's Lynn, Norfolk.

Mixed Sources
Product group from well-managed forests, controlled sources and recycled wood or fiber
www.fsc.org Cert no. TT-COC-002303
© 1996 Forest Stewardship Council
FSC

About the Author

Mandy Haggith first studied Philosophy and Mathematics and then Artificial Intelligence and spent years struggling to write elegant computer programs that could help to save the planet. A decade ago she left academia to pursue a life of writing and revolution, and has since travelled all over the world researching forests and the people dependent on them and campaigning for their protection. In 2003, she returned to Glasgow University to study for an MPhil in Creative Writing, gaining a distinction.

A pamphlet of her poetry, *letting light in*, was published in 2005 and her first full collection, *Castings*, was published by Two Ravens Press in 2007.

Mandy lives on a woodland croft in Assynt.

For more information about the author, see
www.tworavenspress.com

Acknowledgements

I would like to thank Bill Ritchie for believing I could write this novel and helping me take it from a gleam of an idea all the way to publication; my family, particularly the Cohen clan, for food, shelter and love; Graham Harthill for getting me started; Tom Bryan for getting me restarted after I had given up; Tom Leonard, for insightful criticism and encouragement during the agony of the rewrite; the many other staff and students of Glasgow University's Creative Writing MPhil who read, booed, cheered and offered editorial advice, as appropriate; the Northwest Highlands Writers for camaderie; staff at the National Museum of Scotland for research support over the years; Jane Alexander, Kate Orson and Margaret Elphinstone for reading the complete manuscript and giving invaluable guidance towards the end; and Sharon Blackie and David Knowles at Two Ravens Press for bringing it to fruition.

CONTENTS

ᚺ

Beithe - Birch

'Once upon a time, long, long ago...' Frigga began, tethering the shaggy cow to a birch tree, patting the calf, and stumping out into the sunny glade. She breathed in the fragrant crush of meadowsweet and early brambles and let the story spill out of her.

'...there was a fierce he-bear who began troubling people when they were out in the forest gathering firewood. The people grew scared. Then one day the bear attacked a little girl.'

Enya reached for her grandmother's hand. 'Was she hurt?'

'Oh, yes. The bear killed her.'

Frigga felt the tight squeeze on her fingers and smiled down at Enya with her one good eye, the other gazing away as if to some earlier, happier time. 'The village medicine woman, who was called Drumanach, decided to do something about it.'

'What did she look like?'

Frigga had no idea, so she said, 'She was beautiful.'

'As pretty as Brigid?'

'Yes, just like Brigid.'

Enya seemed pleased. 'Is she here?'

'Brigid? She'll be out in the woods somewhere, unless she's sleeping.'

The old woman led her granddaughter up to the gnarled alder that flanked the forest clearing, and they peered into the wooden shelter Brigid had created for herself beneath it. A bundle of skins and fleece was tucked inside, and a skull was hung over its doorway. They tip-toed round to the other side of the tree and sat down, their backs to the trunk. Warblers hopped and twittered in the foliage above them, and somewhere nearby a blackbird sang its glittering song. Frigga was tired after the long walk down from the shielings with the livestock, and with the shock of seeing just how badly the forest on the loch's far side was scarred by burning and felling. It had been comforting to reach the Coile woods with its brambly tangle of willows and hazels.

1

She realised Enya was looking at her, waiting for the story to continue. Her shoulders unclenched as she leaned back against the alder. 'Drumanach came to this tree and cut herself a big round shield from the trunk. Then she went to seek out the bear. She found him deep in the forest in a cave. He came out and attacked her, but she was protected by her shield. He was very angry and wanted to kill her, but whenever he tried, she hid behind the alder shield and was safe.'

Enya's eyes were brown, shiny mushrooms.

'Did he growl?'

'Oh yes, he growled and roared. Ggrrrrrrrrr!'

The mushrooms grew bigger.

Frigga stretched her legs out and stroked her thighs. It felt good to sit down. 'Eventually the bear stopped fighting and took to sulking in his cave and Drumanach sang to him from outside. She picked berries and left them in heaps by the entrance. She brought him tasty fungus. She even raided a wild bees' nest to steal their honey and took him lovely, sticky, sweet honeycombs.'

'Why? Why was she so nice to him?' Enya plucked the leaflets one by one from a frond of bracken.

'Because she wanted to make friends.'

'But why? He ate that girl.'

Frigga untangled a fly from Enya's hair, then began tugging out knots with a slow, gentle rhythm. 'Yes, but Drumanach thought that if she was kind to him then he might stop being nasty. If you're cruel to someone they're not likely to be good to you, are they?'

Enya appeared to think for a while, then nodded. 'So she gave the bear presents to try to turn him into a good bear.'

'That's right,' Frigga said.

'Did it work?'

'In the end it did. In the end he let Drumanach be his friend. He stopped being grumpy and fierce and allowed her to come right up and stroke him. Then he let her come into his cave with him at night and they'd snuggle up to sleep.'

'Was she not scared?'

Frigga shook her head. 'At first, but not when they'd made friends. She got to like sleeping with him, and when he holed up for the winter, she stayed there with him, and when they woke up in the spring she was pregnant.'

'What's preg-nant?'

'It's when you grow a baby inside you. The next autumn she had a baby girl, the daughter of the big he-bear.'

'How?'

'That's just what happened.' Frigga crossed her arms, defying challenge.

'What was her name?'

'Beithe.'

'The same as Brigid's cow?'

They both looked across at the contented cow and her calf, their heads buried in lush woodland herbs. A rich stew of grassy, foggy smells wafted towards them, deep and fat and warm. Frigga's arms relaxed. 'That's right. Now, the daughter of Drumanach and the he-bear –'

'Who, Beithe?'

'Yes, Beithe.' Frigga frowned, wanting to get to the point. 'She was the most powerful healer the Braes had ever known, and when she grew up she had a daughter, and then her daughter had a daughter, and they kept on having daughters all the way down until Brigid. So that's why our medicine woman is always the shaman of the bear, and that's why this tree is called the Shield Tree.' Frigga took a deep breath to signal the end of the tale.

Enya tilted her chin up and rocked her head from side to side. 'So can Brigid talk to bears and stroke them and things like that?'

'You'll have to ask her.'

Enya gazed around as if Frigga was looking at someone else. 'Where is she?'

'Who knows.'

Enya ripped the remaining leaves from her fern and squashed its stalk into a ball, then threw it aside. Frigga went to stroke her hair again, but she tossed her head free. 'Was Ma preg-ant?'

Frigga closed her eyes and took a deep breath. 'Pregnant. Yes, but her baby died with her.'

She felt Enya's head pressing into her ribs and hugged her close until a wood pigeon's sympathetic coo-coos began to rankle. The sun had dipped below the trees and the air was chilly. She got to her feet. 'We'll have to go now, Enya. We've animals to feed before dark and your father will be hungry. Come on.'

'But Brigid's not back.'

3

'Maybe the priest's curse is stronger than I thought.' Frigga looked up at the sky, marbled with bruise-coloured clouds. 'Never mind, you'll get some other chance to see her.'

'Why does Brigid not have a baby?'

'Questions, questions, questions.' Frigga grimaced. 'She just doesn't; and she will not, stuck out here on her own, poor thing. If you ask me she should have had Bjorn's child when she had the chance and to hell with the consequences.'

Enya looked doubtful. 'Bjorn the headman?'

'That's right. They used to carry on like two pigeons in spring. You're too young to remember. We all just assumed Bjorn would marry her, but his father insisted on a Christian wife and Brigid quite rightly refused to convert. She wouldn't give up being the shaman. I think they both missed out in the end. I used to like to see them together. Ach, what am I saying?' She scrutinised Enya's face but the girl gave nothing away. 'You'll not say anything to your father about us being here, will you? There are things best kept between women, you understand?'

Enya nodded, lips tight closed, eyes wide. She kept her next question to herself and let Frigga tug her up to a standing position. The old woman stretched, then hirpled across to the birch tree where they had tethered Brigid's cow. It had only been a short diversion from the path down from the sheilings, and delivering the cow and her calf had seemed like a good excuse to break away from the crowd and visit their banished shaman. She checked the knot in the rough heather rope, making sure the beast had length enough to allow her to graze the flower-rich undergrowth with its scattering of auburn leaves.

'Goodbye, Beithe,' Enya said, ruffling her fingers in the hairy black coat. 'Brigid'll be here soon. You tell her we had to go. Goodbye, calf.'

The cow ignored them, chewing her cud while her five-month calf suckled. Both were fat and glossy from grazing up in the mountains. Frigga patted her, gently. 'Take care of Brigid for us. May the Mother Bear protect you.'

Then the crone and child slipped away among the lengthening shadows, their legs growing weary as they plodded along the lochside, through the ferns, briars and twisted willows, towards the huddled huts of the Braes.

4

❧ ❧

'In the language of the trees, Beithe means beginning.' Frigga's voice
was as cracked as the bark on the birch logs she was humping across
the floor. She dragged a rough wattle basket to the fireplace with a
groan and knelt down on the reed mat in front of it. She was tired
after the big walk the day before. She set about making a fire, her
voice accompanied by snapping of twigs.

'You'll be feeling the cold here, Mistress?' she asked, though it
was a statement rather than a question, and without waiting for an
answer she carried on. 'We'll soon have a good warm fire going for
you. Begin the fire with birch bark, that's the beginning magic of
Beithe. We begin our lives in a birch cradle and every morning with
a birch spirtle in the oats, and we begin every fire with birch bark.
They even say you can begin a baby by moonlight under a birch
tree!' She chuckled at this thought, and the first flames flickered
into the bark strips from her tinder box. She fed them with twigs,
tossing on first one handful, then another. They crackled, then
caught. She placed two logs at the sides, then laid across them sticks
that soon were blazing.

She sat back on her heels. 'Come closer and warm yourself,
Mistress. It's a raw morning out there. The mist gets into your
bones.'

Margaret, who was standing by the oak door, stepped forward.
'Thank you; you're very kind.' She reached out her hand, and
continued, 'Please call me Margaret. "Mistress" makes me feel
like a stranger here.'

Frigga looked at the smooth, pale hand but did not take it.
Margaret's southern accent was strange, her Gaelic the formal
dialect of the aristocracy which sounded shrill to Frigga's northern
ears. 'Well, we can't have that, now. You're the new mistress here
and Bjorn says I'm to make you comfortable. Margaret it will be
if that's what you wish, though it will turn some heads when they
hear me say it. It's not the manner of address we're used to.'

'Well, these are times of change. And what should I call you?'

'I'm Frigga. I've been housekeeper for thirty years, my dear.' She
pushed herself to her feet. 'I was born in this house, you know,' she
said, straightening up like stiff leather. 'My father was headman
before the Norsemen came and Bjorn's grandfather took the Braes.

5

I was no more than a baby then, you see?'

Margaret nodded and Frigga went on. 'It was Bjorn's father, Eirik, who built the house into what you see now. This room used to be a grain store, but he wanted a private room, so he added the fireplace.' They both looked up to the sturdy oak beams and rafters and around at walls made of a bewildering collection of uneven stones – though those around the wide fireplace were laid perhaps a little more evenly than the others. In the opposite wall, there was a shuttered window.

'He doubled the size of the hall too, so there's a separate place for cooking,' Frigga continued. 'He was a good man, Eirik. He and Ailsa were always fair to me, and I looked after the place well when they were gone, which was most of the time. I imagine you and Bjorn won't spend a lot of time here, either.'

Margaret stood in the middle of the room with a fixed smile on her face. Frigga pointed her towards the warmth, her own face hardening. 'I'm talking too much as usual. You have a seat here and I'll leave you in peace.'

Margaret sat down on a stool and leaned in towards the flames which shone on her smooth white skin. She felt their heat on her face and breathed in the wine-sweet smell of the birch. She smiled, rubbing her hands and stretching her fingers out. 'That's good,' she murmured, her posture softening as the glow crept into her.

After Frigga left the room, Margaret unclasped the linen bag at her feet, and brought out a tall beeswax candle which she poked into the flames to light. Then she stood up, holding her woollen skirt at a safe distance as she balanced the candle in a bronze candlestick beside the hearth. Kneeling down on the mat, in a murmuring voice she began to pray. 'Our Father, who art in heaven, hallowed be thy name...'

After the final 'Amen' she remained on her knees, head bowed, the room hushed but for the tapping and breathing of the fire.

When Frigga bustled in a few minutes later, she found Margaret in the same hunched pose. The old woman stopped in the doorway and gasped.

'Mistress Margaret, whatever is the matter?'

Margaret turned her head, her long hair swinging, and said, 'Nothing, nothing at all. I was simply praying.'

'Praying? Here in the bedroom? Is there nowhere this newfangled god won't stick his prying nose?'

Margaret stiffened, wrinkled her nose, and in a low voice said, 'Forgive her, Lord.'

Frigga held her gaze. 'Do you want me to go?'

'No, you're here now. My peace is broken,' Margaret muttered.

'I was just coming to check that the fire was still alight.'

'Perhaps in future you can knock on my door before bursting in on me so rudely.'

Frigga grunted, stomped out and banged the door behind her, leaving Margaret alone again. She got to her feet, blew out her prayer candle, and crossed the room. She looked out of the window and watched the wind toss a flurry of amber leaves from a birch tree. Here on the wild north-west coast the birches were small and twisted, not like the graceful white-skinned silver birches of her lowland home. But these dwarf trees had a certain beauty nonetheless, she reflected, especially as the alchemy of autumn turned their leaves to gold.

For a while she sat in a pool of light by the window, embroidering flowers. They were not real flowers. They were fantasy blooms, the stitches tiny flecks of shining silk, all colours of the rainbow. A posy of six blossoms, each of the most exotic form she could imagine, burst out from six heart-shaped leaves in bronze and green.

'Finished,' she whispered to herself, biting the thread off neatly against the back of the fine linen cloth. She smoothed the fabric out across her lap and admired her work. A smile softened her thin face. She picked at a thread, long elegant fingers seeking perfection, her head tilting first to one side then the other, watching the threads glinting with different colours from different angles. As she moved her hair gleamed in the sunlight, shinier even than the silk stitching.

She got up and went over to the bed. It was big, built of oak timbers now darkened with age and curtained all around with a strange plaid she had never seen before. The effect was daunting. This was where she must sleep for the rest of her life. It was dark and smelled strange, musty and masculine.

She pulled back the curtain and reached in to cover the big bolster pillow with her embroidery, but it was too high, so she had to clamber up and kneel on the mattress in order to smooth the delicate linen down over the pillow. It was not the simple, elegant act she had anticipated. She managed to tuck in one end of the cloth then splayed herself, her feet dangling over the edge of the bed, stretching ineffectually to reach the other side of the bolster. Her pendant crucifix tugged at her awkwardly until she stuffed it down under her collar. It felt wrong to put her shoes on the bedclothes, so she kicked them off and scrambled about in her stockinged feet on the bed to finish her decoration. She squatted, stroked the material and admired her sewing again, but its magic seemed to have faded. It looked incongruous against the rough curtains and woollen blankets, but she hoped perhaps the design brought something feminine, even exotic, to the bed.

She thought forward to night-time. She and Bjorn would have their heads on the cloth, their hair loose over the fantastic flowers. Perhaps they would give her the courage to tell Bjorn of her feeling that she might already be pregnant, blessed by the miracle of conception. She felt the heat in her face as she realised she was looking forward to lying with her husband again, with his body next to hers, feeling his skin, his hands touching her, the smell of him like a rutting animal.

She twisted round into a sitting position and stepped down off the bed, her skirt crumpled, and quickly slipped back into her shoes. The floor of this big room was cold. The whole room was cold: the wood in the hearth had already burned down to a smoulder that gave out no real warmth. She shivered, straightening her skirt and trying to re-establish some poise. Then she set off to the kitchen in search of someone who might relight her fire.

bonny old birch
white bark silver lichens
auburn dress and golden slippers
Lady of the Forest
do you dance?
come one moonful night
dance with me
dance with the loneliest bear in the woods

ᛂ

Luis - Rowan

High above the loch, Bjorn sat in a rowan tree, watching the world below. The rowan's contorted trunk was nearly horizontal, growing straight out of the rock face, and he straddled it as if riding some wild sea creature. Nothing much but lichens could endure the winds on these exposed crags – only a few hardy rowan trees, their roots buried into cracks, trunks and branches carved into sculptures of agony by the repeated battering of storms. Their last few leaves flapped and fluttered in the stiff breeze, like red hands with many nervous fingers. Most of their berries had gone to the wind or the birds, but a few tenacious clusters hung on.

Headman of the Braes, master of the big house below, Bjorn was admired by most of his people for his generosity, but feared also for his unpredictability. His mother Ailsa, an Orkney princess, had married Eirik, a Norwegian jarl, as part of a complicated agreement over land and fish, religion and inheritance, seafaring and war; so he had spent his childhood in many places – Iceland, Greenland, Norway, the Hebrides – moving as his father and mother moved. But he had always lived by the sea, for his father was a great seaman: a lord of the Northern Ocean who had built and retained his power by wielding force from the water – trading, fishing and shipbuilding.

Bjorn had curly hair the colour of autumn rowan leaves, and piercing eyes to match the sky, grey or blue, their colour changing with the light. His skin was the nut-brown of a man always out of doors. His hands, strong yet lithe and surprisingly small, hugged the grey bark of the rowan branch. His frame was powerful but compact. When still, he had the stance of a warrior boatman; yet when he moved, he was as fluid as a deer.

Sitting in the rowan, Bjorn was an eagle, spying. From where he sat he looked directly down onto the thatched roof of his house, surrounded by its stone outbuildings and the wattle-and-turf sleeping huts of the kitchen women. Below the big house was the village, the cluster of small oval huts of his people, mostly built from stone and all heather-topped. Their fields patchworked westwards

9

across the machair grasses behind the dunes and down to the short tidal channel where the loch spewed into the sea. The trunks of newly-felled trees littered this eastern half of the bay, where they had been washed in from the wooded peninsula to the north by the westerly wind. Some had been tied into rafts near the beach below the village where a new longship was taking shape.

To the north of the uighe, sheep-dotted pastures bled into woodland. The forest formed a great swathe between the loch and the mountains to the east, its green mottled with ochres and russets. Here on the craggy south shore of the loch, between wooded gulleys, gneiss cliffs sheered down to the water's edge. From afar they appeared to be a uniform grey, but close up their lichen covering displayed a complex mosaic of delicate colours: black at the tide line, bright yellow where salt water splashed them in storms, and above that, pink and green.

A group of five merganzers on the loch took off, and their flapping, splashing flight drew Bjorn's attention to the shore just to the east of the big house, where three people were gesticulating. No, it was more intense than that. They were struggling.

With a twist, Bjorn swung himself from his perch and clambered up the crag, gripping the heather that grew from cracks to haul himself onto the flatter ground above, where he leaped to his feet and began to run. His was an easy lope, and he sprang from rock to rock with the agility of one used to rough ground. His deerskin boots were as soundless as paws. Before long, he dropped down into woodland and joined a grassy path, soft with mosses and lined with bracken. His pace accelerated on this easy downward path, his auburn hair streaming behind him, his breath rhythmic and powerful. The path was a golden tunnel of birch trees.

As it rounded a corner the path levelled out, and Bjorn could see the three people just beyond the woodland edge. He slowed to a walk to allow his breath to calm, and emerged from between the trees as if idly passing by. The three were struggling down by the water: one, a small red-faced lad, was backing into the loch, his feet slipping on stones under the water; the other two, adults, with their backs to Bjorn, were pushing the howling boy out into the loch.

'Well, well, now. It's a raw day for swimming.' Bjorn startled the two men who loosened their grip on the boy and turned toward the voice.

'The headman!' the boy shrieked.

'Aye, Caphel, going for a dip?' Bjorn asked with a smile, realising that this was the grandson of his housekeeper, Frigga. 'And it's yourself, Eachan,' he added, recognising the man on the left, brawny and with a squint in one eye. 'Causing you trouble, is he? And you too, Angus. Well, well. I thought you would be working on the boat on a day like this.'

'Aye, well, I would be if it weren't for this, this...' Words seemed to fail the tall wiry man on the right, his face taut. 'Damned fool,' he eventually spluttered.

'What's he done, then?' asked Bjorn mildly, looking from Angus to Eachan then back. Angus, the village boatbuilder, was known by everyone in the village as 'the Boat'. He said nothing.

'We caught him cutting rowan.' Eachan shook a pointed finger at the boy. 'Bloody menace. On the harvest moon, too. He'll do us all in. Curse the whole glen, won't he?'

'Cutting rowan, Caphel?' Bjorn looked at the boy who was stepping from foot to foot in the cold water, trying to edge out of reach of the two men who still blocked his route from the shallows.

'The priest said to, sir.' He mumbled it, as if knowing that it would be awkward for Bjorn to hear.

Bjorn examined the stones at his feet, while his mind raced. What outrageous idea was this? How could his new wife's brother possibly order the cutting of rowan, the magical tree?

'Don't you know that rowans are protected by the spirits?' he asked the shamefaced boy, who nodded bleakly. Bjorn went on. 'There's always a price, even if you take branches for a weapon or a ceremony. Only a madman would cut a rowan without getting help from one of the wise ones. Are you mad?'

'No, sir.'

'Then what do you mean by this?'

'I'm sorry, sir, but he told me to cut them. He did, sir, I swear. He said I'd be damned if I didn't.' The two men turned back to him, incredulous.

'But you know fine well you're damned if you do,' Bjorn prompted.

'He said that's just heathen lies,' Caphel replied, in a low voice. At this Eachan lunged for the boy and punched him down into

11

the water, where he splashed, flailing like a beetle on his back, slithering as he tried to get some purchase on the slippery stones. The big man's foot followed but the boy was too far out for the boot to make contact, and Bjorn barked, 'Leave him, Eachan.'

Caphel got a grip on a stone and pulled himself to a kneeling position, panting. The big man made to lunge again. 'I said leave him,' Bjorn repeated. Angus laid a restraining hand on Eachan's arm.

'We'll see about punishment later, once we've got to the bottom of this. Caphel, you come with me.' Bjorn pulled the two men aside and grabbed the boy by his shoulder, propelling him out of the water and setting him half-running up the shore. He strode after him without a parting word to the two men, who followed slowly, shaking their heads.

'First you show me what damage you've done,' Bjorn said to Caphel, falling in beside him. 'Then we'll see what will be done about it.'

Dread rose in Bjorn. Eachan was right. Tonight was an auspicious night: the harvest moon fire would be burned. Today was the day for sharing out the corn and hay and peats that the villagers had worked together to produce over the summer: the beginning of preparations for the winter. To incur the wrath of spirits on such a day was dangerous. And if James, his wife's pious brother, was behind this new crisis, then that would make it all the more difficult to resolve.

As Bjorn and Caphel neared the big house, the boy's pace slowed to a slug's and his head hung lower and lower. Beside him, Bjorn fumed. 'Where is it?' he asked.

In a strangled whisper, Caphel replied, 'In the graveyard.'
'One of the Seven?'
Caphel nodded. Bjorn frowned and stomped on.

Sure enough, in the walled area below the big house, where for centuries the people of the Braes had been buried, a rowan stood maimed, one huge branch cut away. The ground was littered with the debris of the felling. Beside where the severed limb had crashed to the ground, an axe had been flung aside. The tree stood wounded, not killed, but disfigured, as if a wild animal had torn off a limb in a starving fury.

Bjorn winced to look at it. It was one of seven sacred rowans that protected the dead. These seven lichen-encrusted ancients formed part of the structure of the big house, with their roots embedded in the stone walls. They were mentioned in the songs of the bards, their berries were used for the sacred wine for wakes and weddings, and they had been clung to and mourned under by all the grieving people the Braes had ever known.

And now this. Bjorn shuddered at the sacrilege.

'Tell me again, Caphel, why did you do this?' It was all Bjorn could do to keep his voice even.

Caphel started crying. 'I'm sorry sir, really I am.'

'It's a bit late for that now isn't it, Caphel? Tell me again, what on earth possessed you?' Bjorn hoped suddenly that it was just the rash act of a young, thoughtless boy who could be easily punished. At the same time, he knew this hope was futile.

'It ... it was ... it was the priest,' Caphel stammered. 'He called me to him this morning, when I was bringing the cows round after milking, and he asked me if I feared God and I said yes, and he told me the rowans were trees of the devil and that there should be no trees in the graveyard if we want the souls of the dead to find their way to heaven.'

He stopped and looked pleadingly at Bjorn, who said, 'Go on.'

'Well, he asked me if I wanted my ma's soul to go to heaven,' Caphel sobbed. His mother, Beathoc, Frigga's daughter, had died less than a year before.

Bjorn put a hand on the boy's forearm.

'You've said and done enough today. Go home and tell your story to your grandmother and your father before everyone in the Braes tells them different.' The boy looked at Bjorn with eyes as wide and wet as a calf's, his mouth gaping in disbelief at the mercy being shown him. There was a look of sad kindness in Bjorn's face and the grip of his hand on his shoulder was warm. 'Come and find me again in an hour, Caphel, and we'll see what's to be done,' Bjorn said, as he let go of the boy and gestured him away.

'All right,' Caphel mumbled, still stunned. Then, looking down, he walked awkwardly away, as if he too was wounded, before breaking into a scampering run. Bjorn stood watching him leave, then turned to the tree. He shook his head once again.

13

'James, you weasel,' he muttered. Taking a deep breath, and settling himself firmly on his shoulders, he strode into his house in search of his brother-in-law.

He found James in the hall: the heart of the house and the only big room in the building. He was sorting the tithe. There was a hillock of dried fish, a teetering cliff of wooden stakes, a mound of tangled ropes, and a crag of cloth. A scree of pottery, basins covered with fabric, beakers with wooden tops and jugs with birch stoppers was heaped against one of the walls. But most striking were the mounds of deer hides, antlers, and furs of beaver, wolf, seal – even bear, a rare prize these days. They were on such a scale that the floor of the hall seemed to imitate the mountainous landscape outside.

Bjorn stood in the doorway and looked around him in disbelief. He had never before seen such an extravagant display of wealth in this hall. James was browsing among the opulence, pausing here and there, picking up items that caught his eye, then letting them fall back onto their piles.

Poised in the fulcrum of the hall, to the left of Bjorn's throne-chair, stood an oak lectern carved in the form of an eagle's wings, reaching roofwards on its stone rostrum. James stepped up onto it, uncorked a bottle, dipped his quill in, brushed it on the lip and with a flourish began to write into the huge leather-bound tome on the lectern, murmuring as he wrote. Bjorn padded close enough to listen.

'On the seventeenth day of the ninth month of this year, nine hundred and eighty nine years from the birth of our Lord Jesus Christ, this humble servant James of Brand records the first tithe of the people of the Braes.'

All of this tanned, fired, smoked, woven, stitched and bundled harvest would be entered into the ledger, reduced to scratched hieroglyphics, tallied, totalled, tabulated.

'Did God tell you to steal all this from my people?' Bjorn asked, stepping into a pool of light from an open window. James peered down at him like a magpie.

'You are a wealthy man, Bjorn. Be proud! Behold this fraction of your peasants' harvest. Look! Skins, furs, honey, twine. The land you rule is awash with the gifts of the Lord. See what happens when your people show their gratitude to him!'

'Don't lie to me, James.'

'Bjorn, you are a man of harsh words. This is a day of joy.' James tapped his quill on his book.

'It's a day of robbery. It has taken years for my people to gather these goods. And you take them for nothing.'

'I pray one day you will learn to recognise the gifts of God.'

'Do those gifts include trees?'

James nodded. 'All gifts of the Lord.'

Bjorn sighed. 'I don't understand, James, why all of these "gifts of God" must be killed and cut down.' He found some of the phrases James used strange compared to the simple words he exchanged with the local people. Most of them had to learn a second tongue in order to trade and deal with outsiders like himself, but James spoke with the fluid elaboration of the Scottish King's court.

'In order to give thanks, we must sacrifice. This is the way of the Lord. We must harvest gratefully and accept his gifts. You should try to be a little more thankful, brother.'

'Don't call me that.' Bjorn stepped a few paces closer. 'I've always harvested and I've always given thanks, but I've never massacred, and I never cut without reason. There's no joy in such destruction.'

'Quite so; you are of a stewardly nature, Bjorn. It is commendable. But you should recognise the true *bounty* of the Lord, the generosity of his gifts. God has made you rich. It is God's wealth that we gather in order to praise him.'

Bjorn shook his head. 'It's carnage and slaughter. It's an attack on our land. The loch is full of dead trees.'

'Those fine timbers in the loch will build great ships for men such as yourself to captain.' James spoke quietly and smiled. 'Where would you be without such wood?'

Bjorn looked away, out of the window, down to the shore where Angus had begun fitting the basic framework of Bjorn's new ship to its keel. The stack of wood he worked from was the result of several years of careful selection and seasoning of the region's finest timber.

'The people here have only ever taken from the forest what was needed. This purposeless felling, for the logs simply to float and sink in the loch – this is no way to praise a god.' Bjorn thrust both hands, palms up, towards James. 'I cannot support it.'

'Bjorn, Bjorn. It is not purposeless. We are producing beams here that will form the roof of the finest monastery ever dreamed of. The rafters of God's roof will come from this work, please don't forget that.'

'It's hard to forget, James, with you here.' He took a step forward. 'Now, tell me, do the rowan trees in our graveyard have a role as – what did you call them – "the rafters of God's roof"?' He tried to keep his voice steady. His brother-in-law lifted his eyebrows and grimaced down from the rostrum.

'The rowans? No, they must go. They're tools of the harlots, the rafters only of devilry, if indeed they rise to such lofty heights as to be the rafters of anything. I have ordered their removal.'

'Their removal?'

'Yes.'

Bjorn crossed his arms. 'You have no authority to order any such thing on my land.'

'I have the authority of the Bishop of St Andrews…'

'Do you have any idea what will happen if you have them cut down?' Bjorn interrupted.

James became enthusiastic. 'Yes, yes. Without their shadow, there will be direct communion between heaven and the troubled souls below. We have to remove these devil-ridden trees.'

Bjorn stared at him in bafflement. 'But the folk of the Braes revere them.'

'And they are now, fortunately, learning to revere the Lord God,' James retorted.

'But James, they still worship these rowans. Their dead are buried among their roots. Their mothers, their fathers, brothers and sisters, their dead children, James. Don't you see? You cannot cut them down. The forest trees are one thing. People can understand that. But the Seven Rowans are different. There are links between the people and these trees, spiritual links…' Bjorn found his voice weakening.

'Those who worship trees will be damned.' James' voice was silken but terrifying. Bjorn seethed: this man had an air of authority about him that was difficult to challenge.

'The boy you set to tree-cutting this morning risks being drowned in the loch for his sacrilege.'

'Nonsense. He was grateful to clear the passage of his mother's soul to heaven.'

'You underestimate the people here at your peril, James. You have done enough damage already. There are ways here. Ways by which things are done; patterns to follow. Respect must be shown.'

'Indeed, Bjorn, respect must be shown.'

'You misunderstand me.'

'I don't misunderstand you at all. The boy has proved his love of God by trying to cleanse us all of the heathen tree. His was an act of piety, Bjorn: something I cannot expect you to understand. Those who complain,' James thumped his lectern, 'are cursed by their own doubts.'

Bjorn paced amongst the piles of hides and pelts until disgust overcame him at the animal toll that was needed to yield this volume of skins. He became aware of the smell of the tanned carcases: the stench of dried death. Countless deaths, stretched, pinned, smeared, scraped, then gathered, counted and bundled, and finally brought here, to be gloated over in the name of God. From deep in the innumerable animal skins, shreds of vitality, particles and patterns from their animal pasts, sparks of their living intensity converged on Bjorn. He saw the wet curiosity of the seals among their desiccated skins, felt the sure heartbeat of a bear pounding its rhythm from a motionless pelt, and heard the howl of wolves emanating from their silent furs. His anger mounted.

'You have desecrated the sacred rowans. Your violence towards the spirit world here makes life difficult.'

James gripped his pulpit and raised his voice, shaking his thin, bald head. 'There is ONLY the Holy Spirit. All else is devilry.' Then, more quietly, he cajoled, 'Don't pressure me, Bjorn. I am already concerned that the heathens have their hold too tightly upon your soul. You must learn to challenge their tangled justifications.'

'These people make no justifications. But they do have their own beliefs. They're believers in your God, but they also follow the forces of nature. Surely their spirits are compatible with your teachings. Let them be. Don't try to make everyone change overnight. It won't work. It'll only make them turn against you and your gospel.'

'But I must cleanse the land for the Lord.' James' voice was shrill.

Bjorn found himself fighting an urge to climb onto the rostrum to attack him, but with shaking self-control he made himself remember his wife, James' sister Margaret, herself a pious woman but also gentle. He liked to think of her as a delicate flower. It was for her that he was trying to endure this unbearable man. He would speak to her: perhaps she could soften her brother. Bjorn tried one more time to make his point.

'You are going too far, James. I warn you. The rowans are sacred. They cannot be cut. As headman, I forbid it. Your instruction to Caphel has blighted our day of harvest celebration. You've manipulated the boy and put him in danger, and I think badly of you for that. You may be close to God, but I'm closer to these people. Work with me, James – or I'll have to ask you to leave.'

James stood chewing his tongue in an insolent silence, leaving Bjorn's plea to fade into the quiet mounds on the floor of the hall.

FEARN - ALDER

From the knoll that sheltered my hut from the brunt of storms, I watched the harvest festival. On the south side of the loch, silhouette people danced around a fire. In any other year of my life I would have been there. When I was little I used to help my mother run the ceremonies, and in recent years I had led the sacred dancing. Now, banished from the village, I was no longer even part of it.

Sounds and scents tugged from my memory. Drumming. Rhythms for dancing. Birch wood smoke. Roasting meat, the taste of mead, the smell of sweat. Dancers twirling and stamping. I scrutinised the images for details: the shine of wet skin in firelight, green and blue flames sparring in the heart of the blaze.

I knew exactly what it was like to be beside that fire, under the full harvest moon. I could picture how the dancers' boots were laced, and the stitching on the drummer's bodhran. I could hear the cheers and see the smiles on the dancers' flame-eyed faces. I would never forget the pattern of sparks as we threw the pine branch on to signify the end of the dancing.

Even from here I could see it was a big one this year. Since the villagers had begun clearing the woods for pasture in what James the monk called 'improvements', they seemed to have been overtaken with a frenzy for burning, and the fires marking the seasons had grown ever bigger.

Across the loch, the fire shuddered and swelled. The flickering movements of people stopped. I guessed that the ceremonies had begun. The villagers would be giving their harvest offerings, figures and animals twined from barley straw. Mothers would be encouraging their children to hurl their corn-creatures up to be consumed by the highest flames. They would be giving thanks for the food that had nourished them and their animals through the summer, thanks for the grain and hay now safely stored in the barns for the winter to come, thanks for the heather honey that would heal their wounds and salve the bitter times ahead. The great cup of mead would be passing from mouth to mouth, to remind everyone of the sweetness of Mother Earth as they blessed her for the harvest gifts.

I cursed to myself. Now that the ceremony was led by the monkish James, I could only guess what was done and said. But one thing was for sure: it would not be Mother Earth to whom thanks would be offered. It would be the new god, the god of the night sky and underground fires, the god of heaven and hell, of mastery and power.

A great copper bowl engraved with the sacred bear had been the drinking vessel for as long as anyone could imagine. I shuddered at the thought of it being used to toast this cruel new god. I wondered if Bjorn was there, joining in the Christian prayers.

I looked up at the sky and tried to calm my anger by gazing at the moon, dodging cloud creatures chased in from the sea by the west wind. I called out to her, 'At least no priest can overthrow you, Sister Moon. They can steal our sacred things, destroy our sacred places, take over our ceremonies, but they'll never silence the rhythm that you dance to; they'll never still your tides.' I felt better after speaking out loud, and smiled as the moon shone through a scampering cloud and the motion in the sky made her glide and roll. In her light I could make out Beithe and the calf lying by the shore, chewing the cud.

The fire on the far side of the loch damped down. That would be the peats. I had been there in the spring for the peat-cutting, and helped to stack the turfs so they would dry over the summer months, but I would miss the sharing out of the precious fuel after tonight's moon fire.

In the traditional harvest ceremony, the burning of the peats was always the moment of deepest worship. They were a gift direct from Mother Earth, slices of her very flesh, to keep us warm through the winter. I did not like to think what the priest would be saying to the villagers at this moment. Til the hunter, one of the few villagers I ever saw these days, told me that the priest encouraged them to sing the old songs of praise, but that he insisted that they change the words. It was always the father, not mother, who should be thanked. Instead of earth, it must be heaven. Instead of trees, their branches full of the patterns of life's struggles, it must be crosses, upright and regular, cut by man at his meanest.

I sighed. I was chilly, but the memory of the peat burning had galvanised me. 'I, at least, shall honour the Earth,' I declared, and turned away from the loch towards my hut.

It was little more than a lean-to shack, pulled together out of stones and sticks and some scraps of wood I had managed to salvage when I was banished from the village. It was sheltered by the Shield Tree, whose wizened trunk formed the supporting wall. Two crooked beams were wedged against it and held up its ramshackle sloping roof.

I remembered my mother telling me the story of the Shield Tree when I was a girl, but I don't suppose either of us ever expected I would end up sheltering under it. Now I was the only one left to tell those stories, and I had no little one to tell them to.

Revered as 'Father Bear,' Drumanach's he-bear skull had been handed down through all the generations of medicine women. It hung, grimacing, on a peg in the tree trunk above the door of my shack. I reached up and lifted it off, then laid it down gently on a flat stone next to the smouldering remains of my earlier fire. Beside the stone were my ceremony tools – my clarsach, small copper jug and cup, a bowl of rowan berries, my whalebone beaker engraved with a bear, a few peats and the straw figure of a man, decorated with ivy leaves. I poked a strip of birch bark into the fire, breathed it into flame and fed it with birch twigs until it crackled and flared. The skull seemed to smile as the warm light flickered over it. The huge branches of the alder gleamed like the beams of a great hall in torchlight.

I was wearing my long woollen robe dyed in browns and greens, the colours of autumn, and over it my spirit cape, patchworked out of the skins and hides of forest animals. I took off my boots so there was nothing between me and the earth, and sat down beside the fire to sing. At first my voice seemed faltering and quiet, and it felt odd to be alone. I poured some mead from the jug into the cup and took a drink, then placed it in front of the skull, with the bowl of rowan berries beside it.

'Join the feast, Father Bear,' I said quietly.

Gripping the whalebone beaker and holding it stiffly in both hands, I lifted it towards the sky, touched it to the ground, and finally in a sweeping movement encircled the skull on the stone, chanting as I moved.

> '*Sister Moon, Mother Earth, Father Bear.*
> *I am your gift and I gift myself to you.*
> *Teach me what I need to learn.*
> *Bind my humble spirit to you.*'

With this incantation I took a deep swig from the beaker, my face scrunching into a fist at the foul taste, and swallowed.

I fed the fire until it blazed, then picked up the straw man and stood up. Singing with my face to the moon, my voice gained strength as I sent the traditional words of celebration to her. Shouting my final thanks, I tossed the man onto the blaze where he lay wreathed in flames, then blackened and caught fire. The ivy leaves smoked and curled while the straw burned. I stood, watching the man being consumed.

'Sleep well, Green Man.'

Squatting down, I began laying the peats on, starting with a ring around the edge, then working inwards. The firelight dimmed. The sounds of burning hushed as the peats damped out the flames. Stillness settled.

In the distance a stag moaned. Then, nearby, a short-eared owl shrieked. Smoke wreathed upwards, spiralling as it found a breeze. The giant alder tree seemed to shudder. The skull glowed, milk in the moonlight.

I began to sing again, and this time a low and gentle melody emerged. The space beneath the tree filled with my love song to the Earth, my lullaby to creation. The sound floated, hovering, like a firefly.

My voice quavered as the tune began to diminish. Then there was quiet. I sat silently, exploring inside myself, acknowledging my inhabitants, my griefs. Childlessness, estrangement from my people, loneliness.

A few flames curled around the peats, and their smell wafted into the space the song had created. I sniffed, breathing in their scent, the fragrance of winter.

Beyond the peat smell, a growl of musk. I lifted my nose and sniffed again. There was no doubt. A female bear. A twig cracked in the woods. A dark form slid into view between the trees and stopped. I was no longer alone.

I got to my feet and padded gently towards the shape in the

shadows. Stopping just before it, I knelt and emptied the contents of the beaker I had drunk from onto the ground between me and the bear. Tiny mushrooms spilled out.

'I have drunk their blood, Sister Bear. You can have their flesh.' There was a quiet growl from the shadows.

I retreated back to the fire, where the peats were starting to burn. I took a sip of mead from the copper cup to wash the revolting taste from my mouth, and then settled myself, my bare feet tucked into my warm robe, my hands in my lap, eyes on the shadows. The bear had not moved.

I reached for my leather clarsach bag, with its worn patterns of leaves, probably as old as Father Bear. I took out my harp, took a few deep breaths and began to pick notes, one at a time. Each had to be more beautiful, more delicate than the last. The silence between the notes shone. The great alder made room amongst its branches for the sounds. A nearby aspen's leaves fluttered.

The bear edged out from between the trees, licked up the mushrooms, then retreated.

A cloud scudded over the moon bringing an eerie gloom. I found myself tugging shorter notes from the harp, their tone darkening. A breeze brought an alder leaf that fluttered onto Father Bear's skull then rustled into the bowl of rowan berries. The alder leaf became a face, frowning, so I sweetened the notes again until it smiled. The smile widened and widened, the cheeks swelled into round mounds, and the eyes shrank away. Then it was a leaf again.

'Thank you, Alder Tree.'

Thank you, Alder Tree, a voice repeated.

'Sister Bear!' I whispered.

Sister Bear, repeated the voice. It was soft, deep, furry.

'I will not hurt you. I wish you no harm.'

I will not hurt you. I wish you no harm, came the reply. *Winter is coming.*

'Winter is coming,' I found myself repeating.

I am chased from my home.

'I am chased from my home.'

I have no offspring.

'I have no offspring.'

I am alone.

'I am alone.'

The bear began a growl that opened into a roar. Hairs lifted on my neck. *I am angry. People destroy our woods. They dig up the trees.*

'What shall we do?'
What shall we do?
Sleep and dream,
love the earth,
be true to the moon.
'Sleep and dream, love the earth, be true to the moon,' I sang.
Tell me your sorrows.

'Men have come with a new god. I fear he wants to conquer Mother Earth,' I said.

A long time passed. I became old, then I became young again. Eventually an answer came.
The moon dies every month
and every month is reborn.
We take ourselves away to die each winter
yet each spring we re-awaken.
Don't fear our Mother dying, little sister,
for death may not be the end of her.
The bear approached the fire.
We shall endure pain, loneliness, longing.
We shall sleep and love and dream.
Our spirits will shine in the wild wood.

I began a slow dance tune. I let the loping notes begin to skip and skip. The bear pushed her snout amongst the peats, and emerged head flaming. I howled and faltered on the harp.
Play. It was a command.

I played. My fingers tore at the strings. The bear's feet pounded the galloping rhythm of the dance. Soon both front paws were also ablaze, the flames whipping and furling like ribbons. I moaned at the madness of this grotesque creature with flames coursing over her pelt, turning, twisting, spinning, blurring. My eyes filled with tears. Smoke from the fire blew into my face. I had to take my hand from the harp to wipe my eyes. When I opened them again the bear had gone.

A cloud pulled over the moon and a cold wind sneaked under the canopy of the tree. A shiver grabbed and shook me. I reached for the cup of mead.

Uncurling my feet from under my robe I stood up and peered out between the trees for any sign of the bear. Nothing.

I turned towards my hut, with one last look at the fire. It would be safe. I carried the skull back to its place above the door, yawned and groped my way into bed.

dreaming
digging into warm darkness
seeking thunder
wonder of another bear
tight lightning teeth
tumbling whirling
rolling
dreaming

Seallach - Willow

Bjorn had a restless night after the moonfire. He woke in the early hours and lay in the dark, stewing. Doubts curdled in his brain. The fire had gone to plan, but there had been something lifeless about it. Was he the only one whose heart was not fully in it this year?

He couldn't get the picture out of his mind of Caphel carrying wood to the fire. Had it been an appropriate punishment for the rowan-cutting? The boy had worked until he almost collapsed with tiredness, dragging heavy branches from the new pasture that was being cleared beside the big house. All afternoon he had struggled down to the shore with logs of hazel, birch and willow and scratchy bundles of blackthorn, his face clenched with exertion, refusing to make eye contact with any of the men who were helping to build the fire. At the celebration he hadn't joined in the dancing, hanging back with some older boys, looking sulky.

From Caphel, Bjorn's thoughts turned to James, the cause of the punishment, and then circled back to Margaret and the news she had given him when they came to bed after the fire. He would be a father. He would have an heir. He rolled onto his side, hugging the idea of a child to his chest. But he could not settle back into sleep. To avoid waking Margaret by turning again, he slid out from under the covers. He had to talk to someone.

It was still dark as he made his way across the hall but there was a glow from the fire in the kitchen. A figure sleeping near the hearth unrolled itself from a fleece, and with pleasure he recognised Til, the hunter and harpist.

'Don't disturb yourself on my account, Til. I can't sleep.'

'It must be nearly dawn, anyway; I should be getting back to my dogs,' Til replied, stretching his long arms up behind his head. 'Were you pleased with how it went last night?'

Bjorn pulled a sturdy four-legged hazel stool with a wicker-work seat up to the kitchen table and, with his chin in his hands, sighed,

'Not really.'

Til got to his feet and opened the door, letting in the faint grey of dawn. 'No?' He fetched two wooden mugs and filled them with milk from the churn, then sat opposite Bjorn and handed one to him.

'It's not the same without Brigid.'

'No, it's not the same.'

'I mean, Til, do you think – ach, perhaps I'm just being sentimental…' Til sipped while Bjorn struggled to find the words. 'Should I have done more to prevent her going? Did I do wrong?' He looked searchingly into the hunter's long, calm face. Til met his gaze and finished his milk before answering.

'You know my opinion, Bjorn. Now that her mother's dead, Brigid's our medicine woman, and she's my friend. I wish there was a way to reconcile what she believes with the new priest's way. I feel that a heart stopped beating in the Braes the day she was banished.'

Bjorn nodded but said nothing, and looked down into his cup. Eventually, he spoke. 'I miss her. She always reminded me of my grandmother.'

'How?'

'My grandmother was a northerner, a Sami, and her mother was a medicine woman just like Brigid's. But she gave up the chance to follow in her mother's footsteps when she married my grandfather. He took her to the King's court, and she lived there for the rest of her life.'

He looked up at the rafters, as if pulling down memories.

'She never went to sea, hated ships, loved only the forest, so she always stayed at home when my grandfather went Viking. But she was known as a wise woman. The men took her hunting: she could follow animals better than any of them, and she sometimes cured people of illnesses with plants from the forest. I think she might've cast a few spells as well, though she always denied it.'

He fell silent.

'I miss Brigid too,' Til said. 'Anyway, Bjorn, life must go on, and I've got dogs to feed and traps to check.' He started to get to his feet. 'I didn't mean to sleep here last night, but you lot had me playing so long I was too tired to face the hill. Not that I mind, you know; it's always good to play the old tunes.'

'Aye, we had a good ceilidh after the fire, right enough. Thanks

27

to you and your clarsach.'

'It's no bother,' Til turned to the door.

'Wait,' said Bjorn. 'Before you go… Would you help me with my plan for the boat?'

'Me? I'm a hunter, not a fisherman.'

'But you can write?' Bjorn asked.

'Aye,' Til replied, guardedly.

'Wait here.' Bjorn got up and went out into the hall. From an oak chest in one corner he fetched a roll of vellum tied with a leather thong, a silver ink pot and a white goose-feather quill. He returned to the kitchen and spread them out on the table. In the dim light, he and Til pored over the detailed drawing of a ship. It was long and narrow with a sharp, shallow keel and a dragon's head at the bow. Every rib and plank that would be needed to build it was shown.

'It's impressive work, that's for sure,' said Til. 'You drew it?'

Bjorn nodded. 'With Angus. I can do the drawing without a problem, but I want to list all the parts too. I could do it in Norse, but I'd rather have it in your script. Can you help?'

'But I won't know all the technical names.'

'Don't worry – I know all the words. It's the writing I need your help with.'

'Well, I'm not sure. Where would you want it written? Here?'

'Yes, to the side of the drawing, alongside my marks. That's the timbers, then there's the metal work like the iron rivets – it needs three hundred of them – then that's all the ropes and sails that we need.'

'What's that one?'

'Willow fenders for the mooring.'

'You should start there.'

'Why?'

'Well, willow's meant to inspire poetry.'

'Is that what the bards say, is it?'

'It's what I believe. All the trees bring something out in us, and with willow it's a feeling for all the meanings woven together within words.'

Bjorn sat back. 'At this stage, all I need is a list of parts. You can write the Ode to the Boat when it's ready for launching.'

Til raised his eyebrows. 'You might be lucky.'

They exchanged grins.

'So will you help me?'

'Aye, all right. As long as you tell me what's what.' Til took out his knife and began sharpening the quill.

'Thanks, Til. I'll be in your debt.'

'Ach, don't be daft.'

Til dipped the feather into the pot of ink, giving it a stir.

'So, fenders.' The quill was poised. 'How many?'

'Four.'

'Well, there's a coincidence: fourth letter of the alphabet.' Til scratched down the symbol for willow, one vertical stroke like a trunk, with four branches growing out of its left side.

Bjorn watched with interest. 'How do you mean, coincidence?'

'The letters of our alphabet each represent a tree. Birch is first, with one branch, then rowan, then alder, then willow.' Til pointed to the symbol he'd just written, following it with a four-stroke tally for the buoys.

'You old bards don't make anything straightforward, do you?'

'Not if we can help it.' Til smiled. 'Everything's connected. Writing's just our way of bringing it all together.'

'It's similar to the runes we use, but it looks more like a wee tree. Are they all like that?'

'Aye, every symbol we write is a mark of respect for Mother Earth.'

'Try telling that to James,' Bjorn muttered.

Til sat with his hand poised to write. Bjorn looked off, lost in thought, then shook his head and turned his attention back to the plan.

That morning, Caphel also woke early. He lay quietly in the dark, snug under his wool blankets, anticipating the coming day, and as soon as the first signs of grey began to filter under the door he got up. His grandmother, Frigga, was still sleeping and his seven-year-old sister Enya was curled up against her, with her dark hair limp across her face. Careful not to disturb them, Caphel rolled up his rush mat and deer hide and tucked them with his blankets into a corner. Then he tiptoed past them to the door, cringed as it creaked open, and closed it gingerly behind him. He sat on the big stone outside the hut to lash on his boots, then sauntered down to the bridge to see who else was coming. Before he got there, Enya had caught up with him.

'Where are you going? Can I come?'

'No.'

'Oh, go on. Are you going to the fire? I'm good at lighting fires.'

'All right, but don't tell Frigga. She'll get angry.'

'No she won't; she heard you and guessed already.'

'Huh.'

Donald and his wee brother Giric were already waiting, throwing pebbles at the crack willow tree that towered over the river bank. Both he and Giric were fair-haired and bright eyed, with more than a little Viking in them. Donald was a bit older than Caphel, and he had started to shoot up in height, towering a full head above the others.

Soon they were joined by Ruaraidh from the mill, a fidgety red-head, and Lachlan and Groa, the twin sister and brother from the top of the Brae. They were a small, dark-haired pair, and though they were older than Enya their mute closeness made them seem younger.

The seven of them set off down the path that the entire village had used the night before, back to the loch and the remains of the big fire.

They soon had a blaze going with scraps of wood that had been missed in the darkness. They sat around pretending to stay warm but it was cold so early in the morning, and after a while Lachlan and Groa needed to go home to help their mother with the cows, and Ruaraidh decided he needed his breakfast. The others agreed to prowl for some more sticks to keep the fire going.

'Maybe there'll be driftwood at the shore,' Donald said.

They made their way down through the woods to the loch and found a coracle lying unattended in the shallows, tied with a heather rope to a willow tree that hung over the lochside. Some of its branches trailed in the water. The little boat bobbed as ripples lapped the shore.

'Whose do you think it is?' Donald asked.

No-one answered. A wren trilled from a crooked aspen.

'Maybe it's for fishing,' Caphel suggested.

'Can we go out in it?' asked Enya. 'I love fishing.'

'No, we can't take it,' Donald said. 'What if it's the head-man's?'

'Or the priest's.' Giric used the awed tone he always kept for ghosts, devils or the priest, who was as near to the spirits as he could imagine, and at least as fearsome.

'Nonsense, priests don't fish,' said Enya with absolute certainty. 'I think we should take it. I think we were meant to find it, so that we could go fishing and catch something to cook on the fire.' Her mind was made up and she looked to the others for confirmation.

Donald looked uncertain but a grin was growing on Caphel's face.

The coracle bounced like a puppy pulling on a string. The temptation was overwhelming.

'Come on, Caphel, help me untie it,' said Enya, seizing the initiative and pulling her brother along with her.

'But we can't!' Giric was holding back.

'No, Enya, hang on, we really can't,' Donald remonstrated.

'Don't be soft, Donald.' Enya grinned at him. 'We're not stealing it or anything, just borrowing it for a wee while.'

She and Caphel ducked under the grey twisted willow branches and Caphel began tugging at the rough rope tied to a stem, soon unleashing the few hitches that held it. Enya picked her way across the rocks to the boat and, steadying it with both hands, she stepped into its curved hull and sat down on the single thwart.

'Come on, Giric,' she urged. Her smile was infectious and he found himself grinning back to her and then in a rush he was dipping under the willow branches and hopping across the stones. The coracle rolled as he grabbed it and tried to step in.

'Give us a hand,' he wailed to Enya, who had shifted to one side to make room, tipping the boat away from him. She leaned over and held out a hand and he scrambled aboard, flustered and panting, then with a grin he called to Donald, 'Are you not coming?'

Donald shook his head. 'I'll wait for you here. We'll never all fit.'

He was right. The flimsy vessel was full already with Enya and Giric and now Caphel was making his way across the rocks with the rope. He wobbled his way onboard, but there was no room for all three of them to crush together on the thwart, so he perched on the gunnel. The coracle reared awkwardly and spun as Enya tried to push away from the rocks with a dilapidated paddle. 'Help me, will you?' she screamed to Giric who obediently pushed at the rocks with another oar. They began to float off.

Giric's face broke into a broad smile as he began pulling at his oar and singing a song they all knew about a Viking saga.

'*Crewmen on the mighty ocean...*' he warbled.

Enya giggled and joined in.

'*Sailing off to find our fortune...*'

'For God's sake be careful,' Donald shouted, watching as Caphel clung to the back of the lurching coracle. Enya looked round and shrieked instructions to Giric to row in time with her, not to splash. Her own haphazard stirring did not help and they spun round in circles. Yet somehow they persisted in manoeuvring themselves out into the loch, where a stiff breeze was blowing, lifting the water from the top of the ripples. The wind helped, giving them a false sense of progress and of competence with the oars.

'This is great! Let's go to the island,' Enya urged.

They were already in deep water. They needed to steer down the loch to reach the island, but the wind was taking them directly across. Enya bellowed instructions to Giric, who floundered with his oar. Tempers flared. The boat lurched. Caphel, giggling on the edge, found himself slipping sideways. As he tried to right himself his foot broke through a join in the skin hull. Water started pouring in. He screamed. Enya and Giric turned to look and the little coracle tipped up and emptied them into the water.

The children floundered, struggling to cling onto an oar, onto each other, anything. Enya and Giric latched onto the coracle, and kicked for shore.

Caphel was swimming, his arms splashing, but he was not a strong swimmer and with his thick winter plaid wrapped round him it was hard to keep to the surface. What had seemed like ripples from the boat had now become engulfing waves. He tried to keep his head up, but swallowed water instead of air. His flailing arms seemed to get weaker and weaker. The distance between him and the two others lengthened as they got into their stride. He tried to call out to them but another wave smothered him as he opened his mouth. Then he was under the water, sinking, the noise of the slapping, lurching spray silenced as the black cold water gathered him into itself.

Enya and Giric reached shallow water and when their feet touched bottom, Enya looked around for her brother. Her screams brought Donald running. He saw the two terrified faces of the children, standing soaking wet in the shallows of the loch with the upturned coracle.

'Caphel?' he asked. 'Where's Caphel?'

Giric started to cry.

'What have you done to Caphel?' Donald shouted. 'Where is he? Where is he?' He was wailing now, looking desperately out onto the water of the loch. 'Help him!'

'How?' Enya gulped for breath. 'He's gone!' Behind the anger in her voice, tears were smarting.

'He can't be gone,' Giric wailed. 'He was just there, behind us.'

The three children argued senselessly on the bank. They stared out onto the water, looking for some sign of Caphel among the deceiving patterns of the choppy surface.

At first they did not notice the dot on the far side of the loch, growing steadily bigger as it approached. But finally Donald understood what he was seeing: the shape of another coracle with the regular rhythm of someone confident at the oars.

The figure onboard shipped the oars and leaned over the side, lowered something into the water, watching intently. The boat turned and rolled in the waves, then a shape broke the surface of the loch and the stranger on the boat, with much tugging and heaving, hauled a body over the bows and immediately crouched over it, pummeling the chest and breathing into the upturned face.

The children watched from the shallows, motionless and silenced in amazement. Eventually the mysterious figure straightened, reached for the oars, spun the boat towards them and with a few strong pulls, brought it into the calm of the shallows. They hardly recognised the rescuer with her hair tucked into a goatskin cloak and hidden by a woollen hat. Her green eyes turned on the children.

'Quickly, help me get him onto the shore!'

Tossing a rope to Donald she jumped overboard to help tug the boat towards the rocks. Enya and Giric stared with horror into the boat where Caphel lay, limp and pale.

NION - ASH

A querulous voice spoke the fear we all shared. 'Is he dead?'
'He will live. He is strong.' I hoped to reassure the frightened
girl crouched beside the lifeless body of her brother. She looked
up at me. I had taken off my hat to wring out my hair and must
have looked like a wild creature. I wrapped the boy in my cloak
and set about gathering sticks and throwing them onto the fire.
It looked as if the children had been playing with it already, and
flames came easily.

'It's a good thing you came here to keep the fire going this
morning,' I smiled. 'Don't worry. We'll have this young man
warmed in no time. You two,' I gestured to the two fair-haired
lads who were standing staring at me, 'perhaps you had better run
to the village and get help.'

The two boys nodded vigorously and sprinted off.

The girl did not move and said nothing.

'What's your name?' She glanced at me uncertainly as if she
wasn't sure if it was safe to speak to me. Then her eyes rested on
her brother, who looked as near to death as anything could. She
stayed silent.

'No need to be frightened. If you can't tell me your name, perhaps
I can guess. Is it Inga?' She shook her head.

'Then maybe it's Icicle?' Again she shook her head, but with half
a grin this time. Who had ever heard of such a silly name?

'So in that case it must be Enya,' I concluded, to her amazement.
She nodded at me. I grinned back.

'I thought so. You look just like Beathoc, your mother. She was a
lovely woman – a beautiful gentle woman. I still miss her. I expect
you do too?'

Enya dipped her head again. I suspected she wasn't used to
being talked to like this. It took her a while to respond, but I was
happy to wait.

'You knew my ma?' she said. She was gazing at me. 'You're
Brigid, aren't you?' Her little eyes were wide.

34

I patted her on her bent knee. 'I might just be. Your ma and I were friends right up until she died. My mother and hers were always at each other's hearths. It'll be your grandmother who takes care of you now, I suppose?' Enya nodded gravely. 'And your brother.' She nodded again. 'Caphel, isn't it?' I knew fine well, but it seemed friendly to ask. I was surprised Enya hadn't remembered me more clearly; it wasn't so very long since Beathoc had died and I had been a frequent visitor at their house.

'Well, you're in good hands with Frigga, that's for sure. There is no wiser woman in the village, and she's a kind soul too. Is she good to you?' Enya looked uncertain. 'Ah well. I'm sure she's strict. She was always strict on Beathoc, much more than my mother. And she's suffered so many losses, poor woman. I'm sure you're the most precious things in the world to her, so you are. Especially a wee beautiful girl like yourself.'

As I spoke I was steadily feeding the fire, gathering the few stray sticks that had escaped the previous night's bonfire and the children's play. When a warm blaze was achieved I turned my attention to the boy, rubbing him with my cloak and checking his chest and wrists and eyes, but keeping up my talk to the crouching girl.

'She'll make you go to bed before you're ready, I guess,' I said with a wry smile. Enya gave a tiny tilt of her head. 'And she'll be aye sending you off for herbs and making you watch her in the kitchen while she fixes them, I'll bet.' I got a slightly more definite sign of assent.

'And then she'll tell you so much about them that your head spins and she'll make you stand on the stool till you remember it all.' Enya started to laugh as if she couldn't believe a strange woman like me could know all these things. 'But if I know Frigga, she's always got something nice in her apron pocket.' More nods.

'You must think I'm a witch that can change into a mouse in your kitchen to know so much of what goes on within your walls!' I smiled at Enya, who didn't know whether to answer or not.

'Are you a witch?'

'What do you think?'

'You seem too kind to be a witch and not nearly ugly enough.'

I laughed. 'Well, I'm going to act like your granny now and send you off for some things to help me get your brother back on his feet. I'll need ash. You know ash?'

'Yes,' Enya said, definitely.

'I need half a dozen twigs, nice long thin ones if you can get them. And some rosehips. There'll be plenty around just now. Have you a pocket?'

Enya showed me her pocket. 'Good. Fill it with rosehips for me, will you?'

'All right.' Enya looked pleased to be taken so seriously.

'And now, do you know yarrow?'

'Of course,' Enya answered proudly.

'It'll be hard to find just now, it's finished flowering, but if you can, then bring me eight yarrow leaves. Don't worry if you can't find any, just bring what you can.'

Enya nodded. 'Six ash twigs, eight yarrow leaves and a pocket full of rosehips,' she said gravely. 'Six ash twigs, eight yarrow leaves and a pocket full of rosehips,' she repeated to herself.

'It sounds like a witch's spell already.' I laughed, and Enya looked at me with a sparkle of pride and shared humour so far beyond her years that I was sure I could see Beathoc smiling out from behind her eyes.

'Run along now, I'll boil some water ready for your potion.'

Enya scampered off and I rummaged for my whalebone beaker in the cloak wrapped around Caphel who sighed and twisted with the disturbance.

'Good, you're showing signs of life, Caphel. You're a strong lad, aren't you; you'll be up and back in no time,' I encouraged him. Then I strolled to the lochside and back to fill the mug, and placed it gently on the edge of the fire.

'I hope you appreciate I'm risking my favourite beaker for you, sir. If it cracks I'll be round and asking you for a new one.'

I thought I detected the faint edge of a smile nudge onto the pale face. I stooped over him and gently massaged his temples, stroking his face and neck and then rubbing his chest in a strong circular motion, feeling the warmth of my hands reach into him.

'You can come around now, wee man,' I murmured, as I saw Enya approaching. 'Your sister Enya's got something for you.' His eyes began to move in their sockets.

'You'll be having a dream before coming home, I suppose.' I smiled down at him.

Enya trotted towards us.

'You were quick. Did you find anything?' I asked her.

In response, Enya thrust six slender ash twigs and a handful of feathery yarrow leaves towards me and then dived into her pocket which was bursting with rosehips.

'Oh, well done, Enya, that's perfect. Put them here.'

I dunked the yarrow into the steaming beaker by the fire and began to split the rosehips and scrape out the seeds with my thumbnail. Enya watched intently then began to copy, more slowly but soon getting the hang of it. The split rosehips went in with the yarrow until it was nearly overflowing.

'That'll do for now,' I told her, and I picked up the ash twigs and twined two of them, then joined in a third, winding them around each other. Then I lifted Caphel's arm and wound them around his wrist, joining in the fourth, fifth, then sixth, and wove them into a knotted band bound snugly around his lower arm. I tucked the ends into the weaving. It took a few minutes, and Enya watched wide-eyed. This was a kind of magic she had never seen.

'My mother taught me that,' I said, seeing Enya's interest. 'I'm sure she would have liked to teach you too. Ash is the healing tree, you know?'

Enya looked uncertain.

'If you want something good, you say it to the ash and if it can, your wish will be granted.' I looked down at the boy. 'Now Caphel, you are alive and well,' I said in a positive voice.

'You say it, Enya.'

'You're alive and well, Caphel,' Enya said doubtfully.

'Oh, you must really mean it. You're alive and perfectly well.'

'You're really, really well,' she asserted.

'Wake up, Caphel, you're alive and well.'

And to our delight the boy opened his eyes and blinked hazily at us.

'Welcome back, Caphel,' I said. 'Your sister's pleased to see you. She'll make a good witch, will Enya. Now, I've a cup of tea I want you to drink. It'll not taste nice but it'll warm you up. How do you feel?'

Caphel looked at me and shivered.

'I'm cold,' he said in a small voice.

'You'll be fine,' I assured him. 'Sit up against me here and drink some of this. Enya, can you gather some more sticks? We need to keep this fire going nice and warm.'

Propping Caphel up I held the beaker to his mouth and he sipped, wincing at its bitter flavour. 'I know, it's horrible. I'm sorry I've no honey here. I'm sure Frigga will give you something much more tasty when you get home.' He shivered again, then taking hold of the beaker he drank some more. He examined the beaker with its carving of a bear, then turned and looked at me.

'Who are you?'

'I'm Brigid.'

Sitting up on his own away from me, recognition spread across his face. 'Brigid of the Bears?' He looked horrified. I nodded.

'But you're banished!' he whispered. I nodded again, more slowly. Enya was returning.

'And you're better!' He looked down at the cloak wrapped around him. 'I'll leave you that, and the cup. You can return it to me somehow if you want.'

'What?' He was confused.

'You're better now. And your friends are coming, with half the village. I'd better go. You'll do fine, Caphel. And you too, Enya. You're a grand wee girl, you are. You give your grandmother a hug from me, won't you?' I patted Enya gently on the head, ruffling the brown hair that reminded me so much of my old friend Beathoc, and with prickles in my eyes I strode away down to the shore, quickly untied my coracle and pushed off.

'Don't go,' came a little voice.

I turned to see Enya, standing watching me leave. My heart quickened for the tiny motherless girl.

'I must go. I'm not allowed here any more.' I put oar to water and worked my heavy way across the loch.

By the time Donald and Giric returned with their posse of villagers, Brigid's boat had faded to a smudge among the trees on the far side of the loch. 'What trouble's this?' said Donald, the blacksmith, Caphel and Enya's father.

The boys were amazed. When they had left Caphel he was, they assumed, drowned. Now he seemed to have been miraculously brought back to life, and the performer of the miracle was missing. 'You look all right to me, Caphel,' said big Donald. 'These two said you'd drowned. We were expecting a corpse.'

'I did drown. I think so, anyway. But I'm fine now.'

'And how did you manage that? Who helped you? The lads say there was a woman rescued you. Where is she?'

Caphel pointed across the loch, and a look of anger and amazement crossed Donald's face. 'Was it Brigid? Has she been messing with you?'

'I don't know who it was,' Caphel lied. 'By the time I came round properly she'd gone. She just left me with this on.' He stretched out his arm and showed the crowd his armband of woven ash. There was an audible gasp at the clever work.

A plump dark-haired young woman peered to have a closer look. She was Ishbel, who worked in the kitchen of the big house. 'I've not seen one of those healing bands since her mother died, rest her soul,' she whispered.

'That's her all right, the handiwork of the witch!' James the priest stepped forward. 'We'll soon get rid of this sorcery. He reached for Caphel's hand, but he wasn't fast enough, and Caphel withdrew his arm into the cloak. This goaded James, who towered over the boy.

'What's that you're wearing?' he demanded. 'I smell the coat of the witch. Is it hers?'

Caphel nodded.

'Off with the evil rag!' He tugged at it. 'Look, it's unclean. We must burn it!' The man seemed mad, desperate to take centre stage in the drama.

Caphel pulled back. 'But I'm cold,' he remonstrated.

'There are plenty of good Christians here, I'm sure, who will lend you something to keep you warm.' James beamed at the crowd. 'Who will volunteer to save this wee boy from the witch's fleas?'

Elma, a slight woman with one blind eye, another of the kitchen women, stepped forward with a length of plaid.

'Frigga gave me this in case you needed it,' she said to Caphel. He felt unwilling to give up the soft cloak. It was old and the goatskin was cracked on the outside, but inside it was fluffy and thick, not at all rough, and it smelt good, and felt comforting, full of the warmth of the kind witch-woman. But all eyes were on him, so he reluctantly shrugged the cloak off his shoulders and got to his knees to release it from where it was wrapped under him. He let it fall while he reached for the thin plaid, shivering. James lunged at the cloak, snatched it from him and brandished it at the crowd.

'This infested rag will burn,' he said, and tossed it onto the fire, which it almost obliterated. A huge belch of smoke engulfed him and Caphel, who started coughing and choking as he struggled away from the fire towards Elma.

'Elma, you take the boy home and tell Frigga she's to ensure he's washed thoroughly of the hag's filth. And cut off that cursed trinket, boy.'

Caphel looked around at the fireside anxiously, remembering Brigid's beaker. She had wanted him to return it. But the lovely warm cloak was on the fire and the strange whalebone vessel was gone.

┤

Huath - Hawthorn

She is becoming drowsy. Days are short and nights are long. It is time to hibernate, to put away the world and its smells, the feeling of wet fur, the numbness of cold paws slipping on rocks. The salmon have stopped running, so days at the river are futile. Most of the berries are over, only the most difficult to reach remain and too many of those are riddled with maggots. Mice have stolen all the nuts and acorns with kernels in them. Fungi are melting in the frost. The urge to sleep is strong.

It has been a good year, a summer of plenty. She has caught lots of fat fish, though it has taken more time than it used to.

There are changes at the forest edges. The villagers are cutting down trees with a great noise of metal on wood. They build smoking mounds which stink of evil. She fears them.

She is lonely. She has no mate. She wanders the forest seeking her kind, hoping to catch the scent of a bear between the trees. But there is nothing. The most promising trails lead only to badgers. Occasionally there is the stench of a wolf pack roaming, though they come here rarely now. One day she chased a lynx from its roe deer kill. But never a bear.

She has no young, only a longing for a cub to feed at her belly, warm in her den. Instead, her sleep will be solitary, and no cubs will be born in the dark this winter. It will be like all her other winters: empty. Yet she must sleep. Dreams call her.

She lumbers down the hill between birch trees. As leaves fall, the trees begin to show how firmly they are attached to the earth. She rubs up against an aspen tree to let its scaly bark scratch her rump. Its roots grumble beneath the ground, between the rocks, burying themselves into the moss and down into the earth, disappearing under the soil. Down there, the roots are as big and complex as the trees above, with branches that explore the wet darkness, sniff down into the comforting depths. They wriggle into crevices between rocks, stretch out beside underground water courses and rest in the deep quiet, rumbling, stroked by the ripples from distant branches that move in the wind.

She finds herself at the edge of the trees. Water stretches away and the forest scents are washed through with salt and seaweed. Freshwater gurgles nearby, where a loch spills down a gully into a muddle of bladderwrack. It is slippery, soft and slimey and as four wet paws squelch through it, the stench is intoxicating.

Over the channel and up the rocky shore she scrambles. It is exposed here, open in all directions. The wind is cold. This is a strange place, the rocks are steep and wobble with a hollow rocking sound. A seal slithers off a skerry and bobs off-shore. Then it slaps a flipper, splash, and is gone.

She turns up into woodland again, to the comfort of moss and leaves under foot, the brown soil with roots digging into it, back under aspens, frantically shaking their last circle-leaves at the sea-borne wind, defying it to rid them of the glow of summer.

Clambering up the hill, she finds climbing an effort. She is fat these days. Tired, ready to sleep now.

At the top, she can almost roll down the other side of the hill. The water stretches out on the right, far away out into nothingness, away to an empty nowhere that smells of winter and tastes of fish.

The wind is making the trees dance. Down a wee bit more, around a big rock, the sea out of sight, and into the dark wood's heart.

The floor is a bed of soft rustling leaves, settling down for the season. The holly tree is here, the only one awake now, the guardian of this grove, its three strong trunks each with long, shining green foliage, hardly spined at all. Its berries are dropping now. Bitter but tasty, every year they are nearly the bear's last mouthful. Nearly, but not quite. There is one last food to find.

Beyond the holly is her winter hiding place, under a giant rock where a rowan tree grows. Its roots pierce the stone, giving it a toehold so strong that it can lean out over the sheer cliff, festooned with leaf, proffering berries to the birds as if it is ready to fly off with them from its precarious perch. Every year it scatters leaves and twigs at the entrance to the den, just where she needs them. It is all bare of leaves now; a silver skeleton keeping watch.

Sniffing around the edge of her hole, she peers in. It is a small cave formed from a scatter of huge boulders. It looks quiet; only a few bits of hair from the summer residents, the mice, who will soon scuttle off once they see she's back. An otter has been visiting. Smelling its cat-musk, she leaves her own scent on her entrance stone, so whoever needs to know she is home will know.

She scratches the ground and drags some leaves and sticks from the entrance into the den, along with grass and moss. They are not dry but they will do fine to lie on. There are still some old leaves in there from last year.

Now she seeks out her final meal, snuffling up the bouldery scree to a big oak tree, and up a bit more to the foot of the crag. It is awkward, but she reaches her target, a hawthorn tree. Not that it has many thorns: there is no need of them here in the rocks. She can hardly reach its branches, but eventually manages to bend one bough and pin it down with a hind leg so that both front paws can reach out for the ends of the twigs with their buds and haws. It is a difficult tree for a stiff old bear. She pulls the twigs to her mouth and chews, her mouth filling with sticky bark and gummy fruit. The hawthorn will make her feel as if the summer has come back and she can snooze with a full belly in a warm spot. She does not take much, then gently she lets the branch go and crumples back down onto four legs. She will be back in the spring to chew on a leaf or two.

But first she trundles down past the oak, makes one last stop to empty her bowels, then lets the hawthorn settle with a yawn.

In her sleepy hole she nestles. It is dark and quiet inside the earth. Her breath slows. She is back in the womb. Although she cannot be a mother she can at least give birth to herself every year, every spring become a reborn bear, a cub. Now she feels very old, very tired. Her eyes close. It is time to doze, cradled in the depths of the long night, to return to the time before birth, to dream with the shadows and rummage with the tree roots into the heart of the mother bear.

anger in the sky
fury in the earth
when fear is blinding
loud as thunder

mother bear will kill
her offspring cower

underground
shadow bears
teach again
forest lore
the first-and-last
forever more

❦ ❦

Sometime after winter had settled itself into the Braes, after it had bitten in with a few frosts that sent all the sleeping animals to their dens, thrashed the grasses to the ground and cleared the air of autumn scents, after the world had acquiesced to the cold, a storm burst out of the northwest sky. It began with a raw wind that dug deep, sending the people of the Braes indoors, driving the beasts into huddles in the woods, and emptying the loch of birds.

As night fell the trees shivered.

One by one the squat stone huts closed up as the cattle were brought in with their warm smells. Tallow lanterns were put out, the glimmers under doors fell to darkness and the last hints of firelight escaped through the cracks between beams and walls.

At first a crescent moon shone, low on the horizon, but the wind sent clouds to muffle it and put out the stars.

Soon the only light burning in the Braes was the watch light at the big house. The wind grew and gathered and grew more, as the world retreated into its burrow. The deeper the night became, the wilder the storm grew. The more folk tried to sleep and creatures huddled, the greater its fury.

So it raged and rampaged, crashing and thundering among the trees, lashing and tearing at the heather thatch roofs of the clustered houses of the Braes, scooping up water from the loch and hurling it at the big house, howling at the simpering souls below to come out and fight.

People lay awake in their beds, and in their fears roof-beams became kindling sticks, light enough to blow away. Cattle lowed

44

in fright as the storm accelerated beyond a gale to the deadly race of a hurricane.

In the big house, Iain Kay drifted off to sleep to the sound of James praying in one corner of the hall, while Bran and Eachan sat up by the fire drinking and cursing the weather. Bjorn lay awake in his bed worrying at the wild roaring of the gale. Margaret lay beside him, sleeping peacefully, full of her secret joy at being pregnant, her pale skin shining and healthy.

⊰⊱ ⊰⊱

Fury struck in the middle of the night, using the hurricane for cover. It came down from the high corries and cold tarns of the distant mountains. I was the first to sense it.

I had been lying awake in my shelter under the alder, reckoning my chances of surviving if the shuddering tree should fall. I was fully dressed but there seemed little point getting up; fire in this kind of storm would be more danger than help. I fingered an amulet carved out of hawthorn root and chanted charms to the mother bear; cave magic is always a comfort in a storm and hawthorn protects against lightning strikes. After a while I simply lay and listened to the power of the gale, wondering what deep wrong could have angered the earth so.

A rhythmic creaking began in the tree above me. I curled up and cringed as each squeak was followed by the sound of ripping timber.

A wind sang in the forest with the voice of the mustering ocean. I recognised the Fury. I felt as if I was shrinking away beneath its vastness.

A howl of pure violence announced the arrival of the panting, pattering wolf pack. It passed close to my shack, leaving a wake of smell like a warrior ship. I sat bolt upright, my breath drawn tight into my throat, my shoulders lifted.

I could hear an animal sniffing outside the door, an outlier from the pack, exploring. My eyes swivelled in the dark.

There was a crackle of twigs, then a panting and a rustling as it pushed through the bramble that grew at the back of my lean-to. Through a gap between the wattle hurdles I glimpsed the shine of an eye. I willed it to leave me alone, to turn tail and join the pack.

But the eye glowed and there was a deep growl. My wall thinned to cloth, just a tattered rag between me and the wolf. I was defenceless. My only weapon was strength of will.

I drowned the wolf's mind with desire to return to its pack, to be among its own, trying to reflect back to it the Fury it was pulled by.

Then the ancient alder tree gave a quaking tremble, racked by a huge surge, and a nauseating cracking noise wrenched me to my feet. My mouth filled with the taste of nettles.

'Be strong, Shield Tree!' I rushed to the wall of my room that was formed by the trunk, and hugged it. The cracking was followed by crashing and my home began to fall apart.

I shrank to my knees and clung onto the tree. The composure of the shaman left me. I felt no braver than a little girl, alone, out in the dark.

The far wall of my shack collapsed, and the din of its splintering timbers was followed by smashing of earthenware jugs and pots and bowls, as the contents of the shelf hit the floor.

In the strange hush that followed, the wolf whined and backed away, scraping the ground. Then it swung its head and turned, loping off to regain its kin.

The Fury led the pack away.

I wept, and then felt better, able to sit hunched with my back against the tree. I could vaguely make out in the dark the branch that had fallen through the roof and speared where I had been lying on the bed.

Then I heard the rain begin and soon there was water lashing through the tree, pouring into my shattered shelter. I pulled a blanket and a deer skin from under the collapsed branch on my bed, wound them around myself, and sat in a daze watching as the floor turned to mud and my home disintegrated around me.

⊲⊳ ⊲⊳

The pack went on its way, rounding the loch, quiet but for the panting and pounding feet of the wolves. Ignoring the village, it swept up the lochside to the big house, which it circled once then slowed, gathering itself into a focus. The wolves stopped running and sat panting, their sleek bellies pumping, eyes shining.

The dog at the pack's head sat up straight, and as the wind eased temporarily he released a shrill warbling howl, an invitation to the others to join him in a song. It began with a few yaps and swelled into a stone-weakening chorus of yowling. Lights went dim in the big house. The howling stopped as suddenly as it started.

Then the wolves began to sniff, as if a stench had begun to pour in an angry seep up walls, under doors, seeking its way into every crevice and crack looking for weakness. Some got up to circle the big house, homing in on the stable building, jumping up at the wooden door, yapping excitedly at the ponies within.

As the storm's breath oozed into the big house, a wind with ferocious power got up, racking the stone walls, wrenching at woodwork. It ripped the thatched roof of the stable open like the lid of a casket and tossed it sideways. Beams and wall imploded. Terrified horses lunged, kicked, desperate to escape. They jumped over the crumbling wall and fled out into the yard, and the wolves flowed around them like a toothed tide. Four beasts leaped into the stable and harried the two white ponies housed in the most sheltered, but now most trapping, corner. The ponies whinnied. In a panic they crashed their way out of their stall and, with a leap, out over the stone wall. The wolves followed, focusing on the smaller and daintier mare; they surrounded her in a hostile ring, forcing her to a quivering standstill. As another gust blasted the remainder of the stable wall, the wolves attacked. The horse's screams were drowned out by the sound of falling masonry as the wolves pulled her to the ground and demolished her in a frenzy of claws and canines.

<figure>⋖⋗ ⋖⋗</figure>

It was still deep in the night when the storm began to ebb and the inhabitants of the Braes began to fall fitfully to sleep. Some, with roofs ruined and houses awash, picked their way to neighbours after tying up their traumatised animals. A few straggled up the hill to take shelter in the big house. Most chose to wait it out until morning to survey the damage.

Dawn crept into the sky with a resentful grey.

Bjorn had hardly slept and eventually, unable to lie inactive any longer, he slid out of bed. Margaret was still asleep, murmuring to herself in some dream. He stumbled in the dark as he made his way out into the main hall, where he found several of the men sitting awake around the fireplace, wet and cold, struggling to keep the fire alight. As he walked in, they turned to him with eyes full of expectation and faces tense with fatigue. He lifted his eyebrows and donned his easy smile.

'There's a wee breeze this morning,' he quipped.

Moran, always the first to grasp a banter, brought back, 'Aye, I think there might have a been a gust stronger than Eachan's farting for a change.'

'That'll make it a legend, then,' Bjorn laughed, and the dour mood was broken.

'Is there a brew on?' he asked. 'Some of you look like you've been taking an early dip in the loch.'

As he spoke, Frigga came in from the kitchen with a kettle and a basket of bread, which she laid on a table nearest the men. 'Get yourselves a warm drink and some food, lads. There'll be a day of hard labour ahead of you.' Seeing Bjorn she grinned. 'Good morning, Bjorn.'

'Morning, Frigga. The storm woke you early too, I see.'

'I never slept a wink. You can't sleep through a Fury like that with wolves sucking the life out of the place!'

'The wind did sound like wolves at times,' Bjorn agreed.

'That wasn't wind, my boy,' said Frigga. 'That was the thorn dogs. You'd better take a look outside. There's been an evil spirit at work, there's no doubt about that. The wind did its share, and the rain, but it's bad spirits that do this kind of work, not just weather. Did you not feel the malevolence of it?' She put her hands on her hips and went on. 'It was pure Fury, bringing wolves to do its dirty work. But what's behind it? You'd better ask yourself that, Bjorn: what's behind it? And what'll be the consequence?'

Without waiting for an answer she stomped off to the kitchen, leaving Bjorn bemused. He reached over the shoulders of the guzzling men and grabbed some bread. Moran offered him a steaming mug, which he took. It was mint tea with honey, and it cleared his head. He opened a shutter and stared out with amazement at the ruin which, a few hours ago, had been the stables.

'By the gods!' he exclaimed. 'What demon caused that damage? Moran, Til, when you've eaten, join me out there.'

He turned to leave, and called back, 'Eachan, get a few lads together to gather up the animals.' He slugged back the last of his tea, wrapped his plaid around him, and headed out to inspect the wreckage.

In the morning grey, the trees around the big house looked grim, shuddering in the still-strong wind, surrounded by a litter of twigs and broken branches, limbs torn off by the storm. Two oaks lay slumped and broken, ripped from the ground by the wind, their trunks like corpses, their roots standing vertical with the wounded soil exposed. These great oaks, once sheltered by a thick crowding of hazels, birches, rowans and willows, had stood briefly alone after the smaller trees had been cut out and grazed back for pasture. But alone they could not withstand such gales.

Til joined Bjorn, looking at the wreckage. 'The wind has spoken. This is no climate for grand, solitary trees. Here trees only survive in packs, huddled together for support.'

Bjorn nodded. 'They're no different from us. Only the close-knit can endure it here. Those who stand alone will fall.'

ᛏ

Darrach - Oak

Bjorn surveyed the oaks, awed by the power of the wind to wrench them from the ground. Then he turned to face the house. A few shutters were ripped off, but the roof looked intact and the stonework was undamaged. It was an impressive building. Not large, but built with skill. He made a promise to congratulate and reward Iain, who had come to him last summer and asked to work on the housetop, pointing out where the rafters were rotten, where the thatch was leaking, advising on a double thickness of heather and extra purlins where it was most exposed. He was known as Iain the Bat, as he spent so much time up in the rafters and eaves of the houses of the Braes. Many would be thankful for his skills this morning, Bjorn reflected. A man who kept roofs over people's heads on a stormy night was one to treasure in a community.

Next to the big house were the outbuildings, the foremost now in chaos. Little more than a ruin remained of the stable, and its wreckage was strewn over the yard and down the meadow to the lochside. Timbers that had held the walls in place were fractured. Heather thatch was spread in clumps over the field as if some child-giant had ripped open a cushion and thrown handfuls of its stuffing about.

The stables demonstrated what happened when a roof came off. Without it to deflect the power of the wind up and over the building, the dry stane front wall had buckled. Behind it much of the back wall had followed. With their collapse, they had pulled down most of the gable ends. Doors and stalls had shattered under the falling stones. Bjorn reflected on the days of work that a team of men needed to build these walls of gneiss and sandstone rocks, and on a wind that could devastate them in a single blow. He looked again at the big house. It was the same construction, but somehow the building as a whole had been stronger.

He took a deep breath, realising how weakness in one part could lead so rapidly to a total collapse of the whole. He took it as an omen to himelf as a leader of people. 'I need to look for the weakest corners of this community.' Bjorn nodded to himself. 'They are the small holes that could let a gale in; the weak rafters that could allow a wind under the roof and blow open our world.' He picked his way among the wreckage, pondering and muttering. 'Where is that hole that needs filling? Where can I lend some strength, help to patch up a breach?'

He thought of Frigga's family, with its recent loss of Beathoc, the mother of Caphel and Enya. Caphel now seemed open to any suggestion of the priest and was given no guidance by his drunken father, Donald. Enya, his little sister, was perhaps suffering even more from the loss of her mother. Their grandmother Frigga was strong, but her housekeeping duties kept her often up at the big house. Bjorn felt a twinge of concern for the little girl, the most vulnerable girl under his authority. He would seek her out.

Margaret woke up slowly, cosy in her warm bed. She lingered in the solitude, unwilling to step out into the cold room and venture out into the big house, where everyone knew everyone except her, where she was the strange friendless woman from the south. She missed her old friend Maitlin, with her assurances that no matter how long they were apart they would still be close, even if their contact was limited to infrequent letters. She reflected on her parting words. 'Don't tell yourself off. Remember me when you feel lonely. I'll be missing you too.'

Margaret pushed off the blankets and furs that had kept her snug, drew back the thick curtain around the bed and stepped out into the room. It was cold and she reached hurriedly for clothes, wrapping herself up in layers of soft wool: a dappled blue and grey woven skirt with a rosepink smock and a waistcoat of intricate plaited and woven strips of doe-skin. Her taste in clothes had always been idiosyncratic. When most women of her age were wearing plain belted dresses, she took to patterns, dressing like a minstrel, always seeking out the finest work of weavers, commissioning intricate leatherwork and odd garments from skin.

Slipping on warm sheepskin slippers over woollen socks and pulling a deep blue wrap around her, she knelt by the simple altar she had set up in the corner of her room. A bowl of rosewater and a candle stood in front of her treasured Celtic cross, with its beautiful knotwork engraved in a piece of oakwood by her brother's first teacher, Father Angus. It reminded her of home, and of her mother who had taught her to love beautiful things and appreciate the skills of craftspeople, to read and write, to sing and explore her imagination through embroidery and carving.

How little of that she had done since she had come to live with Bjorn, she realised. He was always up at dawn, off to live his outdoor life. He had little time, it seemed to her, for the arts. And yet he did appreciate finely-wrought objects; it was one of the things she had immediately liked about him, that he would remark if she wore a well-woven belt. He would look closely at embroidery on a cloak or a skirt, finger it and express what he thought of it, picking out the unusual, admiring the skill of the maker. At her home and at King Malcolm's court, he had danced and been a keen audience of visiting players, but here in Bjorn's house it seemed to her that there was hardly ever music in the evening, apart from Til the hunter who occasionally got out his harp and sang a saga or one of the strange Pictish songs of the locals. Bjorn's men ate heartily, drank with vigour then slept early, the life of hard workers out of doors. She suspected that Bjorn's joy at the courtly arts was fueled by nothing much deeper than novelty.

Bringing her thoughts back to her cross, she began to pray, taking her mind through its pattern of phrases and rhymes, letting the rhythm of familiar words of worship fill up her consciousness, immersing herself in the comfort of prayer.

So when Bjorn sought her out, he found her kneeling by her shrine. He stood in the doorway not knowing what to do, feeling awkward at interrupting her. But she turned and smiled.

'Morning, Hunter,' she said.

'Good morning, Rainbow.' His nickname for her had arisen from her colourful wardrobe. 'I can't believe you managed to sleep soundly through that storm.'

'I heard the wind howling at one point. It was wild!'

'It was ferocious.' He shuddered, walked over to her and drew her up to a standing position. 'Margaret, listen to me. This storm has wreaked a terrible damage. It wasn't just the wind howling. I don't really know how to tell...' He stalled, lifted his hands from her shoulders, and held them out, palms open, as if hoping they might speak for him. He turned away. 'I've something to show you.

Prepare yourself. Dress warmly.'

Margaret looked at him quizzically then shrugged, belted on her wrap and changed her slippers for leather boots. She tugged her fur coat off its hook in the corner and followed Bjorn.

He went straight through the hall and out of a side door that they rarely used, which took them out right next to the ruined stable. She gasped at the sight of the building.

'My God! It's as if a beast attacked it.' She shook her head, bewildered.

He turned and put an arm around her, hugging her. 'I can't believe you slept so soundly,' he repeated.

Then a dawning crossed her face. 'The horses?' she asked. 'Our ponies?' The two white horses were their wedding gift from her father, a gesture of unexpected love. Her mare was her pride and joy. 'Lightning. And Thor. Where are they?' The names of their horses seemed now to be ridiculous, as if they had asked for trouble.

'I'm sorry, Rainbow.' Bjorn's voice was gentle. 'I don't know about Thor; the men have gone out to try to round up the animals that escaped. But Lightning – well, I'm afraid there were wolves in the storm.'

He led her round to what had been the front of the stable, into the yard. The mangled remains of her mare lay where the wolves had torn and feasted. The ground around it was blood-stained. Bones jutted through clotting gore.

Crouched nearby, its fur prickling, was a single wolf, a young adult male, seeming to guard the carcase. Bjorn lobbed a stone at it, but it flinched and growled, then limped back to the body. Its eyes were fixed on Margaret, who stood stunned, staring at the remains of her treasured pony. The wolf whined and she looked across the carcase at it. It put its head on one side and gazed, then took two steps towards her.

At that, Bjorn sprang forward and lashed out, kicking it away with a swift boot between its legs. It growled at him, suddenly a killer, eyes narrowed, fangs showing under a curling lip. Bjorn aimed another stone, then another.

Margaret felt her throat choking. 'Stop it!' she muttered. 'Leave it be.'

Bjorn merely grunted and continued his barrage of stones till the young wolf turned on its tail and slunk off into the woods.

Margaret, sickened at the sight of the dead horse, the ruined stable, the defeated wolf, turned back to the house, her eyes awash with tears, her shoulders twisted.

'Margaret!' Bjorn called after her, but without turning back to him she stumbled in through the oak door, which banged shut behind her.

❧ ❧

The wolf hung around, hiding in the fringes of the woods behind the big house but venturing forth into the yard whenever it dared. It skulked around the barn, sometimes howling under the back door at night. The mornings always found it sitting where Margaret's horse had been killed, as if it was waiting for something. The first ones up always stoned it back into the woods.

Bjorn set about plans to reconstruct the stables. He set off one morning to the Braes to seek out Iain the Bat, who he found already hard at work among the rafters of one of the cottages that had been damaged by the storm. Frigga's son Moran, whose house it was, paced around at ground level. Iain leaned and hung from the rafters as if on solid ground, spreading his weight instinctively and twisting and hanging like his namesake, apparently oblivious to his height above ground. When he saw Bjorn coming, he waved.

'Ahoy, Bjorn, you're just in time. I need a wee hand up here and Moran's too feared to climb up.'

'I'm no squirrel myself,' Bjorn retorted. 'And it looks to me like you're taking it down, not fixing it.' True enough, Iain was ripping thatch from the wooden supports.

'I'm just making sure the hole's worth putting a bucket under.' Iain laughed.

'Oh aye, Moran's getting too much sleep these days, is he?'

'That storm gave me a taste for a bit of fresh air in the house,' said Moran with a smile.

'I assume he's planning on putting it back up in the long run.'

Moran nodded. 'In the short run, I hope!'

'Iain, can I have a word?' Bjorn called.

'Aye, and I'll pass it onto God,' came the reply. Iain did not appear to be considering descent from his work place, so Bjorn went inside the house and stood where he could look up through the gaping hole through which Iain grinned down at him.

'Can I interest you in some work up at the big house?' Bjorn began.

'What's wrong with it?' Iain asked, defensively. 'I put that top on only two years ago and I've never built one stronger.'

'I know,' said Bjorn. 'That's why I'm asking you. The house itself is sound, it's the stable, you know the one, the roof lifted clean off in the storm.'

'Aye, so I heard,' Iain said.

'Would you consider a repair job? I'd make it worth your while.'

'Well, I don't know. I might have a problem with that. I'll need to think about it.' Iain's head disappeared back to his thatch, making it quite clear that was the end of the discussion.

Bjorn shook his head at Moran and strode back to the big house. He burst into the kitchen, plonked himself down at the corner table and demanded a mug of beer. Frigga poured one from a barrel and settled it in front of him, then asked him what was wrong.

'First Donald wouldn't help to gather the animals, then Eachan refused to organise the stonework repairs on the stable, now Iain the Bat won't talk to me about fixing the roof. I don't understand it.'

Frigga sat down opposite him with a beaker of hot tea.

'You don't understand it,' she repeated.

'No, I don't.'

'Since when?'

'Since the storm.'

'And you want me to tell you what people are saying?'

'If you will.'

'Bjorn, that was no ordinary storm.' She took a sip of her drink. 'That was the Fury. All the old believers recognised it. The wolves, the ferocity of the wind, the way it picked its targets. No-one wants to challenge the spirits that did that sort of harm. It was mostly the new houses that took the damage: there are a lot of crosses getting wet while we heathens are still sleeping on dry mattresses.'

'But what about Moran's house? He's no Christian. Why would Iain work on his place and not the stables?' Bjorn asked.

'Perhaps you should ask Moran about that,' Frigga said. 'They're scared, Bjorn.'

'Of the wolves?'

'Aye, and the Fury.'

'I can't fight fury, but I can hunt wolves,' Bjorn said. 'Do you think a hunt would help?' he asked. 'Revenge?'

'It might.' Frigga nodded. Then, with a shrug, 'Or it might not.'

'Depending on?'

'That's not for me to say. You're the leader, not me.'

He drank his mug of beer in one long slug, set it down on the table and smiled at Frigga. 'Thank you.'

From the kitchen he marched out into the great hall. 'Get a fire going in here,' he called to Iain Kay and his son Diarmid who were sitting playing toss in one corner, 'and bring a barrel of ale and some whisky up from the store. Then call the men around for nightfall.' At the mention of whisky they jumped into action.

Bjorn went to seek out Margaret, who he found embroidering in the thin light by the bedroom window, with James in midflow.

'...and I'll get Seamus to do the carvings and the altar stone. We'll lay the first stone at Easter.'

'The first stone of what?' Bjorn asked.

'James thinks we should build a chapel,' Margaret said.

'We need a house of God.' James clenched his hands. 'I fear the ruined stable is a sign to us that our beasts are treated better than our souls. I'm going to arrange for the monks of St Andrews to design a chapel from the stone.'

'Will I be able to keep my horses in it?' Bjorn asked, winking at Margaret, who looked unamused.

'I've spent a good deal of time with Niall and Diarmid helping to settle the ponies into the barn. It is quite adequate.'

'Well, that can be decided another day. Rainbow, you've a chance to dress up tonight. I'm gathering the men. We're going to plan a hunt.'

'A hunt for what?' Margaret asked.

'Wolves.'

'You would do better hunting the devil out of your souls,' James remarked.

'And you would do better getting the devil out of my bedroom,' Bjorn retorted, storming out and taking off to the woods.

He walked long and far, right around the fringe of the loch and into the alder woods on the far side. He walked as far as Brigid's hut under the Shield Tree. He found himself at a standstill, looking at the wrecked roof of the shack, the feeble patching that Brigid had managed to apply to keep the worst of the rain out. It was beyond his imagination that anyone could be surviving in such a hovel through the winter. He turned and walked back to the Braes.

❦ ❦

I sensed his presence at my clearing. I had been humming, walking back with a bag of hazelnuts and some late fungi. He was striding away, his shock of auburn hair like a dead fox hanging down his back. I shook my head in time with his rolling gait. I had an urge to run after him, to stop him, challenge him, tug at his hair, let him see my anger. But instead, I just stood and watched him go. When the distance swallowed him, I stooped to gather up some half-dry oak leaves and twigs to rekindle my fire.

I remembered the first time Bjorn and I made love, all those years ago. We were in the forest on the north shore of the loch. It was his lips that drew me to him – their flesh so raw, so delicate within the copper stipple of new beard. When he spoke I found myself gazing at them. It was as if each syllable was a kiss, his voice issuing from somewhere behind us while his mouth sang silent love songs. I glanced up and found his ocean grey eyes on me. The disembodied voice said 'you're not listening to a word I say,' but his lips mouthed 'kiss me.'

He was only one step away. As my mouth closed over his mouth, my pelvis locked onto his. All sense of risk was gone with that first clench. His arm scooped around me. I felt his hand flat on my lower back, my ribs pressing up to his, my nipples brushing his chest through layers of hide and wool. His stubble was gruff against my chin, lips light, his tongue pulling me into the rhythm of our bodies. I wanted to bathe myself in him, not caring if it burned me.

Clumsy and urgent, my hands tugged at his clothes. I swayed as he took his arm from my back to his buckle. Leather and bronze clattered against a stone. Our mouths parted, tongue-tips reluctant, breathing hard. Busy hands steadied each other, eyes smiling, as we pulled jerkins over heads and fumbled with laces until naked legs found naked legs. Then our lips resealed.

I pushed him to the ground among our scattered clothes, pressing his chest with my palm, needing to lie with him stretched out, to wrap myself around him. My legs wound and twisted, feeling his hair, his bones. My sex was wet, scalding. I could feel his penis pressing my belly. I took hold of it with one hand, lifting my mouth from his to look down at his face. He gazed back, eyes wide. I paused, savouring the agony of this precipice, feeling his taut hot muscle pulse under my fingers, squeezing. I watched his tongue curl out and lick his upper lip, breath shuddering, eyelids half-closed, as I guided it down, touching myself with its nudging hunger, letting it nose into me. As he pushed inside and our bodies fused, I opened myself over him, pouring molten gold onto his furnace, rocking and screaming as we blazed.

Afterwards, trembling, I saw I'd made him cry.

TINNE - HOLLY

M argaret lay fully-dressed on the bed but felt restless, and finally decided to go out for a walk. Thinking of fresh air and the health of the baby growing within her, she wrapped up warmly and headed out of the back door, across the yard and around the back of the barn.

A strong path led into the woods. There was a cold breeze which caught her face, and she took the path into the trees hoping to benefit from their shelter. All the leaves were fallen now, and she found herself with memories from her childhood welling up as she scuffed the leaves. Soon she was kicking them up in the air, reminiscing on games she and Maitlin had played in the woods at home. An old song, a nursery rhyme, came to her from those days and she hummed it as she strolled along the track.

The woods were pungent with the bass-note smell of winter earth. They had opened up to a spaciousness impossible to experience in summer when the foliage crowds around and obscures the structures of the branches. She gazed at the folded bronzes of dying undergrowth, and the latticework of leafless trees, wishing she had fabrics of such colours and patterns.

She came to a bridge over a stream. A smaller path went off around the bottom of a crag and followed the burn, which was full after the rains and frothed and bubbled busily down to the rock. Its music attracted her. She had never walked that way, but following a stream seemed a safe thing to do, so she turned up it. As she rounded the crag the woods thickened and the ground levelled; the stream twisted, moving more slowly. The path became muddy in places, but continued to follow the stream. As it slowed, its music faded and Margaret became aware of other noises, occasional birds, the wind in the treetops.

Winding between two big holly trees, the stream opened out into a pool. It was a calm and peaceful place. There were dead leaves floating in a log-jam at one side. Elsewhere the water was clear, reflecting the trees and the cloudy sky. A robin scolded her from a fallen trunk overhanging the pool. She smiled at it and stopped, pausing to take in the mood of the place, delighting in her discovery of somewhere new. It had the feeling of a refuge.

'I can come here,' she said to herself, 'to think, to be calm, when I need to.'

Then, out of the corner of her eye she saw a movement, turned her head and caught her breath. Sitting in the path, staring at her, was a young wolf. She stared back, frozen. The wolf's jaw was hanging slightly open. She stiffened, her mind racing. She began to back slowly away down the path, keeping her eyes on those of the big dog.

'Get away!' she said, her voice hoarse, barely a whisper.

It did not move; just kept on watching.

'They're going to hunt you,' she croaked.

The wolf's ears pricked up.

'Tomorrow,' she said, a bit louder, and this seemed to stir the dog. His head dropped and he swung around and loped up the track, away from her.

She shook her head and breathed hard. Her heart was pounding, as if she had betrayed her husband. Shaking her head, she set off walking briskly back the way she had come, returning to the big house as the gloaming started to gather.

She sat in the kitchen surrounded by the bright light of early lamps, the comfort of a hot drink and the chatter of Frigga and the kitchen women. The fresh air had made her skin glow. She did not mention the wolf to anyone.

A steady stream of people arrived, some passing through the kitchen and others, who had entered the big house directly into the great hall, finding an excuse to stick their heads round the door of the kitchen.

Frigga led the preparations for the gathering, keeping the women busy on all kinds of cooking without seeming to boss anyone around. She was constantly bustling to be helpful, moving from one dish to another, praising as she went, noticing every artful touch or special effort the women made and always commending them, helping where she was asked, dropping hints through anecdotes from her long life in the big house.

At one point a young woman dropped a pie she had been preparing as she shifted it from the fireplace. Frigga leapt in to help.

'Och, Maeve, I saw that jump right out of your hands. Have you burned yourself?'

Frigga checked Maeve's hands and called out to her sister, 'Ishbel, bring some water here and help Maeve cool that burn.'

Then Frigga set to cleaning up the smashed dish and spilled food, complimenting Maeve as she did on how well the vegetables were cut and cooked.

'I'm sorry, Frigga,' Maeve blurted, overcome with shame, tears in her eyes. Food wasted was a crime.

'No, don't you feel bad, my girl, we'll rescue most of it and no-one will be any the wiser out there. It's a clean floor, isn't it Elma?' She winked at Elma, who earlier had got a telling-off for her inadequate sweeping of the stone kitchen floor and had been told to go over it again with a mop. Elma grinned back.

'Aye, Frigga, spotless!'

Frigga proceeded to relate a story that many had heard before, of the time she had dropped the wedding pudding for the marriage celebration of the previous headman. She soon had Maeve and all the other women laughing at her tale of her own disaster, and as she told the story she expertly rescued the retrievable majority of Maeve's dish into another earthenware pot, saying, 'There you are; stick a few more herbs in that and you can pastry it up as good as new.'

A baby started to wail from a crib in one corner. A little girl rocked it, but the howling grew more intense.

Margaret caught Frigga's eye. 'Can I do anything useful, Frigga?' she asked.

'I don't know, can you?' Frigga replied with a laugh. A few of the women tittered.

'I'm no good for anything skilled, but maybe I could chop something?'

Frigga smiled at her as if at a young child. 'Could you help Elma shell some nuts?'

'If you'll show me how.'

'All right, Elma, come and help us. The little one sounds like she needs a feed.' Frigga fetched a bag of hazel nuts, some bowls and wooden crackers. She sat opposite Margaret at the table and demonstrated how to crack them easily and get the nut out whole.

61

Elma lifted the baby from its cradle, and the crying stopped. She sat next to Frigga, the baby suckling happily.

'It seems like a lot of food that you're preparing for tonight. I thought Bjorn was just gathering the men to plan a hunt,' Margaret said.

'Oh, this isn't all for tonight,' Frigga said. 'Come midnight, the men will realise they'll need a feast before they set out, and Bjorn will command it. With a bit of advance preparation like this, Frigga the witch will be able to produce a feast out of thin air, like magic, for the appointed hour tomorrow night. Just you wait and see!'

Standing in the middle of the bustling kitchen, hands on her hips, Frigga continued. 'And they'll need provisions for the hunt, too. There's plenty of smoked fish and meat, but they do like a bit of pudding to fall back on.'

The women all laughed and Elma said, 'Don't we all!'

Margaret looked down at her nut-cracker, fiddling with its awkward screw. It was stiff and difficult to use. The women guffawed to another joke, a wordplay in the local dialect. 'What's tinne?' she asked.

'Holly,' Frigga said, 'but it also means three in the old tongue, or a love triangle, or...'

'What old tongue? You all speak Gaelic.'

'Yes, but the people of these parts didn't always. My mother spoke the old language, as I still do, though many folk have lost the use of it.'

Frigga turned back to her cooking and the blether continued. Margaret interjected when places were mentioned, asking where they were, and also when people's names were used, so the women began to refer to people by title: 'Iain, that's Elma's uncle,' or 'Moran, Frigga's son,' or 'Cormac, husband of Frigga's youngest sister Ishbel,' or 'wee Enya, Frigga's granddaughter.' Many of the people they talked about seemed to be related to Frigga somehow or other.

The social banter came to an abrupt stop when Bjorn walked in through the door from the yard. He started with a barrage of questions for Frigga about food and drink for the evening, and who was here already and who had been told and who wasn't coming. He hadn't noticed Margaret at first, and so stopped suddenly when he realised his wife was sitting shelling nuts at the kitchen table.

'What are you doing here?' he demanded. 'I didn't think I'd

married a kitchen-girl.'

She gave him a foolish grin.

'Will you be joining us tonight, or will you be waiting table?' he asked.

She blushed and retorted, 'I'll have enough waiting to do when you're away hunting. Of course I'll be there tonight, if that's what you want.'

'Well, you'd better get ready,' he said as if to a child, and strode off into the hall, leaving a trail of muddy footprints that set Elma cursing.

Margaret got up.

'Don't worry about them,' Frigga said, gesturing at the nuts. 'Plenty of time this evening. Now, my lady, will you be needing anything?' she asked in mock deference, and without waiting for an answer, she instructed Maeve, 'Take some hot water to our lady's bedroom and don't come back until you're not needed any more.'

'Thank you, Frigga. I wish I had your way with…' Margaret began, but Frigga shushed her, saying,

'You can have your way with anything you please – you're Bjorn's wife, remember.'

Frigga guided Margaret out of the kitchen. Just across the threshold she heard Elma, presumably thinking she was out of earshot, say, 'And if anyone can show you how to have your way, it's him.' Margaret cringed. The door closed on peals of hilarity.

She found herself in the hall, where quite a crowd had already gathered, and headed straight for the bedroom, trying to give an impression of composure. Several of the men greeted her and she nodded at them stiffly, her hair dishevelled from her walk in the wind and her sleeves still rolled up from the kitchen work.

Alone in her room, she stripped off her outer clothes, but it was too cold without them. The fire that had been lit that morning had died away, leaving a couple of half-burned logs in the fireplace. She wrapped herself in her blanket and stood staring helplessly at the charred wood. Seeing a basket of kindling beside the fire, she piled some sticks onto the ashes and blew on them – but succeeded only in getting a lungful of ash. She looked up at the candle burning on the mantlepiece and tried to light one of the thinnest kindlers and set it in the fire, but it quickly went out.

She was about to go down in search of help when a gentle

tap announced Maeve at the door. She bobbed in with a bowl of steaming water for Margaret to wash in.

'Thank you, Maeve. Could you perhaps light the fire while you're here? It's so chilly.'

'Of course,' Maeve replied, reaching for her pocket-knife. 'Just look at this muddle.' She knelt by the fire. She deftly pushed the half-burned logs to the sides, removed the heap of kindling, took a piece and shredded it rapidly. She formed a taper by splitting another kindler, lit it from the candle, and used it to light the shreds. Once they were spitting she gradually laid on a mesh of kindling. It flamed, and she worked up to bigger pieces. Then she moved the half-burned logs in towards the centre and laid one more across the top. Margaret scrutinised her intently, and Maeve turned and blushed at the attention.

'Who taught you to make a fire, Maeve?' asked Margaret.

'I don't recall. I've always done it. I suppose I must have copied my mother in the beginning. Why?'

'No reason.' Margaret looked at the bowl of water and reached for a cloth.

Maeve sat back on her haunches and turned to watch Margaret washing. Margaret looked at her. 'Thank you, Maeve; I'm sure that's all I shall need.'

'Very well – if you're sure?' Maeve got to her feet.

'Yes, thank you.'

Margaret watched Maeve leave, then finished her ablutions. She heard voices outside the room and quickly dried herself. As she splashed on some of her favourite scent, a rose and lavender oil made by the nuns of Saint Andrews, Bjorn walked into the room.

He strode over to her and wrapped his arms round her, burying his face in her neck with exaggerated sniffs. 'You smell like the Queen of the Flowers.' He beamed at her.

She flushed. He had already begun the evening's hunt preparations. She could smell the beer, and his smile was full of boyish play. She couldn't push him away, and he returned to her neck, kissing her, then nibbling at her ear. She squealed. His kisses insisted at her neck, his hands exploring up and down her back.

'Our baby…' she began.

He hushed her. 'Your hair feels beautiful.' He eased his fingers through her hair, giving a little tug with each stroke that sent a shiver into her scalp. She closed her eyes, feeling the skin on her neck and shoulders tingle as the hair brushed it with each movement of his hands.

She opened her eyes and found his, blue and smiling, watching her revel in his fingers. As she began to smile back he kissed her on the lips, one hand on her neck, the other keeping up the rhythm in her hair. She let herself soften under him as he danced her over to their bed, exclaiming and laughing as he robbed her of her remaining clothes.

He didn't wait to remove all of his own, just loosening his breeches, one hand on her skin or her hair at all times, teasing her, drawing her into arousal, and before she was ready he had climbed over and guided himself into her, riding her, his hands still roaming, rushing into a frenzy where he seemed to lose himself, shouting his climax as if in a rage.

Then he was smiling, gentling her face, sliding out of her too soon, kissing her, letting go of her, and lifting himself away.

'I must go, Rainbow; the men are waiting.'

The door swung to behind him. Margaret lay on the bed. A shiver caught her and she pulled a blanket over herself. She listened to the crescendo growing in the hall as the men began to gather.

She heaved herself up, then washed again in the now-lukewarm water, and then sat in her underclothes beside the fire. She put two more logs on and moved one around with a stirring motion, but this only seemed to deaden the fire. She put a peat slab on top. It smoked.

She dressed in dark reds and browns for the evening, and made her way down to the hall where a seat had been prepared for her, next to Bjorn at the head of the table.

The evening was already beginning to be raucous, with beer flowing generously, staunched by a few strategic plates of bread and dripping from the kitchen. Shortly after Margaret appeared, Bjorn stood up on his chair, banging his tankard on the table for attention.

'Men, greetings from your headman and his wife.' His greeting was met with a roar of approval. 'You're all welcome here and I'm proud to offer you a beer under my roof, which, thanks to Iain the

Bat, is still on, despite the storm a month ago.' Another cheer.

'But I know that's not true for you all, and even here in the big house, the Fury that brought the storm wreaked its violence. I'm an ordinary man, I don't go much with superstitions, but you don't need to be a seer to know that there was more than just a wind howling within that storm. There were wolves, and where I'm from that's not something to ignore. I'm not going to sit by and wait for a return visit, to hear stories of the cattle being picked off one here, one there. I won't wait for the day when someone's daughter doesn't come back from the woods where she's been playing. I say we shouldn't wait and let our worries grow. We have to chase the Fury out, hunt the wolves down, send them back to the mountains whimpering. Who'll join me for the hunt?'

The men all shouted at once, roused by the beer and the mention of a threat to their children.

'Does anyone dissent?' Bjorn asked, to a murmur of 'no's.

'I do,' called one voice from the back of the hall.

James strode up to the bottom of the table and stood behind the men, who had to turn their heads to look at him. There was a murmur of disdain, but his poise and the hushes of Iain Kay and his other supporters soon quashed it.

'Very well, James. Voice your doubt, so we can all hear it,' Bjorn said calmly. He had expected this. It was better to have it out sooner than later.

'It is folly, if you ask me, to risk men's lives on a wild chase after wolves long gone. There's nothing to be gained. The men will be missed by their families; they could be more usefully employed repairing the damage from the storm, not chasing a few mangy dogs into the hills. Do you not value your men, Bjorn? Do you want to send them starving into the middle of winter? It's a futile plan whose only result will be hunger and misfortune.'

'So what do you suggest, James? That we all sit around like ducks, waiting to be pounced on? These men are not cowards, they're the bravest in the land. If it's just a few mangy dogs we're after, we'll be home before we've time to get hungry.'

James glowered. 'If you're worrying only about wolves, you've lost your reason. What caused the storm, do you think?'

'I'm sure you'll tell me.'

'It was the hand of God, his furious staff, wielded in disgust at the heathen ways of his subjects. If the wolves return it'll be God's justice, his punishment for this community's wilful ignorance. I say you should save your energy and put it to good use, to build a house here for the worship of God, to honour him and appease his anger. Not go chasing after dogs.'

'It's a good idea, James. I like it. To build a chapel for the worshippers. What do you think, men?' There was a doubtful murmur, but some nods.

'I suggest we do as you say and put our best efforts into building this house for God, immediately after we return from the hunt.' Bjorn was smiling. It was a pushover. 'When the victorious men return, we will celebrate by raising a chapel to thank God for our success, and we will clothe our priest with wolf-skin!' The men roared and banged their mugs on the table.

James sat down, mollified that he'd won all the concession he would get from the mob, and Bjorn rounded off his speech.

'But first, on with the plans for the hunt. I need men to prepare horses. We need to gather our weapons. We need supplies for the journey; all the warm clothes we can wear. We'll spend tomorrow preparing, then we'll feast here at sundown and leave at dawn the next morning. What do you say?'

The men cheered. Frigga, from the kitchen doorway, winked at Margaret.

'I propose a toast to the courage of the men of the Braes. Donald, pass round the whisky. Let's drink to the men who will strike terror into the hearts of the wolves.'

The jug went around the table and its content went into the mugs, which were then raised, ready for the toast.

'To the fearless men of the Braes!' called Bjorn.

'Fearless men of the Braes!' the men replied, downing the sharp spirit.

The hunt was on.

Coll - Hazel

I spotted him approaching along the lochside long before he saw me, and I retreated into the shelter of the trees and watched warily until I was sure it was not wishful thinking. His walk was slower and more awkward than it used to be, but it was still unmistakably the stick-assisted step of the woodcutter – the man the villagers all knew as Coll, but who was just Da to me. The wise old man of the woods, who had delved deeper into the forests than anyone else from the Braes.

Despite being husband to and father of medicine women, he did not live by magic, but had always made his living by his axe and his blades. He knew every tree in the woods with an unmatched intimacy. He knew how every wood worked best, and how to use it to greatest effect. The hazel walking-stick that was tapping along towards me had been cut from a coppice nine years ago and whittled smooth with the knife he had been given by his father, a woodsman before him.

My Da was respected throughout the Braes for his wisdom and knowledge of the woods. As for the spirits: he kept his views to himself, and I suppose that was how he kept himself out of trouble. Unlike my mother and me. But now, with his dear Freya dead and me banished, I could see the strength going out of him and old age rushing to claim its prize.

It was a month since I had seen him last. One time in early winter I had sneaked to his house on a rainy day to take him a bag of his favourite treat, hazel nuts.

The wind was cold out of the north and, though it was clear, the sun was too low to counter the chill wind, and snow clouds threatened over the mountains. I couldn't imagine what would have brought him out to see me on such a harsh mid-winter's day.

I set out and met him as he rounded the rocks where the Coille burn tumbled into the loch. As I hugged him, I was pleased to see he was more vigorous up close than his stiff walking suggested.

'You look well, my little one.' He smiled at me.

'You look well yourself, Da. What brings you here on such a cold day?'

'Aye, it's a cold wind that one, sent by the ice bears!' he quipped, ignoring my question. 'I'm glad of my cow today.'

He was wearing his hairy blond cow-hide coat. My mother had made it for him a few years ago, from our old milking cow, and he had always referred to it as his 'cow' and wore it only when the weather was fierce. 'I think winter's coming,' he joked again.

'Winter's been here for two months already if you ask me,' I replied.

'Well, if you must live in a bird's nest, it'll find you that much quicker,' he said. 'How is it, your treehouse?'

'Oh, don't ask,' I said. 'That storm? Disaster. I took the full brunt. The roof came down in the night and I got soaked. I've patched it up a bit, but it's a mess. It's normally sheltered from the big winds – the south-westerly's no problem, nor the south-east – but that storm seemed to come from all directions at once. I thought it would bring the tree down.'

'Oh, little one, you should have come to stay with me.'

'You know I can't, Da.'

He nodded, and said, 'Well, let's see if we can't get it sorted.'

'You'll be appalled at my patchwork.' I grinned, taking him by the arm. 'But I don't know what to do. I've no tools to speak of, and woodwork has never been my strength.'

'Yes, you'd never guess you were a woodsman's daughter.' He laughed at me. 'It was the same with your mother. I always used to say: if you could sew a house we'd live in a palace and if you had to use hammer and nails to cook, we'd starve! You're just the same. You can do anything with wools and threads and flowers and seeds. A genius with a needle...'

'...and a dunce with a saw,' I finished, sing-song. He'd been saying this to me since as long as I could remember. 'Come on, let's get out of this wind. I can offer you much more comfortable draughts than this. Here, give me that,' I said, taking his rucksack. 'What a weight!'

'It's some things Frigga had me bring for you,' he said, as we set off slowly. 'And she sends you her love, and says her wee grand-daughter – Enya, you know, Beathoc's girl – she never stops talking about you. She's been on for months now, apparently, about the nice lady in the woods, and can she visit you. So Frigga says you and she had better make a plan to bump into each other some day.'

I winced at that. His blithe talk of Frigga, who I'd not seen for months, cut right into me. I remembered the little girl standing by the lochside and saying, 'Don't go' that day, as I fled from the people who had banished me. There was no 'bumping into people' in my position. My eyes prickled and I turned my head away, swallowing. I was determined not to betray to my Da how difficult I sometimes found my new life. He thought I was headstrong and argued too much, and that I should have tried to appease the priest, not challenge him. I hated his criticism.

We approached my shelter under the alder tree, and he laughed out loud at how rough and ramshackle it was. He began to tell me off about it, then stopped. I suppose he realised that this shack was my home; it was all I had to shelter in, and not by choice. His practical instinct took over.

'I'd like to make a project of this,' he said.

I cringed. I didn't want to be one of his projects. Most of them took painstaking years.

'You look thin,' he said, suddenly.

I cracked. 'Leave off me,' I shouted at him. 'What do you expect? Living here. On my own!'

'I didn't mean to criticise,' he protested.

'Yes you did. You always criticise me,' I snapped back at him. The air was buzzing with friction.

'No, I don't!' I think he genuinely thought he didn't.

'You do. You told me not to come here!'

'Well, of course I did. I thought if you could try to make your peace with the priest...'

'With that monster? He killed my mother,' I screamed.

'He did not. You know fine well he didn't.' He looked hurt. He had loved her as much as me, maybe more, and he must have missed her sorely.

'He did so. She was fine until he arrived. He suffocated her, starved her of her spiritual life. He murdered her by breaking her soul.'

'You can't keep saying these things, little one.'

'Don't call me that. You don't understand. I have to keep saying these things. They're true. If I give in, he'll kill me too. He'll kill us all. The spirits will abandon us and then where will we be?'

'Don't you think you can let the spirits decide for themselves? Leave them to their world, and come back to ours, Brigid. Please. Come back to the village.'

'You know I can't do that. They wouldn't have me.'

'You could say you've changed. Agree with the priest for a bit, let things go quiet, just for a while. You don't have to believe it, just say the words.'

I snorted.

'I can't.'

'Why not?'

'I can't say things I don't believe.'

'Of course you can.'

'I cannot, Da. Look at me!' I pulled myself up to my full height and flung my hair back, glaring at him. My indignation surged and I felt strong and free. 'I am the Shaman of the Bear. I dream the dreams of the bears and I speak their stories. I listen to the spirits and I tell what they say. That is my life. I cannot subject myself to anyone except the Mother Bear. I belong to her. You know this, Da. Why do you try to make me deny who I am?'

'You're as headstrong as your mother. I just want you to be safe.'

'I am safe here!'

'I hate to see you hungry and cold out here on your own.'

He looked utterly dejected.

'Och, I'll survive,' I said with a half-smile, realising that I had won the argument and he would push me no further.

'Time for a hot drink,' I said, and gathered some sticks. I lifted the lid of the pot at the edge of the fire to test the water. It was steaming, and before long the fire brought it back to a boil. I tossed some dried peppermint leaves into it. The fresh smell revived both of our moods.

'I'm sorry,' Da said. 'I don't mean to push you. You're a strong woman, and I'm proud of you.'

I blushed, and tears pricked at my eyes. It always embarrassed me when he found himself able to praise, and I was still smarting from the argument. I snorted again, and busied myself with cups.

'I'm just who I am,' I said, sounding more cross than I felt. 'I can't help it.'

He smiled at me. I didn't look at him directly, but I caught his admiring gaze from the side of my eyes. Saying nothing, I spooned honey into his mint tea and stirred it, then handed it to him. He sipped and hummed appreciatively, both hands around the cup.

I poured myself a beaker and he asked me to pass him the bag. He began to bring things out. It was mostly food – a bag of finely-ground oatmeal, a pot of fat, a hessian bag full of dried beans, a precious lump of salt, a few vegetables from Frigga's garden, and a couple of flasks: one of whisky and one of a Frigga special – mead flavoured with sloes. 'The strong one's from me,' he said, 'and the rest's from Frigga.'

'Bless her.'

'This is a pie that came from the big house kitchen,' he said proudly. 'A bit spare from the feast, she told me.'

'What's the feast for?' I asked him.

'Oh, I'll tell you later. That's really why I'm here. It's not just a social call.'

'I guessed not,' I said, under my breath.

'Anyway, Frigga said to ask you if you might be able to do some dyeing of wool, some bright colours? Apparently the new Lady of the big house is keen on colourful clothes, and Frigga thought you would get a good trade with your skills with the herbs and that.'

'It'll be blues and yellows she's after, I'm sure.'

'Frigga mentioned scarlet as well.'

'Oh, that needs crottle and it's hard to find. I'll have to think about that. But I can do a bright yellow with sundew, that's easy, and I've some blaeberries that give a good blue in my copper pot. So tell Frigga I'll be pleased to. I can always do with oats and beans, and the forest is meagre from this time on. Will she want the wool spun too? I've plenty of time on my hands at the moment.'

'She said to ask you that too. There's more wool in the Braes now than the women can spin, since all the new sheep they're breeding.'

'I can't say I'm happy with that. Will they never stop destroying the forest to make pastures? Do they not have enough yet?'

'I don't know, Brigid. I have to say it breaks my heart too, seeing the great oakwoods I've spent my life in grubbed up and burnt for a few scraggy muttons.'

'Fat muttons, surely?'

'Well, I don't know. I'm not convinced the beasts are suited to our weather. They can't get through the winter like the cattle. How is your cow, by the way?'

'She's very well. She had a good season and she's milking well, plenty for me as well as the calf.'

'It must be getting a fair size.'

'She is, fat and happy and loving forest life, though they ran a mile the night of the storm. I eventually found them way down the far end of the loch. They're good company.'

We fell silent, supping our drinks, the essential topics of conversation covered. Except for the big one, the one that had brought him here in the first place. Eventually I looked at him. 'So, do I have to drag it out of you? Tell me about the feast.'

'It's tonight.'

'Don't tell me I'm invited?'

'No, it's not that.'

'Good, because I wouldn't go.' I grinned. 'I've nothing to wear!'

'Oh, that reminds me. Frigga said something about owing you a new coat. And I've got this.' He fished in his pocket and handed me my whalebone beaker with the bear design.

'Wonderful. How's Caphel?'

'He's fine, though more taken with the new religion than ever, seemingly. But it was Enya brought me the beaker. She hid it from the priest when he arrived that day. But unfortunately your cloak wasn't so lucky. I'm afraid he burnt it.'

'I thought I saw a lot of smoke after I left. It wouldn't have burnt well. What a monster he is. That cloak was the one Mother made for me. It was my favourite.' I was crestfallen. 'Ah well. It was only a bit of scraggy mutton, I suppose. I'll make another.'

'Well, I think Frigga and Enya and Caphel may decide that's their responsibility. They're indebted to you.'

'It was the least I could do. Just luck I was out on my boat and saw it happen,' I said. 'Anyway, I'm glad to have my cup back. Thank Enya for that, won't you.' I ducked into my shack and came back out with a tiny wooden bear carving, small enough to enclose inside a clasped hand. 'You can give that to her from me. It's the Good Luck Bear.'

'She'll like that.' He tucked it into a pocket.

'Anyway, what about this feast?'

'It's for a hunt. Tomorrow. They're off to hunt the wolves.'

'By the Great Bear, whatever for? They've gone mad.'

'The night of the big storm, wolves attacked the big house and killed the new Lady's horse.' He told me what had happened that night, and explained Bjorn's plan to take revenge. 'It seems, since getting a wife, that he's losing his good judgement,' he finished.

'Thanks for telling me. You're right, I needed to know. I've heard the wolves a few times recently. They passed here that night, sounding angry, swept along by a Fury. I don't like it. War on the wolves has never solved anything, never brought anything but trouble. I doubt it will be any different this time.'

'I don't know what route they plan, but you don't want to be in their path.'

'Not so they see me, anyway.'

'Don't do anything stupid,' he pleaded.

'I don't know myself what I'll do,' I said gravely. 'I'll need to ask the spirits.'

We fell quiet again and Da surveyed my ruin, then looked around him into the woods.

'We need to build you a new home,' he said, eventually. 'That's just going to leak and leak. Never seal it.'

I felt despondent and must have looked it. The news of the hunt had left me with a sense of doom. I wasn't listening to my Da properly, until I noticed he was getting to his feet. 'Come on,' he said.

'What?'

'I was saying I'll build you a bender. Like I used to use when I was cutting timber deep in the forest. You've plenty of hazel here. Come on. I'll need your strength. Fetch your blade.'

I obeyed him in a daze. He led off towards the nearby stand of hazel trees. It had been regularly coppiced for as long as anyone could remember, for building coracles, making hurdles for animal corrals, weaving big baskets and fishing creels, even walls sometimes. So the multi-stemmed stools, the result of repeated cutting and regrowth from the roots, were well-used and in good shape. Each tree was a bundle of almost straight sticks.

'These are perfect,' Da said. 'You'll have the whole village out here for basket material if I tell them about these. Good hazel's getting short around the village since they grubbed out Coille Ghlinne. But I'll not let on, don't worry.'

'I'm not worried if they do,' I said. 'Actually, you can tell Ishbel I'd love to see her here, and she can come and cut all she wants for her baskets. As long as there are folk cutting them, they'll value them, and let them grow back. The day the people don't need the trees, the forests are doomed.'

He looked at me and seemed impressed by what he heard. 'I wish there was someone saying that at the big house.'

'Well, you tell them, then!'

He nodded. 'I'm not sure anyone will listen to me.' He looked shamefaced. It was probably true. Although respected for his forest lore, he had always been on the outside, frequently away in the forest, a loner. When he was in the Braes, his association with medicine women gave him a distance from the other men. People respected our knowledge of herbs, but feared our connections to the spirit world. We were only welcomed into most people's houses at exceptional times: births, deaths, illnesses, traumas. I supposed most people thought him a bit strange.

His forest instincts seemed to come into play as he moved among the coppice, picking the rods he needed from the stools, cutting them with a few deft strokes of the blade, and then leaving me the tough job of extracting their top end from the tangle of twigs above. I shook, cajoled, twisted and tugged the rods from the clutches of their companions, to a shower of twig ends and nuts and dead leaves. My hair was soon full of debris, and Da laughed at me.

'Now you really are the wild woman of the woods!'

I grinned back. The physical effort was a relief, and the sound of the shaking hazels temporarily drowned out my worries.

Soon we had a heap of stout rods that Da had trimmed of their extraneous twigs. We set off back to the alder with them.

'Where would you like it?' he asked, and together we paced around, choosing a flattish area on the far side of the fireplace. He set about digging holes for the rods with a sharp stone, and sent me off to find some thin willow stems for binding. By the time I got back, he had inserted two rods into holes about ten feet apart and twisted them together into an arc like a rainbow. Now he was forming a ribcage of narrower arches in a row across the rainbow to

75

a height of about six feet. He showed me how to tie the ribs to the spine, fixing the oval structure into place. I watched him, amazed by his skill. He was clearly enjoying himself.

'I've not done this for years,' he confessed, 'but you never lose the knack.' The arches were followed by thinner rods woven horizontally in and out around the structure. As a final touch, he bent a stout rod into a smooth curve and lashed it to two of the uprights to form the frame of a doorway.

'There's your rafters; now all you need is a roof.' He looked at me. 'I used to use a good strong hemp cloth. You could just throw it over and there you'd have it, but it's not the kind of thing you can rustle up, I don't suppose. You'll need to thatch it.'

'I've got skins,' I said. 'Any number of good deer skins. Til brought them to me in the autumn, as a kind of payment.'

Da lifted his eyebrows quizzically.

'I healed his sister, Tess, after she lost her bairn last summer,' I explained. 'She was bleeding terribly. He thought she was dying. Anyway, he was so desperate he came and fetched me one night and begged me to help her. Come and look!'

I led him into my shack. 'I sleep on them. I've nowhere else to put them. I was going to make boots to trade, but I'll keep myself dry instead.'

I started peeling them off the heap, one by one. 'I put the toughest on the bottom. I'll start with them.'

Together we hauled out the hides. Da seemed impressed, both with my riches – deer hide was valuable – and with my connection to Bjorn's chief hunter.

Then he suddenly began to laugh.

'What's so funny?'

'The skins. Just before the harvest fire, James the priest went spare. He was collecting the tithe for the church – robbery, if you want my opinion. Anyway, he'd taken everything he could from everyone: timber, food and skins. He'd more skins than I'd ever seen in one place, all stacked together in the great hall in the big house. Then some went missing. Some deer hides, I seem to remember. A dozen, would it be?'

That made me smile. 'Well, well. Good for Til, stealing them back from the church. He didn't tell me that; said they were his payment for a hunt last year, bless him.'

'That's not what James said. I don't think they ever found out who did it, and I'll bet they never suspected Til. Afterwards, James started branding everything with his emblem.'

'Which is?'

'Ram's horns.'

'That figures.'

We continued to chuckle about my windfall, and began to lay the skins onto the framework. I fetched my bone needle-case and chose a bronze leatherwork needle to lash the skins to rods at strategic points. 'I'll put a covering of thatch on top, I think,' I said. 'You never know who might catch sight of my contraband if I leave it like this.'

'You'll be wise to. Toss a load of bracken over it to start with. Remember the hunt may come by tomorrow.'

'Leave that bit to me. You'd better start to think about getting home before dark,' I reminded him. 'Let's have something to eat first.' We tied a few more lashings, and Da looked at the bender with satisfaction.

'That'll keep you a bit more snug,' he said, pleased.

'Thanks, Da.' I gave him a hug, then turned to my fire and chucked on a few sticks. 'Let's eat the big house's pie to celebrate.'

'Seems appropriate.' Da sat down to join me and accepted the piece of pie I handed him, followed by a beaker of the sloe mead from Frigga. 'Here's to the generosity of the big house and to the hazel trees for my new home!'

'I'll drink to that,' he replied, tucking into the pie with relish and slurping down his first mouthful with mead. Then, after a few more gulps, he said, 'It's good to have a daughter, sometimes.'

I didn't reply at first. He wasn't looking at me, he was gazing into the fire, but I knew what he was thinking, what he was asking me, without saying it.

'I'm sure it is, Da.' It was all I could say. I would not be drawn on the topic. It was too difficult to speak about it with him. My own desire for a child, for a daughter of my own, sometimes threatened to swallow me up. It was never far from me, in my dreams. Sometimes it dominated my thoughts for day after depressed day. I wished endlessly for a daughter to love, to play with, to care for, to pass my knowledge onto. But life refused me that opportunity. There was no-one striding out of the forest to join me. No warm body to hold me at night. No father for my shaman child.

Our conversation foundered. I was deep in thought; his simple remark had wrecked the easy warmth that had built up as we'd made the bender together.

'More mead?' I suggested.

He shook his head. 'I'd better get walking.'

I nodded.

We got to our feet and I thanked him for everything, remembering each of the gifts, reminding him of the messages to Frigga and Enya. I accompanied him as far as the Coille burn, chatting about the weather. Before I turned back, I promised to visit him to collect some fleeces for spinning and dyeing.

As I walked home my mind was churning, already preparing for the ceremony I knew I must perform before the hunt set out, to prepare the spirits, to warn them, to try to appease them, or at least to understand what the Fury was all about and what its next move might be.

Before I set out, I tossed bracken all over my new shelter.

I strode along the path I had worn up through the wooded slope to the brow of the hill at the back of my place, until I met the main path that followed the contours around the edge of the loch then struck off up to the north, leaving the loch behind. It was a strong path, just above the top of the treeline, used by the villagers who drove their cattle up here in the summer to graze on the sweet herbs and seek a breeze to keep away the midges. After a couple of miles the path veered off to the east again, moving to the higher ground – but a smaller path slipped down into the forest.

I paused, watching the sun skirt the horizon, its late afternoon light stretching long and low over the forest to the sea beyond. The light glittered on an inlet, a small sea loch where the ocean cut into the forest. There was another inlet further north, and between them was a distinct promontory of woodland. The people of the Braes called it Ardarroch, for it was an oakwood, though full of a variety of other trees too. It also had an older name: Gremara. A ritual name in the old language that meant 'sleeping bear'. It was traditionally a sacred grove, revered by the shamen as the winter resting place of bears, and feared by hunters for the same reason.

I noticed with alarm that on the southernmost tip of the promontory, the tip closest by boat from the Braes, the forest was thin. The villagers had been felling oaks there. I shuddered at the sacrilege. Was nothing respected any more? No wonder there was Fury loose in the world. The balance was breaking, the old rules being cast aside, too little effort being made to listen to the spirits.

An owl shrieked '!!' nearby. The day was fading. Its mate, further down in the forest, replied with a comforting 'woo-oo-hoo'. There was another worried '!!' and again 'woo-oo-hoo' came back, closer this time.

I felt a tremor of fear go through me, and I imitated the second owl. 'Woo-oo,' I called, a bit hesitantly. Then again, more clearly 'woo-oo-hoo,' trying to get the right pulse into the hoot. The first owl shrieked once more. I replied, and the owl fluttered up, perching on a branch just above me, eyeing me.

'Helloo-oo-hoo!' I said to it, in my best imitation of an owl. The owl blinked, swivelling its head, taking in the surrounding forest as if to signal *This is mine*. I stayed where I was, nodding once to the owl, which continued to stare.

'The people are going to hunt the wolves,' I told it.

The owl shrieked.

'Will you tell the bear, or shall I?' I asked.

It sat motionless, with its cool eyes fixed on me.

Then a voice came from below in the forest, perhaps from the other owl, perhaps from the forest itself. It was my invitation to enter.

I shivered: the sweat from the walk was chilling.

I tip-toed down the path into the forest. It was steep in places and I had to hang onto trees for balance. The ground was strewn with leaves which crunched and rustled as I walked, try as I might to be as silent as possible. Sometimes I caught a whiff of the sea, mingled with the earthy smell of forest soil and rotting leaves. The path wound down the slope in a wide arc to the north side of the peninsula, then curved south into the forest's heart. At a low point it divided again, the main track continuing south-east and a much smaller trail leading off down the peninsula. I took the small one.

When I reached the big holly tree in the grove of hazels, I stopped there and began to chant softly to myself, circling the holly. It was the only tree in the wood with any green leaves left on it, though the hazels and oaks still kept many of their dead leaves and would do so until the spring. It was getting dark. Soon the moon would rise;

it was not quite full yet, not until tomorrow. Of course, I realised, the hunt would run on the night of the full moon. The first star was out. I caught its blink between the holly leaves.

I prepared myself to begin the magic as the moon rose. It would be a simple ceremony. There was danger, a risk in it, I knew. But that was inevitable. It was my task to take that risk, my role as shaman.

The owls hooted again, and a bat fluttered around the grove as if it had come to observe the ritual I was about to perform.

I looked to the horizon, and judged that the time was almost right. Sure enough, through the lattice of branches the moon gave a first glint, its silver blade unsheathing from the earth. I circled the holly a third time in silence, then picked up a handful of berries from the floor under the three-trunked tree. I put one in my mouth, chewed, spat out the seed, and thanked Mother Earth. Then I ate another, and thanked Sister Moon. After the third, I made my request to the bear spirits.

The moon grew round, and as it swelled its pale white light set the trees to shadow casting. I sensed presences ghosting into the spaces between the moonbeams, tall forms wavering and small scuttles among the undergrowth. I could feel their eyes on me.

I took a hessian bundle out of my pocket and set it on a rock. The moon shifted and its light shone on the cloth-wrapped package, making it glow. I took this as the sign I needed from my sister spirits. I began to remove my clothes: first my cloak, then boots, then all my warm woollen layers, until I stood naked in the glade.

I folded all of my clothes into a neat roll, tied it with my belt, and shivered up the slope towards the cliff with the great overhanging rowan. There I unwrapped from the package a honeycomb, dripping and full of the sweetest nectar of late summer heather. I held it in one hand and crept towards the round opening at the base of the cliff.

Hunkering down, I crawled, as quietly as I could into the bear's den, my hand outstretched with my offering for its sweet-toothed sleeping inhabitant.

'I've brought you a gift, Sister Bear.'

Queirt - Apple

When Coll got back to the Braes, dusk was gathering. He didn't stop at his hut. The wind was raw and he was tired after his day's exertions, but he carried on until he reached Frigga's place, hopeful that she might be found there when he saw smoke coming out of the chimney. But when he rapped on the door and pushed it open there was no shout from the great-hearted woman, only two pale faces turning to look at him from the fireside: the two children, Caphel and Enya, alone as usual, keeping themselves warm on this bitter day.

'Where's Frigga?' he demanded, a bit fiercely. The children looked scared of him. He regretted his sharpness.

'Is she up at the big house?' he asked, more gently. They nodded. 'And Donald?' They nodded again.

'Splendid!' he said, trying to sound cheerful. 'Would you like to come to help me find them?' They both looked baffled and shook their heads.

He realised that in their minds he was a strange man of the woods, and he would need to pull off some kind of softener to get them to trust him. They had clearly been instructed to stay put. Fancy Frigga leaving them here on their own on the night of the feast, he thought. Then he remembered the notoriety Caphel had gained from cutting the rowan tree, and his drowning incident. Coll could understand his reluctance to go to the big house. But the little girl?

'Do you know where I can find some apples?' he asked them. They looked even more baffled, and Caphel shook his head.

Then Enya piped up, 'I know!' and jumped to her feet. 'You're Brigid's Da, aren't you?' she asked him.

'I am,' he said, proudly.

'My Ma was her friend,' she said adamantly. 'My Ma's dead now but when she was alive Brigid still lived here and they *cooked things up* together.'

'Shut yourself,' Caphel shouted at her. 'We're nothing to do with her.'

'We are so,' Enya said. 'Ma was friends with her, and, and you're her Da so I'm friends with you.' Her logic was unstoppable and she finished with a triumph. 'There's apples in the barrel in Frigga's byre.'

Donald's was one of the few homes in the Braes with a building for cattle separate from the dwelling hut. It had originally been Donald's hut before he married Beathoc and moved in with her and Frigga, and since then it had served dual purpose as forge and byre. Setting off manic barking from Donald's ferocious terriers, Enya led Coll out to the byre. She opened up the door and hushed quietly to the cattle within, who lowed anxiously at the disturbance. She trotted confidently over to the corner and climbed on sacks to point to the raised barrel in one corner.

'They're in there,' she said. On the barrel were two full sacks of grain, which he had to heave down before prising off the lid. Inside, among sawdust, his fingers found the last of the apples. He picked out three good ones, but Enya was watching him.

'And one for Brigid,' she insisted.

He smiled at her. Frigga was right: this wee girl was smitten with hero-worship. He selected a fourth apple, then replaced the lid.

'Hold out your hand,' he said to Enya, and placed a fruit in her cupped fingers. He put two down on the ground and tucked the fourth away in his pocket. 'For Brigid,' he said with a wink.

As his hand went into his pocket he touched Brigid's gift, and drew it out.

'Look! Here's a present for you from her!'

It was like a magic trick, as if the apple had turned to wood. Enya's eyes widened as he handed her the little wooden bear.

'She thanks you for returning her cup. She's very grateful,' he said. 'You know, they say that's what an apple signifies: give a gift, and your generosity will always be returned.'

This nugget of lore was lost on Enya, who couldn't take her eyes off the bear. She held it with reverence, as if it would break if she squeezed it.

'For me?' she asked with a squeak.

'For you.' He nodded, patting her gently on the head, then turned to toss the sacks back onto the barrel. Picking up the apples, he ushered her out of the dark byre into the gloaming outside.

'Come on, lass, it's cold out here!'

They crossed back into the house and Enya rushed up to the fireplace, giving her apple to Caphel and showing him her bear. Coll proffered her another apple and they all fell to munching, Enya chattering between and during bites about the magical Brigid and the bear she'd given them in return for the apple, a big smile over her face.

All Caphel could say was, 'You'd better watch what you say when Da gets home. He'll have the hide off you.'

Coll winced. Caphel sounded as if he was speaking from experience. Donald's reputation was certainly fierce: he had become a hard-drinking man since Beathoc's death.

They fell silent, intent on chewing their apples. Caphel ate his core, then accepted Enya's offer of hers and ate that as well. Coll threw his on the fire, to a protest from Caphel. 'I would have had that.'

'Sorry, I did it without thinking.'

There was a chapping on the door, then it swung open and a young woman poked her head around the frame.

'Hello there!' she said brightly. 'It's yourself, Coll. How's it going?'

'Very nicely, thank you. And how are you, Elma?'

'You see it all,' she replied. 'Are you watching these two?'

'I don't know. Am I?' he asked them.

'Not really,' replied Enya. 'You're just visiting, aren't you?'

Elma smiled at Enya's attempt to be grown-up, and stepped into the room, shutting the door behind her. 'Well, I've been sent all the way down from the big house with instructions from the headman's new wife to gather all the children and bring them up to join in the feast. There's to be no-one missed out. And Bjorn, you'll be pleased to hear, says he particularly wants to see Enya there. So there you are: a special invitation for you from the headman.'

Enya's eyes lit up. 'Why me?'

'Don't ask me.' Elma laughed, leaning against the bundle of coats hooked onto the back of the door. 'I'm just the messenger.'

'I'm not going,' announced Caphel, turning to face the fire.

'Aw, Caphel, I was told to bring all the children. It'll be a really big feast, with music, stories and everything. You must come, it'll be good fun.'

'Nah,' he scowled.

'Oh, go on, Caphel – please come.' Enya tugged at his sleeve but he jerked his arm away from her.

'Leave me be. I don't want to.'

'Well, I can't force you,' Elma said, dismayed. 'What do you think, Coll?'

'It's none of my business, really, but I'd say let the lad choose what he wants to do. There's no point in him coming and being miserable. Do you have something to eat here, lad?'

Caphel lifted the lid on a pot of stew next to the fire. It smelled good. Frigga never left her hearth empty.

'You'll not starve then,' he said.

Caphel half-grinned at Coll.

'Well, come up later if you change your mind.' Elma tightened her coat around her.

'I won't,' said Caphel.

Enya rushed to get her cloak from the door behind Elma, then reached up for a string of beads that was hanging on a hook on the wall.

'They're pretty,' Elma said as she helped to fasten them.

'They're my wishing beads,' Enya said. 'They make me happy.' She smiled her blithe smile, which seemed to fill her face so easily, and both Elma and Coll beamed back at her. Coll thought of his daughter's words: 'She'll make a good witch.' An enchantress, more like, he thought. Every adult she met seemed to fall under her spell.

'Come on then, let's go to the feast,' Enya commanded. 'See you, Caphel.'

'Bye,' he said, more cheerfully now, looking glad to be off the hook.

'Will you take her up, Coll?' asked Elma. 'I've to round up any other children I can find.'

'Of course. See you later.' So they set off up the hill, the little girl hand in hand with the old woodcutter, the pair of them chatting away like old friends.

By the time they reached the big house, Coll had told Enya all about Brigid's new bender and recounted the tale of when Brigid was Enya's age and her mother had taken her out into the forest to meet her totem animal, the bear. Enya was enthralled by the story of the bear, pushing Coll with all sorts of questions he could not answer.

'You'll need to ask Brigid herself,' he said for the third time.

'But I can't,' Enya wailed.

'Oh, we'll see about that,' said Coll with a twinkle in his eye. 'I've no doubt you've not met her for the last time. But don't you go talking about her in here,' he warned.

'I know,' Enya said, sagely. 'She's banished from our thoughts.'

Where had she heard that, Coll wondered? She glanced up at him, precocious and charming, and he winked back. He could see she was playing with the wooden bear in her pocket, her fingers rolling it round and round.

A big crowd was gathered in the great hall. Coll and Enya were met with greetings from all sides, some people noting with surprise the arrival of the motherless child with the father of their banished medicine woman. Enya ran up to Frigga and received a hug, and then with more reticence approached her father, who patted her hand. Donald was drunk enough to be amiable, joking with the men. He shifted aside on his bench and she sat down beside him, chattering about Coll to him and the other men, who all grinned foolishly back at her.

Coll watched her with amusement. With her charm, she was clearly able to blether with anyone. He slipped into the kitchen to find a hot drink. Then he took his cup back into the hall and sought out a quiet place by the fire where he could watch the throng.

As Enya sat enchanting the men, Bjorn approached their table. He tousled Enya's hair and she turned her unfailing smile on him.

'Hello, Donald. Hello, Enya. I've a favour to ask you.'

Donald beamed, and nodded like a horse with a nosebag.

'I need a pretty girl to be the Queen of the Hunt.'

The men looked surprised. 'What's wrong with your wife?' blurted Eachan.

'Margaret wishes the honour to go to one of the girls of the Braes,' Bjorn lied. In fact Margaret had refused, claiming it was against her religion, siding with her brother in opposition to the hunt. They had had a difficult morning. A strife was building between them that he did not understand. But her refusal gave Bjorn an opportunity to fulfil his desire to approach the little motherless child who so

85

attracted him.

She held out her hand to him and, with a tilt of her head, asked, 'Me?!'

'Aye!' Bjorn scooped her fingers up with both paws. 'Will you be my hunting queen and wish us all good luck for tomorrow?'

Enya withdrew her hand, suddenly shy. 'What do I have to do?'

'Just smile and be pretty and sit with me at the top table.'

She looked dubiously at Donald, who was thrilled. 'Thank you for the honour, sir,' he said.

'It's no honour to you, Donald, it's your daughter I'm after,' Bjorn said, to laughter from the men. 'But no doubt you'll earn your honours tomorrow. Do you accept, my Queen?' he asked Enya with mock stateliness, and she, rising to the role, said pompously, 'I do!' and rose to her feet in her childish imitation of a regal manner, to the guffaws of all around her. Blushing, she followed Bjorn to the high table.

He held her by the hand and asked her, 'Will you wish me luck tomorrow?' She nodded. He was a lovely man when you got close to him, with big blue eyes and a friendly smile, a gentle bear of a man. And he smelled of apples.

A sudden urge came over her. She had a special thing for good luck, which she could let him have, if he really needed it. A doubt presented itself, but she put it aside. Rummaging in her pocket, she found what she wanted, and she reached out her hand and offered it to Bjorn. She said, 'This is my Good Luck Bear. You can borrow him, if you like.'

'Well, thank you,' Bjorn said, with a small bow to her. 'I've never borrowed a good luck bear before. I shall treasure it and make sure I bring it back to you safely.'

He took the little wooden bear delicately between his thumb and forefinger then let it drop into his palm. He examined it closely. 'It's a very fine carving,' he said, impressed by the exquisite detail. 'Where did you get this?'

Enya was dumbstruck. She couldn't tell him it was a gift from Brigid, but she couldn't think of a lie to cover herself.

He waited for her to reply, wondering if she was too young to remember – and then he realised it might have been a present from her mother and therefore a difficult memory. Covering himself, he said brightly, 'Why would you remember? It's no matter. It's your good luck bear and it's very special. I am honoured, Enya. Thank you.'

Relieved to be let off, she gave him her widest smile and he grinned back.

'Come on, let's find a throne for the Queen of the Hunt!' He led her up to the high table and showed her to a seat on his left side, opposite Margaret who was seated at his right hand.

Then he excused himself. 'I'll be back soon. I need a quick word with my leaders before the feast begins.'

Bjorn strode away to a table in the corner where Til, Bran and Iain Kay were deep in discussion. He signalled to Donald to join them and tapped Eachan, who was chatting with Moran, on the shoulder. They got up and followed Bjorn. The seven men put their heads together, Bjorn firing questions, the others nodding to confirm that their preparations had been made, or announcing numbers of one thing or another.

'So, there'll be twenty men on the hunt, with six ponies for carrying supplies, and trophies if we're successful. Are we all ready?' Bjorn asked.

'All the garrons are in good fettle,' said Iain Kay, who had spent much of the day checking their feet and teeth. 'Will you take your stallion?'

'No, it's still too jumpy for a hunt, and the local ponies will do much better on the hill ground.'

Iain nodded. 'I think that's wise.'

'And the men?' Bjorn looked at Eachan. 'There's nothing worse than watching the men walk the soles out of their boots and cripple themselves.'

'As far as I can tell, they're all booted well enough,' Eachan said with a frown. They all knew that some of the villagers had not had new boots for a couple of years. 'But most of the leather I tanned went to the church,' he added grumpily, reminding Bjorn of the complaints the cobbler had made at the time of James' great tithe. 'They all have plaids and gloves and good socks so there should be none of us freezing at least,' he added.

'And hats?' Bjorn asked. Eachan nodded. 'Oats?' he asked Moran, Frigga's son, who came the nearest a man could to understanding the big house's food stores. He was a chubby fellow with twinkling blue eyes, a chuckle always trying to break out over his face at the least excuse. He was Enya's uncle, and had the same cheerful nature as her.

'Aye, and we've enough bread to feed the village, and crowdie and malt loaf. My Ma thinks we'll not find anything on this hunt. She's no faith at all in our skills, so we'll not starve even if we don't catch a rabbit.'

'Fine. Weapons?' Bjorn turned to Donald.

'Enough. We're not going to war.'

Bjorn nodded. 'All the men have a good blade?'

'Of sorts,' Donald muttered, nodding. Some were the sickles they cut their oats with and some were billhooks for cutting wood. But at least the men would all have something to wield if they did get among wolves.

'So, Bran, are we ready?' Bjorn asked, finally.

His blond cousin grinned back at him. He was an ugly man, with a nose deformed from many fights in his youth and one ear distorted by years of wrestling. He was thick-set and formidable, Bjorn's loyal companion and second-in-command. Most, though not all, of the women fled his advances and parents tried to keep their daughters out of his sight wherever possible. He was the father of several of the kitchen children.

'You're forgetting the most important thing,' he reminded Bjorn. 'The dogs. Til's bringing his five hounds and I've Steel and Greybeard.' He was referring to his two ferocious wolfhounds. Til's hounds were fit and well-trained, but mostly used for hunting deer. 'We've Donald's badger dogs and I think two of the other men's dogs might be useful. That's twelve. Til thinks we can get them to work together.'

Til nodded. 'It's a lot of dogs, but we might need them,' he said in his quiet voice. 'Wolves fight hard; you need a pack. We'll need to work them hard together as we travel, get them used to being a team.'

'That's if Steel doesn't just eat them all for breakfast,' Bran joked. His youngest dog was as notorious a pugilist as its owner.

Til shook his head. 'We'll need more muzzles. I've only eight and we need them all to be kept in check or we'll never get anywhere.'

Donald said, 'I've three for mine.'

'I'll ask the Bat,' Til said, referring to Iain the thatcher, whose dislike of dogs was well-known. The men laughed and Til looked surprised, his thin face crumpling into a quizzical frown. 'What's so funny? He'll know exactly who keeps their mutt muzzled. It's the only way to get your rafters mended, believe me!'

Bjorn smiled. 'I love your lines of reasoning, Til.'

Til unwound his lanky frame from the bench and strode quickly over to Iain the Bat, who was playing a betting game with Donny, one of his two teenage sons, and his friend Darach. After a quick exchange, Til strode out to the kitchen and returned shortly. 'Elma says Phitir had one for his old dog and she has it in her house. She's sent her wean to fetch it.'

'Good, good,' Bjorn said gratefully to Til, watching the tall man fold himself back into his bench.

'So are we ready?' Bjorn asked again. There were nods all round the table. 'Fine. Let's get the feast underway.' The men rose and Bjorn jumped onto the table and stamped his feet. All eyes in the hall turned to him as he clapped his hands above his head. Alan, the fiddler, and Cormac, on bodhran, stopped playing.

'Friends, get yourselves to the tables. Let's feast!'

A cheer went up and eighty or so men, women and children began to shuffle furniture and arrange themselves at the hall tables. The men took themselves to their various families, with Bran and Bjorn heading to the top table. 'Join us, Til,' Bjorn said, to a quiet nod from the hunter.

They took their seats, Bran next to Margaret, much to her chagrin. Til was put next to Enya, and they each looked thoroughly pleased with their dinner companions. James completed their table, unsmiling opposite Bjorn, his back to the rest of the room, sitting prim in expectation of a call to lead the host in a prayer before the meal would begin.

To his evident displeasure he was not called upon. Instead, Bjorn waited until everyone in the hall had found a seat, then, to a nod from Frigga at the kitchen door, he jumped once again onto his chair, raised his mug and bawled to the throng. 'Does everyone have a drink?'

The jugs had been traipsing up and down the tables for a while. He was answered by scores of raised goblets, drinking horns and cups. For a brief moment he was amazed that the big house possessed so many vessels, then he realised that most had probably come from houses in the Braes. He regained his focus and smiled at the crowd of excited faces.

'You all know why you're here. Tomorrow, twenty brave warriors of the Braes will follow me into the mountains, where we will hunt down the wolves which brought terror here in the last great storm. We leave at dawn. But tonight we forget fighting and bravery. Tonight is about friendship and merriment. There are no heroes tonight. But there is one special person, one among us who will remind us of summer flowers on this winter night, one who has promised to wish the hunt good luck. She is pure, innocent and kind, the very opposite of a wolf.'

Pulling Enya up to stand on her chair, he went on. 'I name Enya Queen of our Hunt. Let her bring us good fortune in the days to come. So, my neighbours and friends, my loyal and dear people, let's drink to the Queen of the Hunt and then feast to be ready for the adventure at dawn tomorrow. To Enya!'

'To Enya!' came the reply from the mass. The wee lass beamed and blushed and gazed adoringly at Bjorn, the hero chief who had exalted her to this place of honour for no apparent reason. He showed her the bear which he held cupped in his left hand.

Then he got down from his chair and helped her down, as the kitchen women arrived with the first plates heaped high with vegetables and a huge platter with a spitted pig already half-carved and ready for eating. They loaded their plates and ate, passing on new dishes of nuts, shellfish, stewed venison, vegetable pies and leafy greens as they kept arriving from the kitchen, taking what they wanted and passing the rest on down the other tables. Til and Bran did the handing on of plates until they tired of it, and roped Elma in to do the job, which she did much more fairly than they had done.

The roar of talk died to a mutter as the hall feasted, and Bjorn waved to Alan and Cormac to start up again and keep them entertained. The plates stopped arriving after a while, and they finished with bowls of honey, sweet cakes, crowdie and fruit preserves. Enya toyed with a cake, but was too full to make much of it. On both sides of her Til and Bjorn munched apples and she grinned with the memory of the apples that she and Coll had stolen that afternoon.

'Do wolves like apples?' she asked Bjorn, who shook his head.

'Wolves like to eat little girls!' he replied with a wicked grin and a tickle, making her squeal. 'That's why we're going to hunt them. But first, my Queen,' he said, swallowing his mouthful of apple and tossing the core away behind him, 'I want you to start the dancing.'

He waved to Alan, who came over with his fiddle. 'A slow one to start us off,' he said, and pulled Enya to her feet. 'Will you join us?' he asked Til, who looked across at Margaret. She smiled warmly, keen to avoid dancing with Bran, who looked equally pleased not to be pulled in. So Til also got up and led Margaret to the clear end of the hall, following Bjorn and Enya, who looked utterly embarrassed.

'I can't,' she remonstrated. Bjorn simply smiled down at her.

'It won't hurt, trust me!' He bent down and said, 'Put your arm round me, like that, that's it,' and then, taking her other hand, led her off in a slow dance. She allowed herself to be pulled along, gazing up at this dreadful, wonderful man. She cast awkward glances at Margaret who was gliding behind them led by Til, whose tall, slim build gave him a natural grace, but who still looked not quite at ease. He winked at her. Soon they were joined by other couples, and the floor filled. Finally, thankfully, the tune ended.

'Thank you, my Queen. That was a pleasure. Now, I wonder if you'll allow me to dance with my wife?'

She nodded eagerly and almost ran off the floor, followed nearly as rapidly by Til, who asked her, 'Are you as glad as I am that's over?' They grinned like conspirators and he said, 'Do you think the Queen of the Hunt might be able to command some whisky for the hunters from the kitchen?'

She nodded at him. A chance to escape, to Frigga and the kitchen women. 'I'll try.'

'That's good enough for me.' He laughed as she turned tail and trotted off to the safety of skirts and cooking smells, where she contrived to stay for the remainder of the evening. Bjorn soon forgot about her as he danced with his wife and then several of the other women. He would have danced again with Margaret, but he found her embroiled at the table in an argument between Bran and James about the merits or otherwise of the hunt, which took them a jug of whisky and several hours to fail to resolve, by which time the hall was clearing and the fire had died down, and Enya and Frigga were long gone home to their beds.

❦ ❦

I lay in the cave beside the bear. Her soft head rested on her front paws and it was hard to resist stroking her, tickling behind her little ears. I listened to the rhythm of her breath, felt it sweet on my hand as I placed the honeycomb at the tip of her claws. Her nose twitched. Her eyes half opened but remained vacant, then fell back into slumber. The thick pelt on her side lifted and fell, lifted and fell with her slow breaths. I began to think about what Da had told me, about the storm and the hunt, but the warm scent of bear brought memories of my mother. I drifted.

I dreamed that a frog had leapt onto my naked belly and sat there looking at me, intently. I was floating on some kind of raft down a river that flowed deep and green. The river had come a long way, out of a vast forest, and it would soon meet the ocean. On the bank stood brown bears on their hind legs, like a guard of honour, saluting me as I sailed past. Looking behind me I saw my mother following on another raft, her hair loose and her body surrounded by flowers, just as she had been the day she was buried. Behind her came my grandmother, and a line of rafts stretched back up the river as far as I could see, each carrying the body of the previous shaman of the bear. In front of me, the river was empty. As I noticed this, the raft passed the last of the bears. It was smaller than the others. I realised this was because it was hunched, and I saw it was wounded in the neck, gushing blood. I cried out to it, but the river carried me on. There was nothing I could do. The frog jumped down from my belly and plopped into the water, swimming back towards the bear, and then there was only me, and the long line of medicine women behind me, being carried out towards the ocean on the snaking river, through a dusty, featureless plain.

I woke. It was still dark, and my nose filled with musk. I made out the entrance of the cave and stiffened away from the mountainous presence of the bear beside me, who snickered and grunted as if she too was coming round. The honeycomb lay untouched beside her snout.

92

Barely a handspan from my face were her ferocious claws. Horror choked me. I tried to breathe as quietly as I could, but each lungful seemed to rasp and croak and echo around the cave. My body twitched as I tried not to move a muscle, and sweat trickled down under my breast. I became aware of pain in my back. In my sleep I had flung my left arm out behind my head and it was stiff and numb. I tried to lift it back down and it sizzled and coloured sparks prickled inside my head. I lay immobilised, my throat tightening, feeling sick. I called on the Mother Bear to get me safely out.

A deep huff broke my frozen spell and I began to edge myself down the cave wall towards the dull light of the outside world. The bear growled quietly but did not move. Reaching the cave mouth, I grabbed my bundle of clothes and stumbled away, shivering hard, hardly able to balance on my numb legs, my heart pounding, back to the normal human world of fear of large carnivores, as if the trance of communion with the bear had never happened.

I had done all I could.

I had taken my sense of doom to the bear, and through my dream the spirits had given me a message. Understanding it was my next challenge. Was this bear the one I had seen wounded, the last bear on the bank of my dream river? I felt sure it was: each of us the ends of our lines. Now I had to carry my act through to its conclusion. Gratitude must be shown to the spirits. I must not run away.

Few of my line had ever done what I had: slept with the sleeping bear; although my grandmother had told me about how her mother had done so, to learn how to make peace with the first Viking headman.

There was thick mist billowing through the forest just above tree height. I knew the moon must be there somewhere to cast this eerie light and I peered until I made out its disc, glowing dimly through the fog, casting a ring of purple like a bruise in the bandaged sky.

Fumbling, I put on all my clothes and, trying to stay calm, picked up a handful of holly berries. Dropping them one by one on the forest floor I tip-toed back up towards the bear's cave, finished the ritual bloodline between tree and cave with one last berry gift by the entrance stone, thanking the bear spirits for my vision.

Inside, I was sure I could hear the sound of licking. I had disturbed the bear enough for her to detect the honeycomb. I smiled to myself and crept away, following the path by which I had come, up out

Mandy Haggith

of the forest, letting the hard physical work of the slope warm me,
mulling over what I had dreamed, and what I had done, and what
it might mean.

    sister bear
    dreaming
    river flowing
    muddy blood red

    frog jump
    splash!

    ripples…

✝

MUIN - BRAMBLE

The hunt left at grim dawn. The big house was an island in mist. There were mutterings from the men, many of whom had their own internal fog to deal with after their over-indulgence at the feast. It was an inauspicious start.

Bjorn was in good spirits nonetheless, cajoling the men into last-minute preparations, assuring them that the cloud would lift and the trail was strong.

For the first hour they strolled through the woods and down to the shore, past the empty fields that belonged to some of the villagers, then followed the same shoreline path that Coll had taken to Brigid's place. It was easy going, and the men began to relax into jokes. Their plan was to head north-east into the mountains, camping by nightfall and beginning their hunt for the wolves in earnest the following day.

At the Coille Burn, the path branched and they struck on up the slope that followed the burn away from the lochside and away from Brigid's shelter. Some of the men may have thought about their banished medicine woman – all of them knew she was living nearby – but none mentioned her.

The men walked, mainly in single file, Bjorn at the front, strolling with customary ease. Bran stomped beside him, with Donald and Eachan just behind – both strong fit men. Donald had new boots, already starting to rub sore in some places, and his hangover made him even more dour than usual, his eyes dark and his mouth in a snarl. Eachan seemed to be closer to dancing than walking, enjoying the striding out, his hat set jauntily on his head and his stick tapping his way along the track. He kept his cheerful thoughts to himself.

Behind them came Iain Kay leading the first of the ponies, and after him five more followed, carrying their supplies. Moran guided the last pony with a gaggle of men where the craic was best, out of earshot of the leaders. Til, with the help of Lachlan and Ro Moine, two brothers who lived out at a cottage on the south side of the loch and who often joined Til on his stag hunts, brought up the rear with the pack of excited dogs that were muzzled to stop them from fighting.

As the hunting gang wound its way up the twisting path away from the lochside it spread out, the ponies heaving their loads, the less fit men panting and dropping behind the others. Til found the pace maddeningly slow at the back, but whiled his time away observing the marks and scat of animals, or at least, those that survived the trampling of the line in front.

Halfway up the slope he saw a figure lurking almost out of sight in the shelter of a hawthorn tree, watching them. It seemed that no-one else had noticed. He strained to make out who or what it was and then, with a flicker of recognition, saw Brigid nod briefly to him in acknowledgement of his gaze. He marvelled that she could squat so motionless, merging almost invisibly into the trunk of the tree. He got Lachlan's attention and pointed out the figure to him. Perhaps at that moment the mist swirled more densely, but as he turned back he could no longer make her out. Perhaps, having been spotted, she had gone, but he thought any motion would have made her more noticeable, not less. She just melts away, he thought to himself in awe.

'Are you on our side in this?' he asked her in his head. She had every reason not to be, he knew. But if she was following their hunt, he hoped she was not on the side of the wolves.

At the top of the slope the path levelled off and eased along the contour for a couple of miles. This was the track Brigid had used the previous night, the main cattle-droving track up to the summer grazings. Bjorn and the men in front paused by a big ash tree to let the others catch up.

'Try to stay together,' Bjorn hollered. The mist was dense and the land above could be treacherous at any time of year. The ground was soggy beneath their feet, and many of the men already had wet boots. The ponies churned up the wet path and most of the men used the pause to sidle in front of the horses, preferring proximity to Bjorn and Bran to the constant mire that the horses left behind. Only Til, Lachlan and Ro were left at the back with the dogs, cursing the muddy track.

The next two miles were easy going and the men were still fresh. The improved pace kept them cheerful, and most of them managed to forget their wet feet. They passed the place where the path led off down into the forest and towards the bear's den. The mist seemed to be lifting, drifting in thin shreds over the forested peninsula, though a dense bank of cloud lay off-shore. It was relatively calm, but threatening. Til became gloomy. Bjorn looked worried, but most of the other men managed to convince each other that the cloud was clearing and the view out to sea was itself a good sign. Eachan even mustered a song, which some joined in.

Their path veered eastwards away from the sea and steeply up for a while, zig-zagging alongside a burn up a narrow glen. They snaked up this path until it reached a point where the burn flowed down from a hill to the north but the path continued east around the side of the hill and down into a bigger, broader glen. As they started downwards, the singing began again. Soon they were back among trees. The path continued past the summer huts they stayed in when minding their cattle, down to the bottom where a narrow loch stretched the length of the glen, perhaps four miles long. It was surrounded by willows and alders.

In the damp shade of the lochside woods with its gnarled trees festooned with beards of moss, the path was sodden and difficult. They clambered over several trees that must have fallen since this way was last used in autumn, perhaps blown down by the storm. It was a familiar place to most of the men, but only in summer. It was weird to be here in winter, with the ghostly lichens hanging lifeless on the alders.

The men fell silent, the only sounds now the squelching and sucking of their boots in the peaty track and the occasional curse. A blackbird in a rowan tree began to pipe, then fell silent. A woodcock crashed away clucking into the dense tangle of bramble among the trees. The miles closed behind them.

When the woods began to thin they pressed on, the ground rising more steeply away from the loch until only a few meagre birches straggled away up the slope ahead of them. The mist, they realised as they came out of the cover of the woodland, was down again. The path led away to who knew where.

Stopping once again to let the ponies catch up, Bjorn wondered if they should press on up the hill or camp in the valley bottom, hoping for a better day the next day. The men gathered around him, heads lowered grumpily at their sodden feet and legs. A light sleet began to fall. The men looked dismal.

Bjorn was just about to raise his voice in a morale-boosting call to the men, but he was pre-empted by a sound they had not expected to hear so soon, one which widened all their eyes and froze them to breathless statues.

The howl of a wolf in the mountain mist.

Time clotted. One long moment straggled across the glen, and in that moment the sleet began to soak into wool, a chill rose up out of the wet ground and dusk seeped into the minds of the gathered men. A horse stamped and clammy clouds of breath hung in the air, sleet grizzling through them. In this grey moment, which lasted for a lifetime, for generations, the hunt failed, the men lost their valour, became cowardly, thought evil thoughts, became estranged from their summer glen. Their spirits withered. They thought only of self-defence and cruelty. They had no response to the wolf's howl, no way to meet its intense animal purity. It frightened them and they became vicious, greedy and obscene.

It was Bran who broke the silence, producing a stream of expletives like excrement. It stirred the men into their own mutterings, like some sort of religious response, murmurings of filth and fear in echo of a cursing preacher.

Bjorn felt his skin creep, watching his men snarl and sneer, their fear turning them to curs. He wanted to walk away, leave them to their indignity. He wavered, trying to make a decision, the wolf's cry still filling him, freezing his mind.

A deep voice from behind the horses spoke out like light, like a warm glow.

'Are we stopping for the night? Shall we perhaps get a fire under way?'

It was Til, the hunter. Of course, Bjorn thought. A fire, that was what was needed. A fire.

'Aye. We'll make no progress in this light. We might as well get a fire going if we can find something dry enough to burn. And get some food inside us. Take shelter for the night.'

The wolves remained unmentionable. Bjorn realised he was trembling. He turned to Bran and said, 'Get them organised to find wood,' then made his way to the back of the group of men, in search of Til, seeking his strength, his advice, needing his reassurance.

Til was struggling with his dogs, all excited by the call of their wild ancestors. He looked disgruntled, swearing at them, cursing as they tugged on their stays. Bjorn approached warily, their eleven hungry dogs together seeming now to be as much threat as defence. Catching the smell of fear from the men, they too had become vicious, their wildness awakened.

'What's your advice for the night?' Bjorn asked outright. He was too tired to beat about for subtleties.

Til looked at him wearily. 'It's a choice. Safest from the weather in the woods. Safest from the wolves in the open. I'd choose the woods – I fear the weather more than wolves. But will you get the men to go back in there?' He shook his head. 'Build a big fire and huddle is my guess.'

Bjorn stood quietly, watching. The men had erupted into a frenzy of activity, their blades put to use on the nearest birch trees, hacking off branches for a fire. It's a good thing birch will burn green, he thought to himself, as there can't be a dry stick anywhere. The horses were being fed, the fire built, out in the open, as Til predicted.

It occurred to Bjorn that he could order the men into the woods before they lit the fire, tell them to move the pile of branches. But he felt listless. The work was being done, why stop the men in their task? Their faces were full of the relief of a distraction from the cold and wet. He doubted if he would really be able to persuade them into the woods for the night.

He stood a little way from them, observing. Then, drawn to the woods, he wandered down to the track where the men were cutting birches and with outer smiles and nods, walked past them into the darkness of the trees.

The sound of metal on wood faded, muffled out by moss and the quiet sound of the trees hushing as sleet stroked them. His eyes grew accustomed to the dark. A great peace crept over him. Lichens glowed dimly in the darkness. The alders creaked. A shiver shook him and he felt a presence, as if someone was watching over him from behind. He turned, stared into the shadows, but could see nothing. It was gloomy here, but gentle, narcotic. He felt safe. His shoulders loosened and he felt tension lifting from him, a lightness in his head, a sense of sudden freedom. He had an urge to keep walking away from the men, to leave their noise and ferocity, stroll away, back to the safety of the wooded glen, perhaps to wander further, to vanish into the forest, become anonymous, freed of all the burdens of his position. The hunt felt suddenly futile, a pointless gesture of human arrogance. It didn't matter what happened. All that mattered was to be calm.

Gradually, his sense of duty returned. He thought of his cold companions, their bravery, the fire, the effect of his absence. He turned back towards the men, against his wailing instincts.

He stumbled, tripping over a bramble, his hand grappling and sliding on a wet rock as he fell. He felt the jar on his wrist as his weight fell unevenly, his knees wet in the mud. His hand was in something slimy and foul. He felt stupid, and got to his feet, blinking to try to make out the path and any other obstacles. It had been so easy on the way into the woods. A stroll. How could getting out again be so much more awkward? The wet mud on his knees soaked into him and he shivered again. The clarity he had felt among the trees was gone. As he walked out into the open again towards the noises of the men, he tried to pull himself back into composure, to regain his sense of leadership, to return as the big man. But it was hard to ignore his muddied freezing legs, his wet feet, his crumpled pride.

The fire was blazing and the men were buoyed up by it, and by the food that Moran and Eachan produced. Moran seemed to be back to his usual self, his chubby cheeks chewing on an oatcake, busily handing out slices of pie to the men, proud of his mother's skills in provisioning them and proud of his own ability to bring cheer to the men despite the sleet and chill. He had a big pot of water by the fire to boil, knowing a hot drink was what the men needed. At the other side of the fire, Eachan was digging into the leather pannier carried by one of the horses. From it he produced a big flask.

'Go easy on that, now,' called Moran. 'We're not here for a party.'

'We need our wits about us,' Til agreed.

Eachan laughed at them. 'Well, you can stick to water. I know I need a whisky to survive a night like this.'

'Whisky won't help you, believe me,' Til said, quietly.

'You're a doom-monger,' Bran snarled. 'Let the men drink and get warm.' He strode over to join Eachan, who soon had a bevvy of men laughing, passing the flask around, swigging and shrieking for another shot.

Bjorn chewed on the slice of pie that Moran had handed him, watching the rabble of men and following the course of the whisky. He looked away. 'Hold yourself in check,' he told himself. 'They'll sleep the better for it.'

Til had strode off, muttering, to attend to the dogs. When Moran's pot boiled, Bjorn accepted a cup of mint tea and oatcakes with crowdie cheese. He munched by the fire, his wet clothes steaming.

After Eachan's flask, another appeared from one of the other men, and then a third. They became boisterous, telling stories of past hunts, and it was not long before Eachan started up a song. It was snowing now, and the fire was difficult to keep ablaze, but the drunk men did what they could to keep it going. Bjorn dozed by the fire. Moran cleared away the food then retreated to sleep near the horses.

After the first few rousing songs, the men began to fade, the whisky and long walk finally catching up with them. Most slumped, wrapped in their blankets close to the fire. After a while, only Eachan's wiry voice scraped on, until Bran told him to shut up, assuming leadership in his brutal way.

'Our boy leader needs his cradle,' he said, pointing to Bjorn, asleep with his mouth open, his head on his hand, beside the fire. The men who were awake laughed at him.

They made no real effort to organise a watch, and though Bran and Iain Kay and Donald sat up late, arguing about the best tactics to use against the wolves when they found them, eventually they too nodded off and the fire dimmed down to a glow. Til, ever watchful, walked over and tossed on some more wood, then returned to his dogs.

In the bleak pit of the night, when the cold had reached into the sleeping men's cores, but before they had begun to dream, the hunt came to the men. Only Til was ready for it, his five deer hounds with their big gentle eyes waiting with him, alert and expectant, listening, unmuzzled.

At the first howl of the wolves, Bjorn came round, shuddering. He was awake in an instant, unsure if the howl was a dream or reality. The fire was barely glowing, the last sticks thrown on by Til nearly burned through. He got up to reach for more wood and froze at the next howl, much closer than before. His legs felt as if he had to wade through mud to reach the wood pile. He seized some branches and dragged them to the fire, panic rising, realising the camp was unwatched; the fire, their main defence, not burning.

He kicked Bran, and shook him, whispering his name. 'Bran, Bran, wake up, Bran.' Though so often annoyed by the brutality of the man, Bjorn needed the strength of his compatriot now.

Turning to Eachan and Donald, he shook them too. They came around, questioning, bleary and blind in the pitch dark. Their protests fell away, crushed by the next howl that tore into the camp, followed by another, and another. A chorus of wolves, singing their victory over the men, their clarion call before battle.

All around the camp the men were ripped from their sleep, waking to terror. The darkness was absolute. The fire refused to burn, the wet branches merely hissing in the embers, which cast no more than a faint red glow on the few nearest faces, further deepening the black beyond.

The horses whinnied and stamped in alarm. Moran came running from them. 'Help us!' he wailed, already mad with fear, crying like a boy, his face transformed into a gargoyle of fright in the dimness. 'The horses are possessed. The wolves. Help us!' He clung to Bjorn's arm, shaking it, beseeching him.

'Get a grip, man,' Bjorn said, detaching his arm from Moran's clutch.

'Donald, can't you do anything with this fire,' he muttered to the blacksmith. Donald began to blow.

Til sat quietly with his five dogs. The others strained at their leashes, pulling at the stakes that held them. Lachlan and Ro Moine gingerly moved among them, removing their muzzles on Til's instruction, preparing them to fight.

For one quiet moment the men's fear grew and then out of the blackness one of the horses shrieked and with a pounding and stamping the other ponies tried to break their tethers to escape. The men rushed towards the horses, blades out, stumbling in the darkness. Then the wolves were on them, like a black lava flow. Night-sighted fangs struck blind iron, and blood spilled from shrieking, fleeing bodies.

In a blacked-out pandemonium the men blundered in the dark to the squeals of terrified horses and excited barking of dogs. Bjorn's courage failed him. There was no time to organise, no way of seeing enough to co-ordinate, no chance for shouted orders to be heard over the clamour. He stumbled among the carnage, seeking anyone who might help him to calm the situation. He flailed at a black shape coming towards him, he hacked with his sword when teeth grabbed his leg, chopping until the feeling of teeth ceased. At one point he tripped over something and found himself once again sprawled in wet cold. Horror, wild and terrifying, prevailed.

Then he felt a hand on his shoulder, someone pulling him to his feet, and Moran's voice. 'Is that you, Bjorn? Let me help you.' The inexplicable comfort of the helping hand.

As quickly as the din began it faded, the wolves ebbing away like ripples into the darkness. A horse's squeal was cut short by an abrupt gasp, the last bark silenced. Brief quiet.

A groan. Then a voice. 'Is there no-one there?'

'Gather by the fire,' Bjorn called. He blinked into the darkness, making out the glow, and a flickering as someone kicked a stick in, which caught alight.

He strode over to the fire, reaching for a branch of birch from the much-reduced pile of firewood. 'Let's get it blazing!' Moran, beside him still, grabbed another limb and dragged it to the fire. Bjorn felt strength blaze through him as the flames lifted and danced. 'More wood!' he demanded.

In the firelight he watched his men gather, some stumbling, some bleeding. Gradually he made out some bodies lying unmoving, and as the fire lit the dark he saw that one was Bran, his head lolling at a terrifying angle. Beside him, impaled on Bran's sword, was his big black dog, Steel. Bjorn felt a chill go through him. The fury had brought not only wolves, it had set their own dogs against them, driven them to madness with their brothers.

The men who had survived stood or sat as close to the fire as they could. Bjorn called out orders for the unwounded to get sphagnum moss to staunch the wounds of their fellows. The men were cold, traumatised. He ordered Moran to get hot drinks underway, and hand out what food he could find. The panniers had been trampled by the maddened horses and tipped onto the wet ground. Moran took a torch from the fire and retrieved what he could. Donald kept feeding the blaze. Bran and Eachan lay dead, their throats ripped out – by dogs, not wolves, from the evidence of the bodies strewn around them. Bjorn cast around the battle scene with a torch, searching for more wounded men who could be helped. He found Ro Moine lying with mauled legs beyond the horses.

'Where's Til?' he asked.

'Gone. He's gone with the hounds, chasing off the wolves. Only the deer hounds would follow him. All the other dogs seemed to go mad.'

Bjorn was confused. What was Til doing? Chasing dogs or wolves? How? In the dark? Or had he simply run away, as Bjorn had wanted to do?

'What happened to you?' Bjorn asked. 'Was this wolf or dog?'

'Dog,' Ro said. 'Fed with my own hand, tried to kill me. Lachlan beat it off, then followed Til, trying to gather the dogs in again.'

'Lie there, I'll get help,' Bjorn said and retreated to the fire, noting a dead wolf lying tossed aside, presumably kicked in the head by a terrified horse. One horse lay shuddering, bleeding terribly from its neck; another sprawled dead, eyes glassy in the torchlight. The other horses must have bolted, he guessed.

Back at the fire he ordered help for Ro Moine, and sent Donald to put the wounded horse out of its misery. He counted the survivors. Fifteen. Six missing or dead.

Then Bjorn went to where Bran and Eachan lay, sightless and maimed, and stood over them. He felt sick, and stepped away into the darkness. Nearby he heard someone vomiting. He understood. A wave of compassion for his stupid, reckless men, for their fear. He wanted to make up for his failure to lead them, for his madness in taking them into this nightmare. He rallied.

He closed the eyes of his dead friends, gently moved their damp limbs into more peaceful positions and found himself singing an old Norse mourning song he remembered from his childhood, the song his father had sung when his favourite brother had drowned at sea. He stood, singing, his voice lifting through the dark night like the firelight, drawing power from beneath the ground, from beyond the mist, from an earlier, nobler time. His voice, rich and smooth, curved around the sad, simple melody, full of the sounds of the north, foreign to all of them there but him, though comforting in its strangeness, like the voice of clouds. He sang of the sea and the land beyond where the dead souls go. When he finished, he could sense how much he had soothed and strengthened the men.

After a pause Moran began a response, an old slow Gaelic air of farewell, a song they all knew. Soon his weak voice was joined by others, and then they all found themselves in unison, mourning the loss of their friends by the fire like a pyre, blazing to burn the tragic night away.

Bjorn looked around at the hunters, their faces in the firelight looking younger than their age, their eyes shining like boys as they sang. Something nagged at the back of Bjorn's mind, until he realised who was missing, unaccounted for. Iain Kay wasn't there. Bjorn cursed. Iain was a quiet man, nondescript, average in height and in build, always dressed plainly, his hair and beard brown, no features that made him stand out, never leading a song nor starting a fight nor cracking off laughter. But he was always around, there when you needed him, usually tending horses in the stables, fetching water, mending a saddle or fixing a hinge or a hole. So where was he now, noticeable for the first time by his absence?

Bjorn stood wondering while the men sang, and when Donald re-appeared, wiping his blade after his gruesome task, Bjorn beckoned him to his side. Moran passed him a steaming cup which Donald took gratefully, wrapping both hands round it and hanging his head over the steam, sipping and blowing noisily. Bjorn felt embarrassed by Donald's emotion. Donald the hard man, the loud man of oaths and alcohol. He realised he had misjudged his choice of man to put the horse out of its misery. The blacksmith was rough on the outside, but to cut a horse's throat requires a different kind of strength. Now was not the right moment to ask Donald about the missing Iain Kay. So who?

Moran was busy with food and drink. Bjorn's henchmen either lay dead, were wounded or had gone missing. The others were muttering among themselves. He sat in a misery of confusion, his feeling of regaining control ebbing as Donald's despair bit into him. How were they going to get out of this nightmare?

'Bjorn.' A voice brought him out of himself. One of the young men was standing beside him. It was Alan, the young brother of Elma, a handsome youth, and popular in the big house kitchen. Moran had taken a shine to him, Bjorn remembered. Bjorn smiled at him and warmed as the smile was returned.

'Do you think it's safe to call Iain back?' he asked. Bjorn looked at him blankly.

'What do you mean?'

'Iain. Iain Kay. Shall we call him back?'

'Back from where?' What did the boy mean? Death?

'He's in the woods. Him and Niall, they took two horses each when the wolves attacked, to try to hide them. To get them away from the dogs.'

Bjorn felt as if he was going mad. When had this happened? Then relief and hope swept over him and he stammered, 'Yes, yes, call them.'

Let them be safe, he thought to himself.

The darkness was fading. Morning eased in as a faint grey in the sky.

Alan beckoned to two of the other young men, and they dashed off towards the woods. One of them, Bjorn recognised, was Iain Kay's son, Diarmid. What had made Iain put the safety of the horses before that of his own boy?

Before long the shapes of horses and men appeared out from between the trees and the mood by the fire lifted. The horses were tethered and Iain Kay came to stand by Bjorn, horrified by the sight of Eachan and Bran lying dead.

'The boys said they were attacked by their own dogs. It can't be true, surely?'

'It looks that way,' Bjorn replied. 'But quite what happened in the night it's hard for me to tell. I was sleeping. I think we all were. Caught off our guard.'

'Except Til. It was Til sent us off with the horses,' Iain said.

'Wherever he may be,' Bjorn said.

'He's one we shouldn't worry about. If anyone can look after himself it's Til. My guess is he's hunting the wolves. That's what he came to do.'

'Aye, the only one of us with the skill for it, that's clear now,' Bjorn said ruefully.

'What will we do now?' Iain asked.

'Go home. Take home our dead. Comfort ourselves. But first, go home. That's all we can do.'

'I'll pack the horses then,' Iain said, gesturing towards the two dead men, 'and try to make these two comfortable.'

'I fear some of the wounded may need to ride as well. Ro Moine is badly hurt. I doubt he can walk.'

'We'll do what we can.' Iain went to join Moran and the able-bodied men in packing up. Bjorn talked to the wounded, checking their makeshift sphagnum moss bandages. A couple had badly gashed arms and had lost a lot of blood. They looked faint but were all conscious, their pain eased by Moran's judicious use of herb teas. He knew more of his mother's old lore than Bjorn had realised. All but Ro Moine said they could try to walk, and all seemed delighted with the idea of a speedy departure.

All that remained were the two dead horses. Would they take the bodies for meat? Usually dead nags would feed the dogs, at least – or people, if meat was short. But how would they carry it? Would the corpses attract the wolves? In the end, the horses shied away from the dead bodies and the men tired of the attempt to move them. Til could feed the dogs if he so wished if he came back here, or they could return later for the butchering when the weather improved and they were better equipped and less vulnerable. Or they could leave them to the carrion. Either way, the horses' carcasses would not burden them on their return.

The corpses of Bran and Eachan were strapped to the strongest pony and Ro rode the next strongest. The remains of their supplies were packed on the other two, who also looked relieved to be on the move, snorting and stamping, ready to travel. Roped together, with the one carrying the dead in front, Bjorn and Iain led them off back towards the woods. The men followed, Moran bringing up the rear, heavily laden with his cooking gear.

Morning continued to grow light in the sky, but there was no lessening in the cloud. As they began to trudge along the path through the woods, once again soaking their feet and legs with freezing mud, snow began to fall. Soon a blood-stained white blanket would cover the two dead horses they had left beside the smoking fire.

The men kept up a determined stride at first, and at one point even sang a marching song, so the funeral procession made good progress through the woods that morning. But their pace slowed as they emerged from the woods and started up the slope to the pass. It seemed an age since they had come down into the glen. Could it really only be the day before when they had sung their way down here, past the summer shieling?

Bjorn looked at the huts. Why had they not spent the night there?

Mandy Haggith

It was not really so far from where they had camped. For the sake of a few miles they could have been under shelter. Should they stop here now? The idea of getting under a roof appealed. Bjorn chewed it over then rejected it. They were heading back home. They had friends to bury. They should continue.

The men slogged their way up the hill, slipping on the wet, slushy ground, the horses staggering into pockets of snow, the cold blowing into all of their faces as they ploughed their way slowly westwards.

Reaching the brow, they heard the snickering burn which flowed down its narrow gully towards the forest. Normally from here you could look out to sea and see the smoke from the houses of the Braes. But today the view out to the west was totally obscured by cloud, and as they came over the summit they caught the full force of the northwesterly, hurling snow. It was a coarse, mean wind. Although the land sloped down, the weather made the path treacherous and the ponies stumbled and whinnied. Their progress was slow and the injured men were faint and freezing, mustering all the strength they could to continue down. Bjorn urged them on, pausing at the side of the path, waiting for the back of the line of men, giving them each a word of personal praise, encouragement, promising them shelter in the forest at the bottom of the glen. Moran looked grim and frightened at the back. Bjorn clapped him on the shoulder, and with cheer that he knew must seem insincere, said, 'We'll be home for supper!'

Moran was uncharacteristically quiet, not to be led on the subject of his next hot meal.

First Tan, one of the injured men, slipped, hurting his wounded arm and twisting an ankle. He screamed like a snared rabbit. His pain drove some of the men to weeping, reaching the end of their strength. The snow blasted out of the northwest. Eventually he quietened, got to his feet and limped on. Ro Moine had slumped into a doze, but the horse that was carrying him stumbled and he toppled to the right, falling from the saddle with a sickening thump onto the rocky slope.

Iain Kay shouted 'Stop!' from the front, and men and horses jostled and bumped to a halt. Bjorn made his way to the fallen man. Iain Kay hung onto the reins of the front animal and called out, 'Hold the ponies!'

108

They all struggled to cling onto ropes and avoid stamping hoofs. Bjorn, Donald and two others tried to bring Ro back to consciousness. He was out cold, still breathing, but now with a bloody gash on this head to add to his other wounds. Moran helped to staunch the blood, but even he couldn't help to bring Iain round.

'We've got to get the poor soul home,' was all he could say.

'Damn and blast the weather,' Donald grumbled.

The five of them manhandled Ro back onto the shaking pony and strapped him, corpse-like, to the saddle. They set off again, the wind stronger than ever, the snow blinding and vicious, finding its way into hoods, under plaids, into eyes and ears. Everyone's feet were numb, many were bleeding. The men ceased to speak except in oaths. They plodded on down the glen, until eventually the trail reached the forest.

The route to the big house and the village lay straight ahead, through the blizzard. The path to the right led into the potential shelter of trees. The men at the front stopped at the turning, and gradually the straggling line crowded together.

'I say we take shelter in the woods until the weather eases,' said Bjorn. 'Get some food into us, take a rest, maybe even get a hot drink down us if we can get a fire going.'

There were some grumbles about getting home.

Iain Kay spoke out in support of Bjorn. 'It's life-threatening out here. Our only chance is to get some shelter. We've lost too many men already.'

That decided it, and Bjorn led off into the forest.

The path was steep, very slippery and difficult in the snow. But the trees provided some relief from the wind. Their upper branches creaked and groaned with the force of the gale, showering the snow in uneven lumps as if angry at the intrusion of the men. Some of the men disliked the woods, found themselves disoriented not to be in the open, but most of them, Bjorn included, felt safer in their shelter, comforted by the barrier between them and the merciless sky. They drew strength from the sturdy trees with their deep roots.

When the path levelled off among some oak trees Bjorn brought the men to a halt.

'This will do,' he said. 'Let's get some food in us. Moran, Donald, do you think we can muster a fire?' He looked at the scene around them. The snow was lying. What ground was under enough shelter to be free of snow was sodden. There was no sign of dry wood.

'I can always manage a fire.' Moran smiled. 'I've never failed yet.' He produced his tinder box from under his plaid and dug out some dry birch bark from his pack. Looking around for birch trees, he asked Alan to cut some branches. Then Donald spotted a big ash tree down the bank.

'Excellent! With ash you've not just got a fire, you've a hot fire,' grinned the blacksmith, setting off with his blade.

'Who'll fetch some water?' Moran asked.

'I will,' Bjorn said. He had an urge to do something useful, practical, and to get away on his own. He kept thinking of Til and Lachlan. Where were they? Moran looked taken aback – it was not the leader's role to fetch and carry water – but he handed Bjorn the skin and watched him turn his back on the men and stride off down the track, soon hidden by the moaning trees.

Moran continued in charge of the fire while the able-bodied men ransacked the baggage for anything they could find to eat. It did not take long for them to begin bickering. Eventually Moran shouted at them, 'Share it out fairly, for peace's sake,' but they laughed at him until Iain Kay stepped in and, with Donald's help, managed to get some kind of order into the sharing out of food. Before long Moran had a fire blazing, true to his word, and was ready for water. There was no sign of Bjorn.

Moran turned his attention to Ro Moine, who was a deathly shade of grey, slumped lifeless over the saddle. Moran and Iain debated whether they should get him down and try to make him comfortable by the fire. Eventually they decided they should. It took four men to ease him down and fix him a makeshift bed with the saddle and pannier to keep him off the wet ground. He showed no sign of benefit from the move. Still Bjorn did not return.

❧ ❧

He bounded down the track like a dog let off a chain, keen to be alone. The path plummeted down the slope, at the bottom of which was the burn: the same one they had followed down the narrow glen from the pass. It was bigger here, and flowed more slowly along a

110

bouldery course, twisting around rocky outcrops, settling into pools, and bouncing over stony rapids. The path followed the burn.

Slipping on icy mud he muttered curses and spirit names. Down by the stream the trees hung thick with hoar from the spray off the rapids. The water frothed, peat-stained evil yellow between rocks, but downstream, beyond a big boulder, Bjorn found a quieter stretch.

He stepped out onto a stone in the middle of the flow to reach somewhere deep enough to fill the water bladder. The cold numbed his hand, and his legs and back muscles became sore in the awkward hunched-up position that he held, waiting for the bag to swell. His grip had to tighten on it as it grew heavier and slippier from the spray. It was nearly full, when something made him lift his head.

Coming towards him was a bedraggled shamble of a creature. Not a dog: it was too bulky for that, yet it lacked the grace of a wolf. Freezing to his stone, Bjorn registered the approaching animal as bear.

Time slowed down.

With inch-by-inch precision, Bjorn raised the bag of water out of the pool. The bear bumbled on, seemingly oblivious to the man, its drunken zig-zag belying the pace with which it was covering the difficult ground. By the time Bjorn took his first step towards the bank the bear had halved the distance between them, yet still did not appear to have noticed him.

Bjorn took another glacial step. 'The wind is in my face, the stream so loud you cannot hear me. Look up! Look up!' he yelled. He grabbed a stone from the stream bed and threw it, aiming for just in front of the bear to make it look up, alert it to his presence and frighten it off before it got too close, but as he pulled his arm back his leg slipped on the wet rock. The pebble flew wild, landing in the pool behind the startled animal, which heaved its head round and lunged away from the splash directly towards Bjorn, just as he picked himself out of the stream and leapt for the bank. Bear and man careered into each other.

Bjorn felt wet pelt as the bear lashed out at him with one front leg, its face a daggered roar. Instinct pulled Bjorn's sword from its scabbard and his right arm lunged for the soft place between head and shoulder. He felt a paw make contact, grappling down his belly, a searing pain below that, then his legs crumpled beneath him and black numbness washed up from the ground. He fell backwards, hearing the slurp of his blade as it withdrew from the severed neckflesh of the bear. He rolled over and began to crawl away. He tried to shout, but his throat produced only a growl that was drowned out by the pounding, blinding water.

❧ ❧

'Where in hell's name has he gone?' Donald watched Bjorn's footprints down the path filling with snow.

'Damn it, I'm going to find out,' said Iain Kay. 'Are you coming?' Donald nodded. Moran looked relieved.

'I'm coming too,' young Alan said.

Iain Kay's son Diarmid pushed himself forward, but his father shook his head. 'There's no point in even more of us getting lost.'

Alan would not be refused, so the three of them, Donald, Iain and Alan, set off in pursuit of their leader. They didn't have to go far before they found him. He was contorted and barely conscious, his plaid ripped and tattered, a gash down one cheek and his lower torso drenched with blood from a wound in his groin. The three men rushed to him, aghast.

'Bjorn, what on earth's happened to you?' Iain had to shout over the crashing of the stream and the roar of the wind in the trees.

Bjorn's eyes were screwed up in agony and his reply was an inaudible croak.

'What did he say?' Iain asked.

Alan had bent down close to Bjorn. 'A bear? Did you say bear?'

Bjorn gave a weak nod.

'Where?' Donald gawped in disbelief.

Bjorn gestured behind him with one arm and the three men peered in that direction, seeing nothing. Then Alan, drawing his blade, began to creep cat-like down the path. Donald followed with less stealth. Iain Kay bent down to Bjorn to try to staunch his bleeding.

A few steps along the path stood the large boulder. Alan peered around it, saw the brown shape, and froze. The bear lay crumpled, its head askew. Its eyes gazed, glassy and green, into a tangle of bramble.

Donald stepped past Alan and, grasping one furry ear, hacked with his long blade through the animal's neck until its head hung from his hand. A spasm made one of the bear's legs twitch and a weird gasping noise came from the gaping windpipe of the headless creature. Donald began kicking it, over and over.

'I've killed you, I've killed you,' he screeched, the head swinging as he kicked and flailed. 'Die, die, why don't you die, you bastard thing?'

Alan grabbed him by the other arm. 'Leave it,' he said. 'The bear is dead.'

He spoke with a clarity, a reverence, that silenced Donald and stilled him.

Alan turned and walked back to Bjorn, followed mutely by Donald, holding the bear's head limply in one hand. Standing over his wounded leader Alan spoke again, in the same clear tone. 'The bear is dead.'

Bjorn looked up at him in awe, his eyes like a child. Iain, too, gazed up at the young man who seemed, in making this solemn proclamation, to be older than all of them.

GORT - IVY

It was clear that Bjorn could not walk, so the three men carried him, with great difficulty, up the slope to the others. Donald was still carrying the bear's head as a trophy. When they reached the fire, several of the men rushed to help and carefully laid their leader down beside the injured Ro Moine.

Moran took charge. He turned to Donald. 'You'll have to return the head to the body. We cannot desecrate the bear – not if we want Bjorn to live.'

Donald looked resentful that Moran should be criticising him in front of the men. 'I shall not,' he said. 'It's Bjorn's trophy and I'll carry it for him.'

Moran shook his head. 'You don't understand. You have to take it back. Believe me.'

Bjorn seemed oblivious. Iain Kay had returned to the stream to fetch the skin of water. The other men had fallen silent. Donald and Moran faced each other out.

Alan spoke. 'Moran's right, Donald. We should leave the head with the body.'

Donald turned and lashed out with his fist. 'Who asked you, puppy?'

Alan stood his ground, but said nothing. Donald took a step back, then hunkered down, the bear's head between his legs. Moran bent to attend to Bjorn, rummaging in his much-depleted leather pouch for some medicine that might staunch the bleeding from the ghastly wounds to his belly and his groin.

'I can't do anything for these kinds of wounds,' he moaned. 'May the spirits forgive us our folly.'

There were some shocked looks. Some of the men made the sign of the cross at the pagan language, but Moran was past caring.

Iain Kay returned with water, which he put on to boil, then crouched beside Moran. 'Will he live?'

Moran looked desperate. 'There's not much I can do. They're deep wounds, terrible. A claw has ripped his genitals. There's only one person who could try to heal this. You know who I mean. Powerful magic's needed for injuries like these.'

All the men knew who he meant. Brigid was the only person with the power to heal such an injury, inflicted by a bear. But she was banished, outlawed. She was forbidden.

'We can't take him to her,' Iain said.

'But what if the witch is his only chance?' Moran cast his eyes to the two corpses on the horse, and Ro lying unconscious.

'Ask Brigid to help us,' Bjorn murmured.

He turned a watery gaze on Moran, a faint smile flickering on his face as he looked at his friend. His eyes glazed over, then closed.

Donald spoke. 'The witch saved my son's life. I'll seek her out.'

'If it's our only chance, I suppose so,' Iain agreed.

'We're under orders,' Alan pointed out. Moran nodded.

An argument ensued about who should go to seek Brigid. Moran busied himself mixing powders and boiling water, producing a foul-smelling paste which he smeared into Ro's gums. It was a stimulant, mixed from ivy and foxglove. Before too long Ro was moving, his eyes opened and though he looked confused and in great pain, he was clearly very much alive. This act of healing brought strength to all the men, and Moran's confidence improved.

He mixed next a steaming tea of willow bark and yarrow. 'This is the last of my supply of herbs for those with wounds. We must share it out, one mouthful each, no more.'

For once the men obeyed him, passing the cup from man to man, taking one meek sip each, allowing those in most pain the first shot.

The medicine administered, Moran said to Donald, 'Go on ahead and find Brigid, fast. We need her. We'll follow as quick as we can.'

Iain Kay frowned but said nothing.

'I'll go too,' announced Calem, one of those of Alan's age who had escaped injury. Alan nodded.

Donald picked up the bear's head, and carried it to one of the horses that was standing with its head in a nosebag. One of its two panniers had held food, but it was now almost empty. Donald placed the head in the basket, nose down. He ignored the protest from Alan, and tightened his belt and boots. 'Are we ready?'

Calem nodded.

'We'll see you at the Shield tree, or if we find her and she'll come with us, somewhere on the track between here and there.' The two men set off back up the slope out of the forest.

Moran packed up his supplies. Some of the men were getting desperate with cold.

'There are women in the village who can treat all these wounds,' Iain said. 'Not least Frigga.' Moran looked up at the mention of his mother and shrugged. Iain pressed on. 'I think we should try to get the dead and wounded home safely as soon as we can.'

'I'll go with Bjorn to Brigid,' Alan said. 'If you can help him onto a pony, I'll lead it.'

'I feel I should go too,' Moran said.

'Won't we need you to care for Ro?' Iain asked.

'There's nothing more I can do for him. All my herbs are done. And my duty is to my leader.'

Bjorn began to make a strange rasping noise, and urgency grabbed them. The remaining water was thrown on the fire, and the able-bodied men helped lift Ro and Bjorn onto horses. They were both tied, like corpses, belly-down over the ponies' backs, wrapped in plaid. The fourth pony was loaded with all the provisions, dumping what it could not carry.

Alan and Moran headed away up the hill. Iain Kay led off in the opposite direction, down towards the stream, leading the horse carrying Ro, followed by Iain's son Diarmid with the bodies of Bran and Eachan. The pack horse and the eight other members of the original hunting squad followed: shambolic, miserable and exhausted.

⊰⊱ ⊰⊱

After I got back from the bear's cave, the hours ground by so slowly I wanted to scream. I had watched the hunt go out, then tried to focus myself on spinning. But the wheel drove me mad with its rhythm and I found myself becoming tense and frantic.

I made sure Beithe and her calf had plenty of fodder, but even stroking and crooning to her didn't bring its usual solace. So I decided to go for a walk in the forest, despite the foul weather, to watch for signs and be alert. I found myself at the bouldery base of the cliff where the badgers live. I leaned against a rock and listened. There was no sound from the sett, only the creaking of the hazels, rowans, birches and aspens in the wind.

A huge ivy grew up the cliff and as soon as I saw it I knew what it was I needed to do. I scrambled over the boulders to where the ivy was reachable, and began tugging at stems. Most were fixed firmly to the rock, their roots dug deep into cracks. But younger stems hung down and I pulled and twisted, snapping off the longest lengths of leafy stems I could manage. I was surprised how many of them were still full of berries. They would normally have long since been eaten by birds. But there was, no doubt, some reason for it. Nothing happens by chance. Everywhere, the spirits shape the world into the patterns they want.

Ivy berries were not something I had great use for – such a powerful stimulant is only needed in extremes – but I left them on the stems anyway. It was too cold out there for the fiddle of stripping them. Soon I had a big heap of twisting, contorted vegetation and, taking some twine from my pocket, I did my best to bring it under control and tie it into a bundle that I could carry. I strode back to the Shield Tree, full of purpose, and dumped my load down by the fireplace.

All that evening, late into the night, and then again the next morning I sat by the fire, plucking ivy leaves from their woody stems until the ground around my bender and under the alder tree was strewn with a deep-green carpet. I collected the berries in a cloth bag. When the snow really got going I shifted into the bender, and carried on.

The more I plucked, the more agitated I became.

Sometimes I would break off from my plucking and weave the stems into patterns. Some were like birds, some like people, some geometric shapes to represent ideas not things: desperate stars for hope, knots for the connections between us all. I hung some from the Shield Tree, tied some to my bender. Sometimes I made things without knowing what I was doing: when I made the bent cross of death I threw it on the fire, muttering. If anyone had seen me I must have looked quite mad. I made a swan to stand for my childlessness and I took it down to the lochside and flung it far out into the water. Between bouts of weaving I kept on plucking leaves. I did not know what was driving me to do it.

By the middle of the next day, all the stems were bare and I began to weave them into something bigger. I began with its stocky torso, then the crude form of its head. I worked fast, deftly, having become used by now to the rhythm of weaving, to the spring of the ivy. Soon I was working on legs, sometimes using a piece of willow or hazel to keep the structure strong, but mostly working the flexible ivy stems into a dense weave. It seemed to take shape of its own accord under my fingers, as if it was weaving me, rather than me weaving it. I fixed ears and nose to the head, then added two small pine cones for eyes. My bear was complete.

I set it down in front of me and it looked at me, filling me with a dreadful feeling. I picked it up again and clutched it, hugging it, rocking with it, unable to name what was filling me with such confusion. Unable to focus properly, still clutching the bear, I staggered outside among the trees. I was as bewildered as if I had eaten mushrooms full of bad spirits. My guts spasmed. I vomited, retching up poisons, my head spinning. I somehow stumbled back into my bender and collapsed on my bed of skins, pulling blankets over myself, shivering, hugging myself and the ivy bear, stricken with a crisis I could not understand.

I must have drifted off to sleep, because I woke to voices outside. I heard them plotting. They sounded like trolls. They thought I wasn't here, and they sounded confused by all the ivy leaves strewn around outside. Then one of them began to creep into my bender. I heard him fumbling with the skin at the door and the gasping of his breath. I could almost hear him peering at me. I cowered under my blankets but when I felt his filthy paw on me I knew I had to fight to survive. I threw back my cover and spat at him. 'Get out! Get out!' I managed a torrent of shrieked abuse, every curse I could think of. I pushed him out, bludgeoning him with my words. He backed away.

❆ ❆

'Crazy woman,' Donald muttered.

Calem put his hands in his pockets to hide his trembling, looking to Donald for guidance. He was willing to turn tail and flee the mad creature in her strange bracken-strewn tent, convinced now that all the stories about how dangerous she was were true.

'No-one in their right mind would ask her for medicines,' Donald said. The implication was obvious. They must return and find Bjorn and stop him from coming here. 'She'll be no help to him, that's for sure. Crazy woman,' he repeated.

'Maybe she was just asleep or something and you surprised her,' Calem suggested. 'Maybe we should wait and ask her again when she's come round.' Dusk was falling, the light gloomy.

'I'm not going near her,' Donald said, already striding away. 'Let's get moving.'

Donald's authority and age pulled Calem along. He shelved his doubts. The cold was enough reason to keep moving.

They set off back up the track the way they had come, the snow driving in their faces. Calem stopped thinking, putting all his efforts into keeping up with Donald, who was pushing out at a strong pace. He walked with his head down, pounding after the older man, focussing on one step after another.

The blizzard intensified. Snow was going down Calem's neck, his feet were numb with cold and pain. He lost track of how long they had been walking this way. Then Donald stopped and turned a frenzied glare on him.

'Where's the track gone?' he demanded.

Calem shook his head and sank to his hunkers.

Donald exploded with curses, shouting through the gale, flailing his arms, raging at the snow, the wind, and all the people who had had anything to do with the hunt. At length he turned his fury on Calem, wailing and blaming him for their predicament. Calem dodged a kick that unbalanced Donald and the big man fell over, cracking his leg against a rock and jarring his arm. His face crumpled, and he wept, whining about the unfairness of it all, sobbing.

Calem stood above him, his face full of revulsion. He stepped aside, then also sank to a squat and put his head in his hands. The snow scoured them, filling their footprints.

⊰⊱ ⊰⊱

Even from afar the men looked dejected as they dragged their way towards the big house. Frigga watched from the kitchen, frowning, puzzled by how few they were – just three ponies led by Iain Kay, tailed by his son Diarmid, with a straggle of men behind, their heads hanging. As they passed the edge of the village, people were drawn out of their houses, but instead of thronging around the men, they fell in behind. There was no hubbub of welcome.

Frigga called into the kitchen. 'Ishbel, is the fire alive? Some of the hunters are coming, with doom on their backs by the look of them.'

Ishbel set a pan on the range and filled it with a wooden pail.

Then she joined Frigga at the door and her eyes widened as she saw what Frigga meant.

'They're a picture of defeat, aren't they?' said Frigga. 'I daren't think what has happened. Something too dreadful to speak of.'

'I'll get more water.' Ishbel headed to the well with the empty pail, not wanting to watch the dismal troupe approaching.

Frigga went to seek out Margaret, in case she had not already seen the hunt returning.

Soon the yard filled with folk emerging from the stables. People gravitated in from the shore where they had been gathering seaweed or shellfish, or working on the longship. Children abandoned their livestock and ran down from the pastures. By the time the men arrived at the big house most of the village was there to greet them, including Margaret, ashen and dithering, and James, who looked triumphant.

'The hunters return defeated,' he gloated.

'For goodness sake, James,' muttered Margaret. 'Show some humanity.'

She walked forward to Iain Kay and took his outstretched hand. 'What's happened? Where's Bjorn? And the others?' Once she began questioning it was hard to stop. Iain held up his hand.

'I can't answer now, Margaret. I bring you the bodies of Bran and Eachan and many wounded men. Pity us. Give us what help you can. I'll do my best to explain later.'

But Frigga was not to be fobbed off without an explanation. 'There are several others missing. Moran. Til. Where are they? Where's Bjorn?'

Iain glowered at Frigga and then looked at Margaret. 'Your husband was wounded and taken to the medicine woman. There are four men with him, including her son and son-in-law.' He flapped his hand in Frigga's direction.

James stepped forward. 'And was it those heathens who decided to take him to the witch?'

Iain shook his head. 'I argued against it, but he asked to be taken there. It was his own choice.'

'How badly is he wounded?' Margaret demanded.

Iain stared at the ground. 'I don't know.'

James gurned. 'He must be extracted from the witch's clutches.'

Iain shrugged. 'He will no doubt return as soon as he can. I can't imagine him wanting to linger out there.'

He turned and tried to organise the unloading of the horses. A melée of people helped to lower Ro Moine and the corpses to the ground, then carried them into the big house. Margaret went indoors to organise space for the wounded. The pack pony began to be unloaded, and as the panniers were emptied a gasp went up around the crowd. The bear's head, matted and bloody, was lifted out by a young stablehand. He stood aghast with it in his hands, its tongue lolling between canines. People backed away and there were shouts for explanation. Iain Kay stopped his efforts to guide the arrangements for the wounded, and walked over to the boy. Taking the bear's head from him, he held it up and shouted.

'This is the trophy of our leader, Bjorn the Bear Slayer.'

He grabbed a spike, impaled the bear's head on it and, brandishing it above him, strode down to the yard entrance and leaned it against the gatepost.

At the kitchen door Frigga stood watching, shaking her head. 'It's a sacrilege,' she muttered, and turned inside to begin the preparation of pain-killing brews and poultices. She tried to avoid going into the hall. The men disturbed her. Her rage about the desecration of the bear's head grew as the evening drew in. She let the story of the hunt be brought to the kitchen in shreds and snippets, gradually growing in elaboration and detail, pieced together into an exaggerated and convoluted version of what had actually happened, the roles of some men magnified to heroism, others (mostly those who were sleeping) relegated to incidental bit parts in the drama.

It was late when Margaret sidled into the kitchen. She had been nursing since the men arrived.

'Frigga, can you help us? I'm worried about Ro Moine. His wounds are so dreadful and we cannot staunch the bleeding. I worry that he will lose his legs, or even his life. He seems to have a fever now. We need your knowledge, Frigga.'

Frigga felt hardened and tired but Margaret stood before her, eyes begging. With a jolt, Frigga saw that both she and Margaret were waiting for loved ones: Margaret for Bjorn and herself for her son, Moran. They had both heard the stories about the fight with the bear.

'All right,' she said. 'Any word of Bjorn, or Moran, or the others?' She would have heard if there was, but asked anyway.

Margaret shook her head. Frigga followed her into the hall, where a fire was blazing and torches around the walls showed makeshift beds laid out around the room for the wounded men, mostly sleeping now. Ro Moine lay unconscious, his breathing a rasp, his bedclothes soaked in blood. Frigga examined his legs. The wounds were oozing and the flesh was swelling and gory.

'It's bad,' she said. 'I doubt we can save the left leg. I think it's best to admit that straight away or the rot will spread. The right leg may repair, the belly also, if the rot isn't too deep.' She sat back on her haunches and looked at Margaret. 'We need a medicine woman.'

Margaret straightened her back. 'I will not have that witch in my house.'

Frigga took a deep breath. 'But…'

'I will not.' Margaret refused eye contact.

Frigga's shoulders slumped. 'Then tell Iain Kay we need to … to operate on him. We'll need the sharpest saw he can find, and a quiet place away from the other men.' She paused, and then went on. 'But I'll be honest with you. I don't hold out much hope. There's every sign of a curse on these men, and no amount of herbs will bring them through that.'

'What do you mean? James has been praying since they arrived.'

'I doubt the spirits of the bears and wolves will listen to his kind of prayers, if you'll forgive my directness. I don't know what's gone on, but there's a bear's head desecrated outside this house and the best men in the village are missing out there in the snow. I'm fearful, Margaret. That's all I'll say.'

The young woman shook her head. 'Superstitious nonsense,' she snapped, and went off to find Iain Kay while Frigga concentrated on the awful wounds in front of her.

⊲⊱ ⊲⊱

It was a long night. Ro Moine came round as Frigga operated on his leg, and his screams filled the big house. It was as if the stones absorbed the howls and breathed them back out, and all the house's inhabitants were chilled and edgy.

In the small hours Frigga went home, leaving Margaret and Ishbel to tend the men, fetch drinks or herbal brews for them, and keep the fire going.

She stopped for a long time by the bear's head on the stake at the gate, talking to it, apologising, asking it for guidance. She found herself weeping for her son, exhausted by the trauma of the night, feeling old.

⋐⊳ ⋐⊳

The next morning, several of the men were fit enough to go home after a bowl of porridge. Ro Moine was feverish and delirious, but all of the rest were feeling much better than when they had arrived. There was a bustle in the hall as children came to visit their wounded fathers, and those well enough to go home departed, packing up beds and clothes that had been hung around to dry.

By mid-morning an uneasy calm had descended on the big house. There was still no sign of Bjorn, and Margaret's nerves were frayed. Iain Kay paced the hall, and when Frigga arrived she told him to sit down. 'You're making folk nervous, man, with your back and forth. What's on your mind?'

Iain sat down on a bench. Frigga stood with her hands on her hips. 'I'm torn. I want to go looking for Bjorn and the others that are missing, but I daren't risk any more lives in weather like this.' It was no longer snowing, but a vicious wind blasted in from the north, heaping the snow up into drifts. 'That wind's more dangerous than anything: it'd chill through the warmest furs.'

Iain's son Diarmid sat sullen by the door, dressed ready to leave as soon as he was given permission. It was he who had urged his father to send out a search party; his friends Alan and Calem were out there somewhere. Diarmid looked as if he scorned his father's caution, but he did not disobey.

Frigga shook her head. As she returned to the kitchen, there was a burst of shouting outside.

Til and Lachlan had made it back, and they stood at the gate with three of the deerhounds. Til was raging at the bear on the stake, bellowing furious questions up at the house. Lachlan rocked from foot to foot beside him, and the dogs barked excitedly.

Margaret was the first to run out of the big house, closely followed by Diarmid then Iain. Others emerged from the stables to see what the clamour was about. Frigga and Ishbel watched from the kitchen door.

'What in the name of the Goddess is this doing here?' raged Til.

Margaret crossed herself as she saw the black fury in his face and heard his pagan words.

'It's your headman's trophy.' James' voice was cold. He joined his sister and put a hand protectively on her shoulder.

'Trophy?' spat Til.

Iain and Diarmid stood by, aghast. They had never seen Til so fierce. He had seemed the essence of calm at all times, the thoughtful tracker, quiet, attentive, even serene. The man before them was transformed, as if possessed.

'You heard. Bjorn's trophy,' James repeated.

'It's a bloody desecration,' Til shouted. 'I can't believe it of the man. Has he lost his mind? Where is he?'

There was an embarrassed pause. Til looked from face to face. James was tight lipped. Eventually Margaret spoke. 'The men took him to the witch.'

'To Brigid? He's with Brigid?'

Margaret nodded.

He glanced at Iain Kay for confirmation, who nodded too. Then he shocked them all by laughing: a wild maniacal laughter. 'I don't believe it. And you're all just waiting here?' He snorted, reached up to the bear's head and pulled it off the stake, then turned to go, Lachlan with him.

'Wait!' said Margaret. 'Lachlan, your brother Ro ... he's hurt, terribly. He's in here. You must see him.'

Lachlan stopped and turned back.

'Stay with him, Lachlan. You deserve a rest,' Til said. 'I'll go alone to try to right this wrong.'

'I'll come with you.' Diarmid stepped forward.

'And I, too,' came Frigga's voice from across the yard. 'I'm glad to see someone at last show some respect to the spirits.' She came striding across the yard towards them.

'Give that to me,' she said, and took the bear's head from Til. 'No man should ever touch the sacred she-bear.'

She turned to Iain Kay, who stood aghast but limp. She spat at him, then turned and strode off down the track towards the loch, Til and Diarmid close behind, the three big dogs loping like shadows beside them.

nGetal - Broom

At first Moran led the way and Alan followed with their barely-conscious leader, concentrating on keeping the garron on as even a keel as possible. The snow was bitter, the path up out of the woods exhausting, but they made steady if slow progress. When they reached the main drove-track their going got easier, but they kept the pace slow, anxious not to jolt their leader.

'We've enough daylight, and hurrying won't help us,' Moran said. After a while they swapped position, Alan leading the way, Moran guiding the pony. This seemed to be a smoother way of travelling, the animal stumbled less and Moran was happy to trust the young man's sense of direction.

After about an hour they reached the ash tree where the path led down beside the Coille burn. It was steep, twisting and icy in places where the spray from the burn had frozen. Bjorn had fallen into unconsciousness again and seemed oblivious to the unavoidable bumps as the pony slithered and stumbled down towards the lochside. Still the snow fell, but the wind had eased, not that the men noticed, their minds so focused on their descent.

At the bottom of the track they paused. The main route went right to the village, but they turned left onto the small path along beside the rocky shore. When they saw the Shield Tree they turned inland, approaching Brigid's camp with trepidation.

Night was creeping in, and under the shadow of the trees it was gloomy and quiet. There was no sign of life. Alan noticed the footprints of Donald and Calem, and pointed them out silently to Moran. The stones around the fireplace had a deep layer of snow on them.

They were standing forlorn, not knowing what to think, when they heard a quiet voice inside the bender singing a mourning song. It was the same song the men had sung up in the mountains, in the darkness of the dawn after the wolves had struck. A lifetime of walking had passed since then. Had it only been that morning?

Alan looked quizzically at Moran. He had been brought up to fear and respect the shaman. Moran nodded and Alan stepped forward to stand next to the doorway. He bent down and waited, becoming aware of how cold and sore he was. A shudder passed through him and the song stopped abruptly.

'Who's there?' asked a strained voice.

'I am Alan, son of Morag, Irene's daughter.' It seemed strange to find himself using his matrilineal name, but his instinct told him it was the right way to identify himself. He continued, 'I am with Moran, son of Frigga. We have come to ask your help. We bring Bjorn, the headman, son of Ailsa of Orkney. He has been wounded by a bear. Can you help him?'

There was quiet, and Alan felt himself stiffening as he crouched outside the bender. Moran held his breath.

After a long silence, the voice replied.

'No.'

I sat among my rugs and skins clutching the ivy bear. I felt as if there was nothing left in the world except me and it. My mind was clear but my senses were fuzzy. Nothing beyond my bender was real. I would ignore it. Only me and the bear mattered, and the outside world could not help us any more. It had rejected me. Now I would reject it.

To keep the pain in my soul at bay I sang, and what I found myself singing were old mourning songs and laments I didn't even know that I knew. Perhaps I was singing for my mother. Perhaps she was singing for me. Perhaps we were both singing for the grandchildren I had not brought her: my child who had never been born.

A voice outside tried to make me come back, taunting me with the name of Bjorn, asking me if I could help, but I said 'No.' I had no strength even to help myself.

I tried to sing again but now it was more difficult: my voice was croaky. A sadness that would not stay down rose up in waves, trying to wash me away, catching at my voice, trying to engulf me.

Then I felt another voice join mine. It buoyed me up, like a raft on the sea that was drowning me; it sang under me and my voice could float above it, rest on it. It was a deep voice and its bass notes, quiet but true, were somehow the same shape as mine. Their harmony felt like a resting place, a hollow carved to the exact shape of my body.

My hearing cleared, and as I sang with this new voice my other senses also began to clarify. The bear stiffened in my hands and bristled and my fingers tingled as I held it. The ashes in the corner of my bender were cold, but I caught the last scents of woodsmoke. All I could taste was salt and bile and a desperate thirst. Behind that, beneath it, beyond all my senses, inside the other voice, I began to feel a terrible, terrible pain – a wound so deep that it reached into the heart of the earth. It drew me towards it and I seemed to recognise it. The bear scratched my hands, tugging me.

I pushed back the rugs and, holding the bear out in front of me, got up and pulled aside the deerskin which formed the doorway.

The singing stopped abruptly. I blinked into the dusk. Two men stood looking at me, their eyes full of anxiety, their bodies clenched and fearful. They were very wet. I recognised the older of the two – he was Frigga's son, Beathoc's elder brother. A good man. The other younger man I didn't know, but he was shining, despite his soaking clothes. I could tell at once that they were no danger to me.

The bear writhed and I saw the body on the pony and knew that it was the source of all the pain. With a sway of dizziness, I sensed that the voice I had been singing with had come from the soul of this man. It was Bjorn. I had always known he would come to me in the end.

I set the ivy bear down on the ground, then stepped gingerly over to the pony. I stilled it with one hand, and with the other, I touched his body. Nausea belted me and I stumbled aside, retching. There was only bile. I beckoned to the two men, who were standing watching me, and said in a faint scratch that was all that was left of my voice, 'Bring him inside.'

They were instantly at the pony, untying Bjorn and lowering him off. I led the way, picking up the ivy bear as I went into my shelter. Throwing aside some rugs, I gestured them to lie him down on my bed, on his back. He was disturbed by the movement and groaned as they carried him, then let out a deep sigh as they laid him flat. His eyes were closed and his face was cold and clammy.

I lifted his hands and placed the ivy bear in them, then let them drop onto his chest. He pressed the bear tightly to himself and it

127

glowered back at him. There was no point in speaking, nothing to say. I looked at his wet clothes and his wounds, then pulled the rugs over. I lay down beside him, covered us both up with blankets and curled up in a ball with my back to him. There was nothing to be done.

◁▷ ◁▷

I woke to a man's groans. There was a body beside me. I remembered: they had brought Bjorn to me. To pay his due for the slaughter of a bear. To die.

But his soul had sung with mine and instead of striking him down I had brought him into my bed. I felt sick.

I sat up and pulled the blankets back. It was too dark to see, but the stench of blood was revolting.

My home was full of men. In the shadows I made out Frigga's son, Moran, and his young friend, curled up together beside the dying fire. A chill had slunk inside. I sat watching as the young man nudged Moran aside, stoked the fire and fixed the wick on the lamp so he could relight it.

The light was like bramble thorns inside my head, nettle stings on my eyes. I looked at the body beside me and my stomach churned. The young man was staring at me like a roe buck, as if I might attack him. I let my eyes bore into him, testing him. 'Who are you?' I asked.

'I'm Alan, son of Morag…'

I cut him off. 'Him.' I pointed to Bjorn. 'He is a murderer.'

I wanted to weep with fury and confusion, but I knew I must be strong. The young one tried to shake Moran out of sleep.

'Why is he here?' I insisted.

'He is our leader.' His voice was firm. 'We thought you could heal his wounds, the wounds of the bear. We didn't know what else to do.'

'But he killed her,' I shouted. 'He killed my sister bear, didn't he?'

He looked me in the eye and took a breath.

'Yes, he killed the bear.'

'Then he's killed us all,' I whispered, and got out of bed, struggling to my feet, my head swimming with nausea. I had to get out. I

128

managed to stagger out of the door before the wave of retching seized me. Under the moonlit clouds the snow glowed like honey. I sensed the young man at the doorway. I had to get away from all these men.

'Wait,' I heard him call. 'Come back.'

I stopped and turned and said, very quietly and clearly, 'Leave me alone, murderer.'

I watched my words make contact, saw the young man reel as if he'd been punched, and stomped away into the trees.

⪥ ⪤

I walked in the forest, crazed and barely knowing who I was. I crashed through tangling willow thickets, my clothes catching on brambles, stumbling from tree to tree, calling to the spirits to show me what to do.

There was no signal, no help, only the wind moaning in the trees.

I started to doubt that any of it had happened. Stumbling over a rock, I fell, soaking my knees and hands in slushy moss. When the cold bit into me and the snow soaked into my boots, I knew I had to go back, to see him again. Perhaps I needed to face the consequences of his deed before the bear spirits would talk to me again.

I returned at dawn, frozen. Moran and his young friend looked at me as if I was a ghost. They asked me questions but I ignored them.

I stood by the door and gazed at Bjorn for a long time, without saying anything. He stirred, and then opened his eyes. Moran went over to him. He was very weak, but he looked around the bender and seemed to become conscious of where he was. As his eyes reached the doorway they widened, seeing me watching him. I was reflected in his eyes, two of me, my hair matted, my clothes wet and dishevelled, my face full of grief.

We spun around the axis of our stares. My will drilled into him, prising out his guilt. I hollowed him out, but still he stared back. I scraped at him with my eyes, trying to reveal the demon in him. I could see it was agony for him, but he held my gaze.

His face became blurred. I no longer knew who I was looking at. 'Who are you?' I asked, stretching out my arm to point at him with one finger. I was trembling, but I didn't shift my eyes.

'It's me, Bjorn.' He came back into focus. His voice was surprisingly clear, though very quiet. It seemed to cost him a lot of effort to use it.

'Bjorn,' I said. I had his permission to use his name. 'Bjorn,' I repeated. I wanted to go on saying it, over and over.

'And you're Brigid,' he said.

I shrugged.

He squirmed, seeming to rummage for something under his blanket. He tore his eyes away. My breath went jagged and I shook with cold.

'Moran, in my pocket...' His voice faded. He looked beseechingly at Moran, who patted him, reassuring him. Alan began to scrat in Bjorn's clothing hanging by the fire, searching through pockets, laying objects out in front of him on the bed. Eventually, from the breast pocket of his shirt, he produced the Good Luck Bear that I had given to Enya as a gift. Bjorn nodded and tried to reach out his hand. The younger man placed the bear in his palm and he folded his fingers around it.

It was too much. I frowned and shook my head. I would not meet his eyes, but I had to know. Stepping forward, I took Enya's bear from his hand.

'How did you get this?'

He smiled at me, but it was as if taking the bear from him had broken the spell: he was swooning away from consciousness, his head lolling, his eyes glazed and flickering.

I sat by the door with Enya's bear. Moran offered me tea. I refused. I wanted nothing.

Bjorn had slipped into a tossing delirium, moaning and sweating. The morning was dark and grim, more snow was threatening and the wind battered the skins. I sensed the men feeling uncomfortable. The hours drew on.

The men discussed setting off for the village then talked themselves out of it again. Moran rummaged around in my medicine chest. He seemed knowledgeable about the herbs in it. Because I refused to speak to them, they talked about me as if I was not there. Perhaps I would snap out of it, they said. Bjorn was too ill to move. At least they were warm and dry, with a good supply of herbs. The wind was too cold to attempt travel. Their lassitude provided plenty of excuses to stay where they were.

The young one called Alan went out to check their pony, and came back in saying that he'd found my cow and her follower standing looking hungry outside my fodder store and they were now all three together feeding in the shelter of the trees. He had tried to milk my cow, he said, but had a bruise on the shin for his efforts. I tried to smile inside myself at her spirit, but I felt only despair.

⊲⊳ ⊲⊳

It must have been noon when Alan, who was standing by the doorway, shouted 'Til's coming, with two others.' They both dashed out.

When Frigga walked into the bender it was as if a torchlight was brought into the darkness. She was carrying Sister Bear's head. She hugged me and stroked my hair and told me how the bear had been desecrated and needed to be restored. Then she fussed around Bjorn.

I cradled the bear's head in my lap and told Frigga what we had to do. I felt ashen and tear-stained, but the bear made me determined.

She made me dress up in my long black cape and stout boots and wrapped a green scarf around my head. Then she went back outside to the men.

I took the bear's head over to the bed and sat down. I reached out and touched Bjorn, feeling the bear's fur against one hand and his hair with the other. His was softer, fine as down next to the thick winter pelt of the bear. Bjorn opened his eyes and he tensed when he saw what I was holding, then looked up at me.

'I'm sorry, Brigid. I'm so sorry.' His voice was a whisper. His eyes filled up like pools in the rising tide. I saw myself reflected in them. I looked dark and sleek and powerful.

'We'll make amends,' I promised him. He reached his hand out from under the blanket. Our fingers touched, wove, settled.

⊲⊳ ⊲⊳

I left Bjorn sleeping.

It was good to see Til. I leaned against him and he put an arm round me and patted me in a fatherly way. 'Let's go.'

Moran waved the five of us off, Frigga and I in front, the men behind, Til and his dogs bringing up the rear as usual.

We set a brisk pace and made good progress. In less than an hour we reached the shelter of the forest. I stopped and waited, looking around. A wren fluttered up onto a branch of an oak tree overhanging the path and chattered angry territorial chatter. I showed it the bear's head. The wren hopped up the branch and stopped by the trunk. Then it fluttered down to the ground, hopped across the path and flew off into the forest. There was a chatter of birds in the distance, as if the word about the intrusion was being passed around. I waited.

A creep of fear rose up my back. I sensed magic beginning to flow. Diarmid was uncomfortable, fidgety, irritating. Til finger-mouthed him to hush, listening. The others waited calmly. A gust of wind blew snow down from an oak branch above us. Still we waited.

The bear's head was heavy in my arms. I felt tears roll down my face.

Then two ravens flew over, circled, their flights twisting into a spiral. They called, 'craw, craw … craw, craw…' and wheeled overhead. I glanced round at Frigga. Her eyes shone. The two birds banked off, soaring away over the forest towards the coast, soon hidden by the trees. I led off in the same direction, down into the woods.

We passed a fireplace, and Moran whispered that it had been made by the men yesterday. I pressed on down the twisting steep path until it reached the burn. There I slowed, and padded onwards to the pool where they had found Bjorn. I stopped where he had lain, prodding the blood-stained snow with my foot. Then I stepped forward to the boulder and around it.

The decapitated bear lay in a mess of blood. This was the bear I had slept with only a few nights before. Our totem, my fulcrum.

Bringing the bear's head back into contact with her body again, I knelt down and wept, stroking the thick, lustrous fur of the stiffening creature. 'Oh my sister bear, what have we done to you?'

I sat back on my haunches. My hands stilled; I took a deep breath and stood up to face the others. As I rose, I felt a transformation flow through me. I was as powerful as I had ever been. I felt moonlight shining from me, translucent, pearly. I stood tall, head high.

I looked at each of the others in turn. Diarmid cowed. Alan lowered his eyes. Til was smiling and Frigga too held my gaze, her face full of relief. I felt restored.

'Diarmid, I need to ask you to go,' I said. My voice was seductive. 'I need to give the bear her final ceremony. She is our sacred spirit and I will need to use whatever magic I can to try to heal the wounds that have been inflicted here. But I have been forbidden from carrying out such ceremonies, as you know. I cannot risk incriminating you, son of Iain Kay, the priest's henchman, by having you present at the ceremony. I sense anyway that you would rather be seeking your friends. Is that not correct?'

'Yes,' he nodded. He looked relieved.

'Go then, and thank you for your help.' I gave him a smile that I hoped would sooth the discomfort he had been feeling.

'Alan, you too may go if you wish, or stay if you wish. You are already incriminated. You have slept under my roof.'

He looked up shyly. 'I will do whatever will be best for Bjorn. I brought him to you with Moran because we felt sure that you're his only hope. If you can heal the bear, can you not heal him too?'

'Nothing I can do can bring the bear back to life, nor Bjorn, if he is going to die. But if he is not due to die, then yes, my ceremony will help him.'

'And will it make any difference if I stay or go?'

'If you bring your will for Bjorn to live to the ceremony, it'll undoubtedly help. The spirits will respect your loyalty. Give your love of Bjorn to the bear and she will use it. She loves love and she loves life.'

'Then I'll stay.'

'There are some things you cannot watch,' I told him, 'and that goes for you too, Til.'

'I understand. There are things only women can do.' His eyes twinkled. 'But I would stay to honour the bear, if I have your permission, of course.'

'Of course.' We exchanged the smile of old friendship. 'And Frigga, I need your help. I suppose you know that.'

She bowed, as if the ritual had begun.

We said our farewells to Diarmid, then I set them to tasks: building a fire, collecting evergreens, heather, broom, holly and ivy, and cutting reeds from a boggy clearing in the woods. We stacked all of these outside the bear's cave upstream, and built two fires beside where the bear lay, one on either side of her body. Til and Alan cut fresh birchwood for the fires, since all the dead wood around them was sodden. By the time the preparations were complete our hands were hurting with cold, but otherwise the exertion had kept us warm.

I told the men to sit on logs at the bear's feet, while Frigga and I scratched a flame from a tinder box and, lighting birch bark from it, we each lit one sacred fire of birch sticks to honour the passing of the she-bear.

It was a short, simple ceremony. I sang and burnt sage for cleansing the wrong. We said farewell to the bear, and one fire, representing her living body, was put out. The other, the spirit fire, burned on. Together, we carried her up to the cave. Then I asked the men to leave me and Frigga alone, and to wait for us at the edge of the woods.

We skinned the bear, starting with a slit down her belly and punching the flesh from the skin. Sometimes, we had to whittle the skin off with a knife because the body had stiffened. The paws were most difficult, but eventually she lay naked. We left the head intact.

'What will you do with the skin?' whispered Frigga.

'I shall be buried in it, here, one day.'

Frigga shivered.

'We should light a fire here,' I said. 'Start it from the spirit fire.' Frigga set about gathering sticks for this third blaze, while I swept out the cave with a branch of broom, then laid a mat of reeds for the bear to lie on. Together we dragged the naked body of the bear into the cave and curled her up as well as we could on the reeds. Then I covered the body with the green vegetation, laying on the heather, broom, holly and ivy gently and evenly from the head down until all the flesh was completely covered. We blocked the entrance with the third fire, piling sticks on until the flames leapt and crackled.

Singing the final mourning song, tears ran down our faces. I cried partly from a sense that an era was ending, partly from the smoke, and not least from sheer exhaustion. We left the fires to die away in their own time.

Dusk was drawing in and Frigga decided to return to the village along the low path through the woods.

'I'll send Moran home,' I promised her, 'and I'll tell him to come looking for you if you're not back when he gets there.' But we both knew the old woman was as safe in the woods as anyone could be, knowing them as intimately as she did. They were her larder and herb garden, as they were mine.

We hugged and parted on the path, heading off in opposite directions. I began the climb up out of the forest to the drove road where Til, Alan and the dogs were stamping and pacing to keep the cold at bay. The three of us set off back to my camp. The wind had dropped and the sunset over the sea was a flush of pink.

'You've breathed life into the sky, anyway,' Til said.

'Let's hope the same can be done for Bjorn,' Alan murmured.

An owl shrieked behind us. We stopped, and I hooted the response. 'Who-oo-oo, who-oo-oo?' Another shriek, then the response came from deeper in the forest. We walked on, leaving the last bear to wander in the realm of the forest spirits.

❧ ❧

My home was quiet when we arrived. Moran, Alan and Til made their farewells; Alan was reluctant to leave Bjorn but was persuaded by a firm nod from Til. Feeling more composed than I had for days, I watched from the doorway as they set off in the half-dark. Then I turned to give my full attention to the man in my care.

He was awake, his face contorted. 'Such pain,' he croaked. 'I can't endure it.'

I took his hand with one of mine and stroked his cheek with the other. 'The pain is caused by healing. It will need to hurt more before it hurts less. Mother Bear is taking her daughter back. The spirit fires are burning. This is a good time for healing, but you must be strong.'

He nodded.

'I am going to dress your wounds with fresh dressings and treat them to help them to heal. It will be awful at first, but then it will be easier. Don't worry. I think you're strong enough to handle it, if you'll trust me.'

He nodded again, and as we looked at each other, something leapt between us. It was awful to see such pain in those eyes. They

135

reminded me of the sky, full of blue-grey clouds but with a bright winter light behind them, bands of white that glowed almost gold. I could lose myself in them. Despite his pain, I wanted to savour the look of him.

Each glance we shared spoke to me in what felt like my mother tongue, and I realised that with my own movements, glances, touches, I was communicating back to him in the same language. There was no need to say anything.

Turning to the casket of herbs, I set about my medicines, mixing a poultice of selfheal, yarrow, flag iris root, horsetail and butter, and an astringent ragwort wash to clean the wound. I poured him a generous measure of the poppy-willow brew and helped him to drink it, then held his hand again and took Enya's bear out of my pocket, laid it on his palm and wrapped his fingers around it. He smiled, his eyes glazing and pupils shrinking with the opium.

'The little girl, Enya, lent it to me for the hunt. She said it's her good luck bear. I promised to give it back to her.'

'Hang onto it for now, you still need it.' I smiled.

'Was it yours once?'

'The Good Luck Bear is his own. He doesn't ever really belong to anyone. But yes, he lived in my pocket for many years.'

I marvelled that Enya had given it to Bjorn. Perhaps she did have a bit of magic in her.

As Bjorn became woozy with the drug I turned to his injuries, pulling off the dressings that Moran had made as gently as I could. Bjorn moaned, at one point clutching my hair in pain, but I worked patiently, swabbing the wounds clean. There was a big tear in his abdomen where the claws had gone deep. A gash on his penis was still bleeding, and a claw had ripped up and through his scrotum, leaving his testicles mangled.

I went to my casket and took out a bone needle and thread. I soaked them in a bowl of boiling water, then quietly threaded the needle.

I fixed up the belly cut as best I could, then arranged blankets and cushions so I could raise his legs and part them. All my years of sewing had not prepared me for this. I examined the soft flesh where the testes had been clawed open. I had to slice away a flap and stretch the skin to make a neat join. Each puncture of skin seemed as violent as a sword slashing, the tug of the gut thread like a rope hauling a great weight up a cliff. Bjorn's breathing came in shuddering waves. His hands grimaced, clutching the blanket. I stitched to just short of the anus, counting as I went, twenty-one, twenty-two ... The bleeding eased, and as I bathed him with a gentle swab dipped in willow water, he gulped a sob of relief.

Lowering his legs again, I set about mending the cut that ran diagonally across the lower half of his penis. I held it firmly with my left hand, squeezing the wound together and with one swift dive I pulled the first stitch through and tied it off. I swabbed away the blood then stroked the needle through a second time, sealing the base of the cut. Tugging the final stitch tight, I felt a hardening pulse through the flesh in my hand. As I bent my face to bite the final knot of thread he gave a gasping moan. His feral scent was powerful behind the smell of blood and herbs. A single white drop seeped out of the eye at the penis tip. I kissed it away. Its salt made me heavy with tears.

The stitching complete, I applied the poultice to all his wounds, and butter to the skin around them to stop the bandages from sticking, then gently bound them with soft felt. Wiping his sweat away, I stroked his forehead and gradually he relaxed, slipping away into a doze, his face softening.

I studied him, following the contours of his head, looking at the detail of his beard, the wrinkles around his brows. Staring at the shape of his mouth, I toyed with the urge to kiss it. Then, with a jolt, I found my eyes closing.

I put peats to smoulder on the fire and blew out all but one lamp, then took off my dress and eased under the blankets next to him, facing him, close enough to feel his breath on my cheeks. I was asleep as soon as I lay down.

winter cave
lying in a hedgehog heap of leaves
cold wind aching
broken

137

Mandy Haggith

rocks under paws
brambles snagging fur
bracken stems tangling
neck hung
head hanging
broken

nose nudging nose
snuffling
licking
smelling him
wanting him
rolling growling
tumbling

cave full of bears
safe with mother bear
mending

sad to be the last
so sad to be the last
so sad to see the long line
broken

Straiph - Blackthorn

I woke with tears on my face. I had dreamed about the bear. At first light I got up and dressed. Bjorn stirred and I sat by the bed. He looked around bewildered, then recognition spread. His eyes settled on me and we exchanged smiles, our hands reaching for each other.

After the trauma of the past few days we had come to rest, like a boulder that falls from a cliff during a great storm into the loch that has been waiting for it to drop since the rocks were formed.

After the splash, ripples.

Then calm.

Bjorn dropped back into a doze. I set more medicines by the fire, took my broom and swept the hide on the floor clean of yesterday's debris. I opened the doorway to let the watery sun in as it rose glittering across the loch, and found myself singing about a mountain stream that flowed to the sea, carrying stories down from the hills.

Then it was time for porridge, and I woke Bjorn to persuade him to eat. He managed a little, and seemed comforted by the honey-rich oats.

For the next day and night I nursed him. When he woke, we chatted quietly about easier times, drifting back into memories of the summer we had spent together, when Bjorn had first come to the Braes, before his father had installed him as headman. He had been sixteen years old to my twenty-two, but already world-travelled and sure of himself, whereas I had still been learning my craft from my mother and had never been beyond the mountains to the east or the coast to the west.

'You reminded me of my grandmother,' he said. His voice made me think of a wave rolling pebbles over on the shore. 'You smelled of the woods, of wet ivy leaves and mosses and rocks dripping onto ferns. I felt as if I had spent my whole life at sea moving from place to place and here you were, as much part of the forest as the trees themselves.'

'I suppose I am.'

I stroked his upper arm and shoulder, aware of my chapped skin, caloused and rough as aspen bark. He reached up and his fingers rippled around mine. 'It was your voice, too, even before I could really understand what you were saying. I loved listening to it; it's so rich, with all the colours of an autumn landscape: bronze, gold, jade. And when you laugh it's like rowan berries, a sudden burst of red among a forest of greens and browns.'

I giggled at his flattery.

'There, you see: rowan berries.'

I lay down beside him.

'You're wise, like she was, too.'

I felt like I was drowning in his words. 'If I'm so wise, why did you banish me?'

'I didn't.'

'No, you didn't say the words, but you didn't stop them being said.'

'I had no choice.'

'You're the headman. You have nothing but choice.'

'You know that's not true, Brigid.' He closed his eyes. 'I couldn't allow myself to see you.'

'What do you mean?'

'I wanted to be a good husband to Margaret, to look only at her.'

'With your eyes or with your heart?'

'Perhaps I confused one with the other.'

'Perhaps?'

'I'm sorry, Brigid. It was wrong. I was wrong.'

I let the words reverberate.

'Thank you.'

'What for?'

'For saying that. It helps.'

I watched a tear squeeze out from his left eye and trickle down his cheek towards his ear. I stroked it away. My eyes had never felt dryer. 'It was probably good for me.'

He didn't reply, just shook his head.

'The anger, you know, and not having to see you. Her. It was probably good for me.' My voice petered out.

I sat rubbing his tear between the finger and thumb of my right hand, even after it had dried. He reached with his right hand then let it fall onto the cover and looked up at me.

'Will I die?'

'No. The bear doesn't want you.'

'How do you know?'

'I just do.'

Clouds in his eyes cleared. 'I should have married you.'

'It's too late.'

'It's not too late. It's never too late.'

My belly churned.

'Say it again. I want to hear you say it again.'

'What? I should have married you.'

'Yes.'

But we both knew why he hadn't: more stubborn than his grandmother, I had refused to give up my shaman role, while his father had insisted he must take a Christian wife. I had never expected to hear him say he'd been mistaken.

There was nothing else to say, so I kissed him, twisting round and leaning over him so he didn't have to move. His lips were still light, his tongue still strong. We spoke together in that primitive language, the language that has only the present tense, no sense of history, no fear of the future. Then Bjorn lay back. He looked contented. I curled beside him, my face buried in his auburn hair. He smelled of the first gold chanterelles in summer when the sun is high and the leaves form a latticework against a clear blue sky.

After a while I said to him, 'If I ask you something will you promise to be honest, not to say what you think I want to hear?'

'Can I say nothing?'

'No.'

He sighed. 'I promise.'

'Do you love her?'

'I thought I did.' He paused. 'I thought I loved both of you. Does it matter?'

'You aren't allowed two wives.'

'Not at the same time.'

'Ach, Bjorn.'

'Why did you ask, then?'

I looked away. 'I suppose I hoped it was just convenience. Ambition.'

'But you're not surprised?'

141

'No, not really.'
'You're both so different.'
'She's a flower and I'm a tree.'
'Something like that.'

❦ ❦

While Bjorn slept, I set about making a basket. I had to do something calming, something simple and physical, familiar yet absorbing; a basket would be perfect. I had cut willow several weeks back and the withies were stored in a dry sheltered spot under a holly tree nearby. They would have shrunk a bit by now and would be weavable without needing to be soaked. I checked Bjorn was sleeping soundly, then dressed against the cold and set off. It wasn't far to the holly tree but the snow made it hard going. Fortunately the big holly had held most of its snow, so the ground by its trunk was mostly clear. I sorted out a bundle of rods of various sizes, then made my way back to the bender.

Bjorn was fast asleep. I was pleased. The rest would be helping him heal.

I cut eight sticks of willow as long as my shin and with a sharp bodkin pierced four of them in their centre then threaded the other four through them to make a cross. This would form the main structure of the basket's base.

Now I needed long, fine rods for weaving, but as I rummaged through my bundle, I heard Bjorn stir. I blew the fire into life, putting a pot onto the flames to warm the contents. It was a powerful brew, based on Frigga's sloe mead that my father had brought, with broom tops, willow bark and tormentil root. The sloes, fruit of the blackthorn, were for healing the wounds and to protect him from the spirits that bring fever; the broom to purge the evil and staunch the bleeding; the willow to numb the pain and the roots to clean his blood.

As Bjorn came round, I could see that he was once again in pain. The poppy had worn off, as I had expected, and he was sore. I helped him to urinate, gave him a fresh blanket, refreshed the poultice and bandages on his wounds, and when he was settled, gave him a big draught of the blackthorn medicine. He grimaced as he drank it. The mead could not hide the bitterness of the tormentil,

142

nor the bite of the willow, but he was compliant.

'You're doing all right, you know,' I assured him. 'You're bound to feel sore, but your wounds are clean. You're healing.'

'I know,' he said. 'Don't mind my groans. I'm soft with pain.'

I shook my head at him.

He grabbed my hand. 'Look on the bright side, the injury brought me back to you. I'm grateful to the bear for that.'

I didn't pull my hand away. 'They'll come to take you back to your house soon, then you'll forget all about me again.'

'I never forgot,' he said. 'I don't know how to forget.'

'You've taken a lot of poppy and willow and now the broom and mead's getting to you.' Suddenly embarrassed and furious with hope, I tried to free my hand, but he resisted, holding on with surprising strength.

'I'm not feeling the drugs, Brigid. You've relit the fire in me.'

I didn't know what to say. 'The bear has entangled our fates, but I'm not sure why.'

'I'll find a way to be with you. I'm the headman.'

'Shush, you're talking drugged nonsense. It's enough to feel what you feel. Leave planning what you'll do until you're healed and can think straight. I'm forbidden, remember, quite aside from the fact that you're married. There are forces out there that won't take kindly to their Christian lord taking a witch for his mistress.'

'I'm no more Christian than you are, and there are forces in here,' he pointed to his chest, 'that insist that I must.' He pulled my hair with a look of hunger I had not seen for years. I lowered my lips to his to silence him. But the impossibility of our love swarmed around us, biting at me like midgies. I pulled away and Bjorn looked at me, his eyes raging. We sat silently together and eventually the medicine took effect and he seemed to slip into a doze, so I left him and returned to my basket.

As I stepped out of the bender, two people were riding up on white ponies. They were unmistakeable. The man in front carried a big cross of wood. The woman behind him was stiff and upright. Behind them, three other riders halted at the lochside. James and Margaret had not come alone.

A shiver went through me and I stood and watched them approach, full of loathing for the man, but resigned to the inevitable meeting. I braced myself to be civil, unresisting.

143

'Welcome.' I smiled as they stopped. 'I was expecting you. Look, I've even prepared for you.' I pointed at the wicker cross formed by the base sticks of my basket, grimacing inwardly at the irony, or was it good luck, that I had managed to make so little progress with the weaving.

My welcome seemed to set James off his guard. He was clearly expecting a confrontation and looked disappointed, his stony face averted, clutching his cross. I ignored him and looked at Margaret, who appeared relieved at my lack of aggression. She looked feeble and awkward perched up on the pony. The last time I had seen her I had been full of bitterness about the confrontation over my mother's funeral. Now I was rash with confidence.

I spoke directly to her. 'Come inside, Margaret. Your husband is healing well.'

She shook her head. 'I can't.'

'What?'

'Go ... in there ...' she faltered.

'Whyever not?' I feigned surprise.

James recovered himself and launched into a verbal assault, spewing furious condemnation of heathen ways and pagan means. I felt a heat growing inside and a blush of anger crept into my face. Why should I tolerate this? For Bjorn, I reminded myself. I struggled to remain calm and turned away from James to collect myself, then turned back, took two paces towards his horse, and raised my hand, palm forwards. I let the soul of the bear roar in my voice. 'Stop.'

James voice was cut off and he took a sharp in-breath.

I lowered my hand. 'Tell me what you want.'

'Release him.'

'Bjorn is not my captive. This is not a prison. He is free to come and go as he pleases. If he wants to go, he may go. He is very badly wounded, and though he is healing well, I do not recommend travel. But you are welcome to come and see for yourself.' I gestured into my bender.

'We will not enter your heathen hovel,' James spat. Turning on his horse he shouted, 'Men, come here,' to the three riders who had held back. They were leading a fourth horse. As they drew near I could see it had a strange contraption strapped to its back. It was a sort of stretcher. They were serious about taking Bjorn

144

away. The three riders were Iain Kay, his son Diarmid, and the old stable hand, Niall.

Niall had been one of the earliest and most enthusiastic converts to Christianity and was one of James' strongest allies. He and I had a long-standing mutual dislike. I loathed him because he baited badgers, and seemed to obtain pleasure from watching animals tormented or killed. I considered his conversion an excuse for treating his wife, Lia, with endless abuse and I had fallen out with him on numerous occasions after treating her wounds. I was sure Niall was responsible for Lia's unusually frequent falls, bumps, and tumbles into the fire.

Niall spat. Not directly at me, but his feeling towards me was obvious by the snarl on his face. I looked at Iain Kay, perched on a pony too small for him, his eyes averted from me. Only Diarmid made eye contact, full of fury.

'Hello, Diarmid,' I said in as warm a voice as I could muster. Their five horse-height presences were intimidating. 'Did you find your friends?'

'No, thanks to you.' He glowered at me. 'Now I understand why you wouldn't help me look for them.'

'What do you mean?' I was taken aback.

'You know fine well,' said James. 'You and your heathen curses. We hold you responsible for Donald's perishing.'

'Donald's dead?' I thought of little Enya, now an orphan, her childhood blotted again by loss, and of Caphel, already a sad boy, now fatherless.

I must have looked sorry because James said, 'Remorse won't undo what you've done.'

'I've done nothing. I don't know what you're talking about.'

'It's lucky that Calem survived his night in the snow. When he's well enough he will tell the whole story of your murder of Donald.'

'Are you accusing me?'

My question hung unanswered.

Then Iain Kay spoke. Still he did not look at me. He addressed James, but I could tell that what he was saying was intended for me. 'As yet, there's only speculation. There is no evidence of involvement by the witch. We know Donald and Calem were coming here to find her; we think perhaps they did come here before going up the hill. But we do not know if they had any encounter with the witch. There are those who say otherwise. For now, I suggest we attend to the reason we are here. Our headman is inside and it is he that we came for.'

'You are welcome here, Iain.' I gazed up at him but still he wouldn't meet my eyes. 'And I'm grateful for your clarity. Bjorn is healing, but he's badly wounded. The worst is a terrible injury to the groin which I've had to stitch up.'

Iain winced and I heard Margaret gasp. She looked as if she would have rushed into the bender there and then if James had not restrained her. Iain, Diarmid and Niall dismounted and followed me inside.

Bjorn had woken up. When he realised what they were going to do he tried to protest, but they would not be swerved. They threw back the rugs, picked him up and carried him out of the bender. He was groaning in pain as they lifted him onto the stretcher on the pony. I could do nothing but stand and watch, biting back tears.

'You're fools,' I said, catching Margaret's eye. 'I don't know how the spirits of the bears will react to this. Without me you can't heal the bear's wounds. Bjorn, may Mother Bear take care of you and give you courage.'

'Shut your heathen mouth,' said James viciously, lashing at me with his whip and catching my face. 'In the name of Jesus, you will be punished for your witchery.' He spurred his horse and led their train away.

I watched them go, the stretcher on the pony lurching over the uneven ground. I felt sick at the thought. Retreating with my humiliation into the bender, I took the crossed base sticks of the basket and flung them on the fire, then slumped down on the heap of blankets tossed on the floor. They were still full of the smells of Bjorn and his dressings and medicines, even his blood. Burying my face in my hands, I cried into the blankets and when my sobs receded, I pulled them over me and descended into blackness.

But despair could not dominate me for long. A fire began, burning my misery into something much brighter, sharper, keener. Soon I was sitting up, my eyes drying, priming myself for action.

They were worse than fools. I railed in my mind at the arrogance of the priest, at the coy superiority of his sister, remembering Margaret's face, recognising in hindsight the smug look of a pregnant woman. She was bearing Bjorn's child. It would be his only offspring, and she would raise it to be a Christian bear-hater. It was enough to drive me mad.

I clenched my face and hands and started muttering to myself. 'She has everything I once had. Power to do good or ill, influence over important decisions, respect of the people. She has what I most want: a child in the womb. And she has Bjorn.'

But as I said that last thing, I doubted it, remembering the way we had kissed, his vow that he would not forget me.

I found myself wailing wordlessly, my face twisted. I punched the heap of blankets beneath me with frustration.

Noticing the ivy bear lying beside the bed, I fell silent, appalled by my petulance.

Getting up, I set about preparing food, frowning and tense, munching on oatcakes and feeling their nourishment without pleasure. Then I wrapped myself in my coat of skins and set off into the forest to try to find some peace among the babble of my inner voices.

⋖⋗ ⋖⋗

When Frigga saw the riders coming along the lochside with their stretcher, she feared Bjorn was dead and knew she would be needed at the big house. Her loyalty was torn since the incident of the bear's head, but her bond to Bjorn was strong. He had always been good to her and she respected him as a fair and kind leader. No-one else, except Brigid, had the herbal skill to try to heal his wounds. She would do her best, if he was going to survive. If he was dead already she would do her part to pay her respects.

At the big house, Bjorn was taken to his room and lain in the oak bed. He was ashen but conscious and gave a weak smile when Frigga appeared at his bedside. They clasped hands and he said, 'Give me something strong for this pain,' then he closed his eyes. His breath rasped.

Frigga tended him all afternoon and into the night, giving him painkilling drinks and trying to make him comfortable. But as the night deepened he slipped into a fever. Frigga grew frightened. She had been avoiding his wounds, trusting Brigid's dressings, but now she knew she must act. She undid the bandages and saw the full horror of his injury, and the careful stitching of his groin. But it was the slash to the abdomen that worried her: it oozed and smelt rotten. She changed the dressing, but feared the worst. 'The spirits have seen all the wrong that has been done and will extract the price from us somehow,' she muttered to herself.

She found Margaret pacing in the main hall, tending Ro Moine, who was the only man from the hunt still in the big house's care.

'How is he?' she said anxiously.

'I've done all I can,' said Frigga, 'but he's deteriorating. His fever is rising and the gash on his belly is in an awful state. I've put on a new poultice but I don't know if it will help. I cannot challenge the bear spirits. If their anger is strong, only a bear shaman has magic powerful enough to save him. Now I'm tired and I must go to my orphaned grandchildren.'

Margaret blanched at the pagan outburst, but bit her tongue. After Frigga had left, she tip-toed to Bjorn's bedside.

He opened his eyes and she was shocked by their yellow pain, glinting in the lamp light.

'You have to fetch Brigid,' he croaked. 'I am dying of the bear's wound. Only she can cure it. She has a strong medicine for the pain. I need it.' It was a struggle for him to speak.

Margaret stood stiff and began to remonstrate. 'I'm sure it's just the night. You'll feel better in the morning.'

'Fetch her,' growled Bjorn.

'We can send for her medicine, but not her. She's a heathen. James wouldn't...'

'James is not the headman.'

She was silenced.

'Tell me you will fetch her,' he said.

She said nothing.

'So, you'd rather watch me die than cross your brother. I see. Then get Til.'

'Yes, in the morning.'

'I may not have until morning. Send for him now.'

She could not disobey any further, and trembled as she set about finding someone to send to Til's cottage. She felt awkward, ordered about by this sick man who hardly resembled the Bjorn she knew. Outraged that he was asking for the witch, she contented herself by reasoning that his fever was making him behave out of character.

She returned to his bedside.

'Til has been sent for,' she assured him and he seemed to relax and drift into sleep.

The tallow lamp gave out a flickering light, bright at its heart, but small. Margaret continued to sit by Bjorn, her head nodding into sleep. She was woken by a quiet hand on her shoulder. Til was standing there, gaunt in the weak light, seeming taller and thinner than ever, as grey as an aspen tree.

'I'm afraid Ro Moine has not made it through this bleak night,' he said glumly. 'I found him in the hall.'

'But he seemed stable when I last saw him,' said Margaret, 'not so long ago.' She felt a rush of guilt that she had abandoned the man she had been nursing for the past two days.

'His wounds were too deep to withstand the darkness, I suspect,' said Til, looking away from her. 'He sent for me?' He looked at Bjorn.

'Yes, before he slept.'

'How is he?'

'Frigga seems worried; she says he has fever and his wound is festering.'

Til said nothing, but Bjorn was stirring. He opened his eyes, looking blearily at Til until recognition came.

'Leave us,' he croaked to Margaret.

She sat motionless until she saw Til offering her his hand to help her stand. She refused his gallantry and got up. She stumbled at the doorway. Til closed the door behind her.

'Bjorn, you look dreadful,' he said.

'I shall die without her,' rasped Bjorn.

'Brigid?'

He nodded.

'I could fetch her, but they won't allow her in the house.'

'Do they need to know?' Bjorn and Til exchanged a long gaze, weighty with meaning.

'I'll do what I can,' said Til. 'Meanwhile, be strong. You are our leader, and we need you more than ever just now. We have lost four brave men already; our hearts cannot cope with losing another.'

'What did we do wrong?'

'I don't know. But I think we need more respect for the spirits. I feel the need for their support more than that of this jealous new

149

god, who seems always to be angry with us.'

'Be careful what you say, Til.'

'I am, don't worry,' he smiled. 'Now sleep.'

Bjorn nodded and let his eyelids fall, and Til stole away.

He made his way to the kitchen, hoping to find Frigga, but she was not there. So he strode off down to the village. Her house was all darkness and he stood outside, wondering if he should wake her. The sky had cleared and the moon was riding high. Four hours until dawn, he calculated. Not long. He must hurry. He didn't yet know how he would get Brigid into the big house, but decided against waking Frigga and instead set off towards Brigid's camp. The track through the snow was slushy and well worn after all the to-ing and fro-ing of the past few days. His long-legged stride took him swiftly along the lochside.

⬦ ⬦

Til came for me in the middle of the night. I woke to hear him calling from outside the bender, asking if I was awake. I shouted back, 'Come in,' and went to the doorway.

'No time. It's Bjorn. He needs you. You must come now, before light.'

I pushed my hands through my hair.

'They'll never let me in.'

'We're not asking anyone's permission. Bjorn's summons is why I'm here. He needs your medicine.'

I shrugged and sighed. 'Wait a minute. I'll get some things together. Come into the warm.'

He sat on the bed and watched me pack a small bag of herbs and poultices, and a flask of the sloe mead medicine.

'You'll need to climb into the big house, through his bedroom window.'

I shook my head. 'This is ridiculous, Til.'

I threw my cape around me and laced up my boots.

'Ready?'

'Aye.'

We set off towards the big house at a quick pace. We talked little on the way, but at one point Til stopped and turned to me and asked, 'Is the bear at peace?'

I shook my head.

'No, and never will be.'

'Never?'

'We're finished, Til. The angry god cannot tolerate us.'

'But the bear will come back again?'

'Maybe one day.'

'One day?'

'I can't say for sure.'

We walked on in silence. At the village Til took the back alley to Moran's hut. I started to question, but he silenced me. 'You'll need more protection than me,' he whispered, before rapping softly but urgently on Moran's door.

Moran came to the door quickly, as if he was up and about. He didn't seem surprised to see us and ushered us into his one-room home. It was warm, comfortable and tidy, with his bed curtained off in one corner and a fire burning in another.

'Is it Bjorn?'

We nodded.

Til explained. 'Bjorn has asked for Brigid. His wound is festering.'

'So why come here?' Moran asked.

'We need to sneak her into the big house somehow. Will you help?'

'Me, master of disguise?' Moran was back in his characteristic good spirits.

'We were thinking more like a leg-up to the window,' I said.

'And keeping an eye out,' Til added.

'Will a couple of extra eyes help?' Alan peeked out from between the curtains of the bed. Moran beamed a delightedly wicked grin and I smiled back.

'Definitely.'

Alan clambered out, and stood by Moran's chair. He was handsome in the firelight, his black hair shining and green eyes flickering. 'You must wonder what I'm doing here.'

'I can't imagine. I'm just glad to see you again.'

Alan nodded and Moran beamed, 'Well, that's all right then, isn't it?'

Til realised the question was directed at him.

'An extra pair of eyes will be most welcome,' he confirmed.

'And we can all keep a secret tight,' Moran said.

Til smiled. 'Aye, what happens at night will stay in the dark.'

I took the flask from my bag.

'Do you have a bowl or something, Moran? I'll leave some of this with you. It's based on your mother's sloe mead. I can't tell you the rest. I'll try to get it to Bjorn tonight. But if I fail, at least you'll have some.'

Moran nodded and took a small birch bark pot with a wooden lid from a shelf. He held it out while I poured some of the sticky black liquid into it from my flask. Then I untied a cloth package and took out a small wrap of birch bark and gave it to him. 'This is a poultice for the wound.' I retied the package and stowed it with the pot in my bag.

'Perhaps we should leave them with Frigga?' Alan suggested.

'Alan's probably right,' Moran said. 'If something goes wrong, they're no use here.'

Til nodded. We discussed the plan, then got ready to go, and Alan and Moran wrapped up in warm clothes. It was a cold night for hanging around.

'Let's go,' Til said, and we set off, creeping through the village, stopping outside Frigga's hut and leaving the birch bark package and pot by her door. Then we stole up the brae toward the big house. At the gate, we separated. Til went first up the track, then after a minute, Alan, Moran and I crept along the shadow of the dyke to the back of the ruined stable. From there we tip-toed around to the east side of the house, where Bjorn's bedroom overlooked the loch. We waited in the dark cold.

Shortly, the shutters opened and a faint light shone from inside, revealing Til's sillhouette. Alan bent down and I clambered onto his shoulders and then he heaved me up until I could climb through the window. Til hauled me over the sill.

It was not a graceful entry, but I was in, and Til closed the shutter behind me. There was a trunk across the doorway. I stepped over to Bjorn. Burning with fever, his breath came fast and shallow, each gasp sounding like billows. I touched his brow and looked at him, but he remained unaware of me.

I pulled back the covers and reached down to his bandages. I peeled them back to reveal the festering wound across his abdomen, and my carefully-stitched repair to his groin. Whispering requests to Til for hot water and cloths, I set to work on his wounds. I was satisfied with the groin injury, though Til looked horrified.

'He'll never sire children again, that's for sure,' I whispered to him, 'but it is healing. The belly is the one that's causing him trouble.'

After washing the wound gently I applied a poultice of selfheal, golden rod, elder leaves and butter, packed a sphagnum moss pad over it and wrapped the wound in a fresh bandage.

'This must be burned,' I said, giving Til the old bandage. 'I've used moss to draw out the badness, but it must be changed regularly, every two hours, until it is properly clean. Can that be done?'

'I'll tell Frigga, don't worry.'

Bjorn was stirring, and I poured the contents of my flask into a cup by his bed and added some boiling water. 'Til, help him to sit up a bit,' I instructed.

'Bjorn, it's me, Brigid,' I whispered. His eyes were glazed and it wasn't clear at first he recognised me, but a half-smile crossed his face and then he frowned and coughed.

'Here. I want you to drink this all down. It will taste nasty but help you a lot, so drink it for me, please. '

Coaxing him like a little child, I got him to swallow the potion, grimacing. Then we laid him back down, and I sat for a while stroking his forehead with a cloth, holding his hand and looking at his face. He relaxed and his breathing slowed and quieted.

Til tapped on my shoulder and urged me to leave before I was found. I repacked my bag, touched Bjorn one last time and scrambled back out the way I had come, to the place where Alan and Moran waited below. The first grey light saw us striding away from the big house, looking back once or twice, praying we had not been noticed.

Ruis - Elder

In the morning Bjorn's fever abated, and all the next day he seemed to make progress, sitting up, eating a bit. Frigga cleaned his wounds and used the poultice and decoction that Brigid had left. The healing was remarkable.

During the day, the corpses of the dead men were dressed for their funerals – all except for Bran who, being high-born Norse, needed to be taken to Orkney to his family tomb. The bodies were laid out in the big house, and the families visited to pay respects and to mourn.

Lachlan Moine sat by the body of his dead brother Ro for hours, until eventually Til persuaded him to leave, finding some pretext for a walk with the dogs to get him out into the last of the short afternoon. The wind had turned to the west, bringing a rapid thaw. Snow slumped off roofs and eaves spilled a patter of meltwater. Green and brown began to strip away the furious white on the land.

Iain Kay organised the funerals and digging of graves and ordered preparations in the kitchen. Even Coll, Brigid's father, was at the big house, making the wooden stretchers to carry the men to their graves.

Margaret drifted listlessly about, oppressed by the smell of death in the main hall. She was politely guided out of the kitchen where the funeral meal was being prepared, and eventually took up a seat by her husband's sickbed, sitting by the fireplace to sew, working on an embroidery smock for her child-to-be.

Bjorn mostly slept, but when he woke he seemed alert and clear-headed and wanted to know what was happening in the rest of the house. Frigga paid regular visits and he seemed to perk up when she arrived, managing to joke a little with her and banter about the herbs she was giving him and the food that was being prepared for the funerals the next day. It was she who helped him to eat, and soothed him back to sleep. In the evening he even got out of bed for a while, standing up, wobbly, while Frigga let him lean on her, and though he grimaced with the soreness of his healing wounds, she was impressed with his progress.

When Frigga left, he slumped back into sleep, and between her visits there was little interaction between Margaret and himself. As she sewed, she tried to persuade herself that he was ill and she was merely imagining the great gulf that she looked into when he turned his eyes on her. Though he made no comment, she felt a fire had been extinguished. There was no tenderness in his hands and once, when she made a remark about praying for him, his face curled in revulsion. She saw him joking with Frigga and finally, when he asked her to leave him alone with the old woman while he urinated, indignation rose in her throat and she stalked out in search of her brother, passing Til in the hall without acknowledging his presence.

James was not in any of his usual haunts, so Margaret retreated to a corner of the hall where she had set up a bed when the injured men had needed nursing, and sat sewing until dusk began to draw in. She lit candles and prayed, but found no peace, and so she went in search of her brother once again. She found him in the outbuilding he had taken over and was using as his cell, poring over a plan he had drawn up on parchment. It was the sketch of a new chapel. He was delighted to see her, and she marvelled at how high-spirited he seemed. They talked about his ideas for the chapel. It would be big, really more of a church, and as he discussed his plans he embellished them until eventually he was outlining a monastery, serving a congregation of the faithful.

'I'm going to go away to King Malcolm's court in St Andrews, on a pilgrimage to Iona and then a mission to Orkney. We need funds and backing for this plan. I'm sure we can do it. Your son will deserve it.' He patted her belly. 'It will be my life's work: to transform this pagan backwater into a shining home for the Lord.' He was beaming.

Margaret was taken up by his fervour. 'You must have a bell cast, too,' she said enthusiastically. 'I do so miss the chimes in the mornings, and the way everyone would gather for prayers.'

She went to her bed full of thoughts of silks and gold, memories of the splendour of the monastery of her childhood home on Iona, of the majesty of the building, the holiness of the monks and nuns and the safety she had felt among them. This would all come to the

Braes, and it would become truly her home. She looked in on Bjorn on her way to bed. He was sleeping. In her glow of contentment she felt suddenly warm towards him, forgetting the dark looks they had exchanged earlier.

⋖⋗ ⋖⋗

Bjorn slept well that night, and the next day he was able to attend the funerals of Eachan, Ro Moine and Donald. He was carried down to the hall and out to the graveyard in a chair by Til, Iain Kay, Moran and Alan. He did not speak much, but everyone's spirits were lifted by seeing him smiling, crying for his friends – and by the knowledge that he had survived and was healing, that they were not leaderless. The thaw had continued and the day was mild, though grey. The drizzle was not enough to wet the gathered crowd.

Bjorn waved Angus the Boat over to him. 'How's the boat?'

'Beautiful.' Angus looked proud. 'Iain's done a fine job on the detailing. You'll love the dragon's head.'

'So it's seaworthy?'

'Absolutely. Well, there are a few bits to do.' He shifted from one foot to the other.

'How long will it take? We need to get Bran to Orkney.'

'We'll go flat out.'

'Thanks, Angus.' Bjorn turned to watch as James called to the stretcher-bearers to begin.

Frigga stood by Donald's grave, pale but tearless, with Caphel and Enya on either side of her. Enya held her grandmother's hand, her head hanging low, crying. Caphel shook himself free of his grandmother's touch and though he would not make eye contact with anyone, he watched intently as the bodies of the three men were lowered into their holes, and kept an observant gaze on James, Margaret and Bjorn as the last rites were spoken.

James led the funeral prayers in a gentle voice. Bjorn had never heard him so restrained. It was a moving service. Calm settled on the villagers.

Bjorn was carried back to the big house in his chair, and the rest of the villagers followed behind for the funeral meal. After they had all eaten the food that the women had prepared for them in the great hall and toasted the dead with rowan wine, Til was

156

persuaded to get out his clarsach and sing a few songs. Eventually, everyone departed back to their homes. There was a sense that life could go on again.

Bjorn retreated to his bed, asked for something to dull the pain, and slept. Quiet descended on the big house. By the late afternoon, the sun was breaking through between showers. All seemed well with the world again.

⋘ ⋙

But all was not well.

I was feeding Beithe and her follower under a birch. I would rather have fed her under an elder tree, like I used to at home, where the good spirits would look after her. But there were no elders out here in the forest. I was worrying about how long the fodder I had managed to cut for them would last, hoping I'd be able to keep them going for the rest of the winter by grazing them in the forest and only feeding them when snow or frost threatened to starve them. I wished I had a building to shelter them, though to be honest Beithe looked happy enough choosing her own spots under the trees. Even standing in the melting snow she was warm, breathing out comforting clouds of steam.

I didn't hear the horse approaching, so I was taken aback when I turned back to the clearing to find my way blocked.

'What brings you back here?' I said to the hooded rider, trying to sound civil.

'I saw you leaving the house yesterday. I know. I know all about it.'

I felt stones grinding in the pit of my stomach. I had to be strong. I stepped forward, looking the white pony in the eye. It backed off into the clearing, allowing me to come up and stand out in the open, to take my space.

'I am a healer.' I took another step and willed the horse back towards the edge of the trees.

'You're a witch.'

I pushed one more step. 'I am the medicine woman.'

The rider pulled the horse to a halt and glared at me. 'I know what's going on.'

'Bjorn needs me.' As soon as the words were out I knew it was

157

a mistake to say them. Boots rammed into the horse's belly and it lunged, knocking me to the ground. I wrapped my arms over my head and called out to the spirits to protect me.

A lightning bolt hit me and as my spine exploded into stars I struck a curse: *'My innocence will purify the deepest well; your guilt will poison you to hell.'*

❦ ❦

Moran tended Bjorn that night. When his sleeping and painkilling draft wore off he woke feeling hungry. Moran was pleased, fed him soup, bread, a little fruit and nut loaf and some elderberry wine. They joked quietly, and spoke in mourning tones about their buried friends.

Then Bjorn said quietly, 'Moran, I need to see Brigid again. My wound's healing but I'm still full of pain. I dreamed about the bear this evening, roaring with agony. Will you fetch her. Please?'

Moran groaned. 'It's a risk, Bjorn, but I'll do my best.'

It was planned as a re-run of two nights ago. Moran sent Alan off to find Brigid whilst he went to Til's cottage to enlist his help. He and Til waited for Alan at Moran's house. It was a dark night and raining, so they expected Alan to take a couple of hours to reach Brigid's bender and return to the village. After three hours they were growing worried, and Til was cursing that he hadn't gone to Brigid's himself instead of Alan. Moran was beside himself with worry for his friend and guilt for deserting Bjorn's bedside.

Just as Til was about to go out in search, the door of the cottage opened and in walked Alan, shaking and panting. He was distraught.

'What in the world is the matter?' Moran shrieked, to a hush from Til.

'Where's Brigid?'

'I couldn't find her at first,' Alan spluttered between pants, 'but then I did, in her lean-to, but, but...' He was unable to finish.

'What? But what?' Moran urged.

'She's dead,' Alan wailed, shaking his head.

'What do you mean, dead?' asked Til. 'How? Was she murdered? Was it an accident?'

'I don't know. How should I know? She was just dead. Limp,

158

like a dead animal. I don't know. Just dead.'

He began to sob, and Moran put an arm round him and tried to calm him down. He was cold, wet, shivering. Moran wrapped him in a blanket.

'I got there and called her name. No answer, so I tried the bender. Couldn't see her, went in, the bed was tidy, the fire was out, no sign of her. Then I wandered around, not knowing what to do, looking for signs. It just seemed so strange, her not being there. Then I thought maybe she'd already gone to the village or even to the big house. I looked into the lean-to and I tripped over her. She was lying on the floor, in a heap. Honestly, she looked like she'd been tossed in there. I tried to wake her up. I didn't understand it. I went and lit a lamp, tried to see if there was anything I could do, but she was dead. No breath, nothing. What are we going to do?'

'I don't like this,' said Til, quietly.

'What do you mean?' Moran was clasping his hands in front of his chin.

'Was she wounded?' Til asked Alan.

'Yes. I don't know. She's filthy, muddy, it's hard to say, and I couldn't really see. She's got a cut on her face but there's no sign of, you know, a blade, blood.'

Alan was too incoherent for Til. 'I'm going to see for myself. Moran, we must tell Bjorn. Try to break the news gently, maybe wait until daybreak if you can. He'll take it hard.' Moran nodded.

Then Til set off, his thoughts full of shame at his lack of protection of Brigid. He had known she would be in danger for breaching the terms of her banishment, but had wanted some quiet time for himself. He had left her alone there in the forest after she had risked everything to save Bjorn. Why had he not protected her, stayed by her? He strode down the track berating himself, then tripped on a rock and brought himself to a standstill. It was dark and wet.

What was he doing, charging off to the woods like this? What was he going to do when he got there? What was the intelligent thing to do? For once he simply did not know. He just wanted to see her again, to find out whether what Alan had said was true, and if so to try to understand why she was dead, to understand why he, along with everyone else, had abandoned her.

He swithered on the path. Should he go on? He needed someone to talk it all through with, someone else who cared for Brigid, who understood the great changes sweeping their land. Who could do that? Til thought of Tess, his young sister, but decided he couldn't bring her into all this – then of Coll, Brigid's father. He was hiding out there in his cabin on the edge of the forest, not troubling anyone, another loner like himself. But he would be devastated by the news. Or Frigga. She would understand, but she would be devastated too. They all would be, of course, all of them, too shocked and hurt to be any help to anyone. He decided, finally, to go alone. He could always talk later.

So he continued on down the path on his own, slower now, picking his way carefully in the gloom, relying on his feet and knowledge of the path to find the way, and came at length to Brigid's camp. He found her as Alan had said, lying in her lean-to, under the shelter of the old Shield Tree.

It wasn't possible, he thought. Was the magic of the land so weakened that even the great Shield Tree could no longer offer protection to their most powerful shaman?

He crouched beside her and lifted her head onto his lap, pulling her tangled hair, thick with mud, from her face, his hands shaking with the realisation that she had died childless, that there was no successor to her position as bear shaman, no-one there to follow in her path. Her life had been broken off before it could branch.

In his arms she seemed strangely peaceful. He remembered their ceremony with the bear, the skin of which she must be buried in. He resolved to give her a shaman's funeral, no matter the consequences.

He cursed himself for neglecting her, for keeping her at a distance, for never admitting to himself or to her how he really felt. He had always told himself he was too ancient for her, too much like an uncle, just a good friend. He had only ever envisaged himself coming to her as an ancient man, perhaps, for them to grow ancient together. To share their wisdom by a fireside as elders. Now he longed for her, to have been a young man to her young woman. He had grown so used to standing back; knowing how she loved Bjorn. But why had he not come forward when Bjorn had returned to the Braes with Margaret? Why had he hung back? What exactly had he been waiting for?

But one insistent question kept coming back, and eventually he grasped it fully and didn't let go. It stang like a nettle. Why was she dead?

To answer that he needed light, so he crossed the clearing to the bender, smiling grimly again at the good use to which she'd put his gift of hides. He found a lamp by the fire, lit it, then returned. In its yellow pool he saw what Alan had seen. She was muddied from head to foot, her face and legs and hands were grazed, her chin was bruised, her lip split. There were bruises, too, on her legs and shoulders. At first his respect prevented him from looking further, then he undid her clothes and peered at her slim body. He tidied her clothes again, then sat, frozen beside her, racked between shame and anger. She was bruised, especially on her chest, with livid stains as if she had been kicked repeatedly, or even as if, he couldn't bear to think it, as if she had been trampled underfoot.

✟

AILM - PINE

Bjorn's roar brought the big house to a standstill. Margaret reached his doorway just behind Frigga, and they burst into his room to find Til standing by the open shutters, the early morning light filtering in, and Bjorn lying quite still in his bed – an apparent calm at odds with the shout they had heard.

'What is it?' Frigga asked. Bjorn's eyes were closed and he did not open them, simply rolled his head away in a gesture of refusal. She bent over him, but he brushed her away with a growl.

Turning to Til, she frowned. 'What's the matter?'

Til raised his eyebrows and said nothing.

'We heard a great shout,' Margaret said. Til nodded.

'Well, man, what caused it?' Frigga was anxious. 'Has he injured himself?'

'No, the injury was not self-inflicted,' Til replied, cryptically.

'What injury?'

Frigga went to pull down the covers on Bjorn's bed but he clung onto them, then opened his eyes wide and barked, 'Get out, all of you. Go. Leave me alone.'

Margaret backed to the door. His voice was like a stick, pushing her out with each poked word. Frigga stood firm, but Til steered her by her shoulders out of the door, which he closed behind him.

'What in the…?' Frigga stuttered.

'Leave him be. Do as he asks,' said Til, quietly. 'Let him suffer in peace.'

Frigga crossed her arms and would be pushed no further. 'I demand to know what's going on. He's ill. I can't just ignore a scream like that.' She stabbed at Til's chest with her finger. 'What do you know that you're not telling?'

But Til stood impassive in front of the door, blocking her way. Margaret shifted a few steps away, uncomfortable, unwilling to leave the scene but afraid to confront the hunter.

Til stared down at Frigga, saying nothing until her furious outpouring abated. She glowered back, a sense dawning in her that she knew what he knew. Dread swept through her from her feet upwards, like a tide rising, and she swayed as it reached her head. Til steadied her, his hands still on her shoulders. She looked up at him and he nodded and stated the simple fact.

'Brigid's dead.' His arms curled around her, gentle but strong, and he held her, small and birdlike, as sobs shook her. His own tears fell on her feathery hair.

They stood there, united in grief at Bjorn's door, while Margaret dithered and finally turned her back on the pair of them and stomped across the great hall and out of the house.

A few minutes later, Til and Frigga walked slowly across the hall. Niall the stableman entered from outside, saying, 'What's going on?'

Iain Kay was pacing. Elma and Ishbel had broken off from cleaning. Frigga ignored them all and disappeared into the kitchen. Iain and Elma exchanged looks, and Ishbel tip-toed after Frigga to try to find out what had happened.

'There's been a murder,' Til said. Elma sat down. 'Brigid of the Bears is dead. Bjorn the Bearslayer wishes her death to be avenged.'

Iain Kay's cheeks flushed. 'The witch was banished. She was nobody,' he spluttered.

'The witch, as you call her, used her magic to heal our leader and has paid with her life. He'll honour his debt with justice. The murderer must pay the price.'

'Who is the murderer?'

Til shrugged.

'He'll reveal himself. Meanwhile, we have another funeral to organise.'

'We?' Iain looked scornful.

'Bjorn requests the full ceremony that is due to the Bear Shaman.'

'I'll honour no witch.'

'Nor me.' Niall was vehement. Elma looked at her feet, saying nothing.

'There'll be plenty who will. And there'll be suspicion of those who disobey Bjorn's orders and don't.'

With this retort, Til strode out of the big house, whistling to his dogs until they came about. They loped with their master down towards the village, where a small crowd soon gathered around Moran's house, arguing about the news of Brigid's murder, speculating on the perpetrator, and building up a head of steam to hold a funeral worthy of a martyr.

'We should bury her with her mother,' Moran said.

'Both she and the bear have died for our leader. We must honour her with whatever ritual is needed to return her to Mother Earth and appease the bears of the spirit world,' Til reminded them.

He, Moran and Alan were trying to get the crowd of villagers organised when Frigga appeared, looking tired but resolute. Immediately, questions were fired at her. 'Where do you think we should hold the funeral? Should she be burned or buried? When should it be?'

She hushed them and the 'shhh' spread around the crowd, until they were all waiting to hear what she had to say.

She smiled. 'Well, well, what have we come to? It's been a long time since a crone like me was asked for guidance. Normally all you want from me is a poppy drink when you're hurting, or instructions for baking a pie.'

'Go on, mother, tell us what you think we should do,' said a voice. It was Iain the Bat.

'There's been enough bad luck for us all,' chimed in Eileen Moine. 'If there's a way to stop the angry spirits, let's hear it.'

'I can't say, no-one can say, what the spirits will do. But there are ways to respect the bears. Brigid would have known best, but I do know she wanted to be buried with the bear, in its skin, in the cave where it used to spend its winters. But first we must light fires to bring the spirits here, to guide her to their world. And then we must sing to them, of course.'

'Where should we build the fires?' Til asked.

'One at her camp, where she died. One here, where she belonged, in the village,' Frigga said, indicating the swath of meadow and the well around which the houses were clustered. 'And another by the bear's cave where we'll do the burial rituals, though only women can go there.'

'Will it help if we cut wood for you to use by the cave?' Alan asked.

'It would. Birch, fresh, is best. And pine. Moran, will you get a fire going here? A good big one, to burn all day and all night.'

164

Moran nodded and there were several offers of help.

'Til and I will go to make preparations at Brigid's camp.'

'Can I be of any help?' Tess, Til's sister, stepped forward. 'Brigid saved my life too, when I lost my baby. I'd like to pay my respects.'

Frigga nodded.

'And you'd better come too, little one.' Enya looked back at her, wide-eyed. 'There are a few things you're not too young to learn.'

Caphel was hanging back behind Enya, looking sullen, listening. Then he burst out, 'The priest'll not stand for it. It's pagan. She was banished.'

A couple of other people nodded. Their doubts had been voiced.

But Frigga retorted, 'My first loyalty is to our headman, not the priest. And look what the Christian's banishment brought us. We've just buried your father, Caphel, and Eileen's brother, and Eachan. That's enough, surely? Let's make sure we do this burial right before we anger the spirits any further.'

'Perhaps it's God that's angry,' he persisted.

'Well, if you want to think that you can, my boy, but it seems to me that all our problems started since the priest arrived with this new-fangled god. Have nothing to do with the funeral if that's what you want. But the rest of us are going to pay our respects, as our ancestors always have.'

Caphel looked dejected. 'She saved my life, too.'

Til said, 'You're right, she did. Just a few months back. Perhaps we should do something with her boat? Frigga, can we send it after her, in case she needs it in the next world?'

Frigga shrugged. 'When Big Angus died, we built his boat into his funeral fire. I suppose we could do the same with Brigid's coracle.'

'You'd better come with us to fetch it,' Til said to Caphel, who brightened up, his criticism of the event shelved now he had a role. Some of the other boys wanted to go with him to fetch the boat, so in the end it was quite a crowd that set out along the lochside. The day was brightening and low-angled sun glinted on the water. The birchwoods on the far side of the loch stood out as deep maroon against grey gneiss cliffs and the white snow-blanketed scars where trees had been cleared for pasture.

Before they reached Brigid's camp, Frigga stopped the boys. 'The coracle's tied up under a willow by the shore down there. You boys take it straight back to the village, and be careful with it. And when you get there, be sure to find some pine pitch – there's some in our byre, Caphel – and smear it on well so it'll burn properly. Moran'll help you.'

The coracle was small and light and the lads carried it easily between them. They set off, chattering and excited.

The others carried on into the hazelwoods. A little further on, Frigga also stopped Enya, Til and Tess so that she could enter Brigid's camp alone. 'I want to look closely at what I find before we start leaving our marks all over the place.' She did not need to say that she wanted to be quiet with Brigid one last time.

Approaching the lean-to, she was surprised to find Coll sitting against the shield tree, his face streaked with tears, eyes red. He saw her, got to his feet and reached out, and the old man and woman clung together for a while. Wind moaned in the treetops. There was no birdsong. Eventually, Frigga pulled herself away, wiped her eyes and looked around her at the scene of the crime.

'What happened here?' she asked Coll, but he just shook his head, numb, and sat back down. She began pacing around, then stepped into the lean-to where Brigid's body lay broken. She recoiled at the sight. Brigid's bonny face was bruised and swollen around the jaw. The crooked bear's skull looked down at her from its shelf.

'Did she come in here herself?' she asked the skull. It stared back.

Then she noticed tracks in the ground, two furrows from two dragged heels. Frigga followed them out of the doorway where they were trampled by footprints and the hoofmarks of the cow. She looked around and saw that the cow and calf were waiting beside the fodder store. 'The cow's hungry, Coll. Can you give them some food?'

Coll prised himself to his feet.

'What happened here, Beithe?' Frigga asked. 'If only you could tell us.'

The cow gave a low moo as Coll started to tug hay from a sheaf.

Frigga picked the tracks up again where they continued out into the clearing, two clear parallel lines that ran for a dozen yards then stopped among a clutter of footprints and a frenzy of hoof marks, as if a pony had been galloping on the spot.

The hoof prints led Frigga to a picture of the struggle. What could Brigid do if a horse was being driven to trample her? She cringed at the thought and shouted to Til to come. He strode over.

'Look, here, a horse has been going beserk, and look, that's where she was dragged to the lean-to, it must be, her two feet made this trail.' Til looked with his hunter's eyes and nodded, then turned to the hoof marks, bending down, tracing around one of the clearer imprints.

'If Donald were here, he'd know the horse straight off,' he said, setting them both thinking.

'Perhaps we can still tell.' Frigga looked more closely. 'They're big, aren't they? Is there anything distinctive about them?'

'I wouldn't know. Horses aren't my thing. But you're right; I'd say they're too big to made by a garron, or by any of the local horses for that matter.'

'Well, I wouldn't know. Keep quiet about this for now. We'll need to get a few questions answered at the stables.' They looked at each other. Neither of them got on with Niall the stableman.

'It had to be one of the Christians,' Frigga said.

'Well, that's obvious. Who else would want her dead?'

'Who could hate her so much? She was such a gentle soul.'

'She could be wild too, remember? She was no mouse.'

'But she healed Bjorn. Surely they'd be grateful for that.'

'But Frigga, there are several folk at the big house who couldn't stand the consequences of that.'

'What do you mean?'

'Her healing was a threat to them, if the old ways were shown to have power, more power than their one angry god. James is furious. Iain Kay is livid. It undermines them. Then there's Niall. He always hated her, for years. And now Diarmid has turned against her, blamed her for what happened to Donald and Calem.'

'But Calem is fine.' Frigga shook her head.

'I know, but it didn't seem to stop Diarmid calling her every name under the sun. I think he felt humiliated by her.'

'True enough.'

'And then, if we're naming names, which I seem to be, we'd better not forget the pale lady herself. Margaret.' He mouthed her name with loathing. 'After all, if anyone has a grudge to bear…'

'What do you mean?' Coll had joined them and was looking baffled.

'Did you not know?' asked Til.

'What?'

Frigga laid a hand on Coll's arm. 'She loved Bjorn.'

'Yes, I guessed that. But what's that to Margaret?'

'The feeling was mutual.'

'But there was nothing to be jealous of, surely.'

'Oh no?' She lifted her eyebrows. 'You should have heard him howl when he heard she was dead.'

'That wasn't for the loss of a surgeon, I can assure you,' Til added.

'Well, well,' Coll murmured.

'And whose horse has hoofs the size of this? I think it should be Bjorn asking these questions, don't you?'

Til nodded. 'Aye.'

'You'd better go, Til. Tell Bjorn. Ask him what we should do. Meanwhile, I'll try to set her poor body to rest and get her dressed up for the funeral. Come back with some strong men and a stretcher.'

He nodded again and hugged her briefly, shook Coll's hand, then hugged him too, as tears came to their eyes. Frigga watched them, and shook her head.

'We're all getting old,' she muttered, then remembered Tess and Enya, standing where she had insisted they stop, just outside the clearing. They looked cold. Enya was pale and tiny, but had something steely in her small posture, a determination that Frigga recognised. She waved them over, and Enya bounded across to her grandmother like a puppy let off a leash.

'What's happening?' she demanded, burying herself in a cuddle.

'We have to do a very important, but very difficult thing,' Frigga began. 'Poor Brigid needs to get ready for her funeral. It's her last time to be dressed, so she'll need a wash and the most special outfit put on. But I think she'd like to be modest, so I'll wash her in private, and then you can help to make her look beautiful.'

Enya's questions tumbled out.

'Why can't I see her first, before she gets washed? Why's it her last time to be dressed? Where will she go after the funeral? Can I go there too?'

Frigga answered her patiently, and held her while she cried, and then sent her down to the lochside where some gorse was growing, to look for any flowers she could find. The spiny bush, the one plant that has blossoms in every month of the year, would be in flowering mood somewhere.

Frigga, Til, Coll and Tess carried Brigid into her bender and laid her on her nest of fleeces and soft-coloured blankets for the last time. Frigga shooed the men out, Coll to build a fire and keep an eye on Enya, Til to go to Bjorn. Then the two women prepared to lay out the body.

✝

ONN - GORSE

The afternoon was over. The sun had finished its brief low-angled perusal of people's lives, glinted through the entangled branches of the diminishing woods, and slumped feebly behind the hills to the southwest. A band of cloud lay above the Braes and as the sun sank the clouds lit up peach and bronze, like a banner of flame over the loch. As if in response, fires sprouted around the loch as the sky faded to smoky grey: one at Brigid's camp, one on the far side where the harvest fire was always lit, and one in the village itself.

Bjorn sat by his window, watching. His wounds were healing well. He would soon be up and about – maybe not back to normal for a while yet, but he knew the danger was past. Though at what price? He watched the fires being lit and was satisfied, but the urge to be down there beside them was overwhelming. He imagined the stories being shared, the villagers' recollections of Brigid being pooled, the legend being woven from the threads of anecdote and memory. They would be honouring her, he was sure; telling jokes, remembering funny moments, recalling good times. He was missing it all.

He had sent Margaret away, which he regretted now as he sat in the gloaming on his own. With the sun gone the chill air had become uncomfortable, so he got gingerly to his feet and closed his shutters. He went to the door, opened it and bawled, 'Can I have some light in here?' then sat back on the bed, wincing at the movement. He could easily light a lamp himself, but he hoped for some company.

To his surprise, James was the first through the door with a candle in his hand, which he lit from the fire and stood on a stone shelf. Bjorn stifled his disappointment.

'Hello, James. Thank you.'

'I wish I could bring the light of the Lord to these heathens.' His mellowness from the previous day had evaporated, and he was back to his usual acid self. Bjorn stiffened.

'We will honour Brigid in whatever way we wish. I want no

170

interference, James. The local traditions matter to these people, and it is not the Norse way to stop them.'

'Sometimes I fear the Norse way to be as close to the devil as theirs.'

Bjorn sighed. He had no energy for this just now.

'Brigid's no threat to you now.' He tried to sound mild. 'Leave them be. They honoured the good Christians the good Christian way the other day. Now let them mourn their medicine woman.'

'Why should they mourn the witch? That's what I want to know. I should put a stop to it.'

'You will not, James. Who do you think is headman here? I'm telling you, we leave these people in peace and let them do what they will tonight.'

'Or else?' James sneered.

'Or else you'll go.'

'If I had my way I'd leave tomorrow. The Bishop needs to hear of this pagan filth. This place needs a mission.'

'Then go if you wish, James. And give my greetings to the Bishop. But remember, we're not ruled from Dalriada here. Our law is the Udal, our Jarl is Orkney, our justice is Norse. You're a guest of Norway here, and you must obey the Norwegian rules or face the consequences.'

There was an uncomfortable pause as James bit his tongue, then a rap on the door broke it. Til's head appeared. 'Sorry. I'll come back later.'

'No, I was just going,' James said, taking the opportunity to escape and pushing Til against the door as he swept past him. Bjorn lay back on his bed with a sigh.

'What can I do about that man?' he moaned. 'It'll be the best thing for all of us if he does go back to Iona, or wherever it is he wants to go.'

Til drew the chair to the bedside.

'How are you?'

'I'm healing. Steadily. Brigid's magic was powerful, though I fear I'll die of the wound to my heart instead.' He gave a wan smile. 'I see they're lighting fires by the loch. I'm glad.'

'Aye, it'll be some night tonight.'

'And the burial?'

'In the early hours. She'll be carried to the bear's cave by torchlight and buried as the moon rises.'

'I want to be there.'

'It'll be hard on you.'

'I must pay my respects. I must see her one last time.'

'All right. Can you make it to the village? We'll be burning her coracle later, after we've brought her back from her camp. That would be a good time for you to be there. I'll check with Frigga. The business in the cave is really the women's ceremony, you know.'

'Is Enya there?'

'She's with Frigga, dressing the body.'

'Really? She's so young.'

'We're never too young for death, unfortunately,' Til replied. There was a pause, and Bjorn shuffled on the bed. Til waited until Bjorn looked at him again, then proceeded to tell him about the hoof prints and how Brigid appeared to have died.

'They were big prints.' Til stuck both forefingers out to show the scale. 'This big. There's no way it was one of the local ponies.'

'I'll ask some questions,' Bjorn assured him. 'Now you'd better go. Let me know when I should make my way to the village. I'll need plenty of time.'

'You'll see the procession. Come then. Good luck with your questions.' He left Bjorn thinking about what his first move should be.

When Margaret appeared, he told her he planned to go to the village that night. She was displeased, but he was firm.

'You should come with me. She healed me. We must show our gratitude for that, at least.'

She grumbled, but Bjorn insisted. In the end she agreed, and even deigned to dress as the wife of the leader, in full Norse robes. She opened the trunk in the corner of the room, unfolding the long red dress she had been given as a wedding gift by Bjorn's father, and then rummaged for the torcs and brooches that went with it. Her scuffling grew more and more furious.

'What's the matter?' Bjorn was becoming irritated.

'Nothing, I'm just looking for a necklace.'

'Why not wear the one my aunt gave you for the wedding? It was my grandmother's.'

'But I wanted to wear my silver crucifix.'

He laughed. 'Forget it. Let me assure you, that would hardly be appropriate tonight.'

◆ ◆

Frigga led the procession, holding her torch high. It was slow going. The path was icy and difficult where it faced south, having melted and frozen repeatedly in the sunshine and frost of the past two days. No-one spoke. There were grunts from the men who were carrying the stretcher, ice crunching underfoot, and spitting from the torches. Then Frigga began a song in her wiry voice, an old slow lament with an awkward twist in the melody at the end of each verse that suited their walking. Moran and Til, who knew all the old airs, joined her from their position at the back of the stretcher, and gradually the air lifted the voices from all the walkers, and pulled them on toward the village.

As the procession approached, a hush fell on the crowd gathered by the bonfire. They moved aside to allow Brigid's body to be placed on the stone bench nearest the fire, where the light enabled everyone to see her. Her hair was combed out, shining like an otter's pelt in the flames. Her pale face, with subtle painting, made it seem as if she might wake at any moment. Around her neck was a beaded band, but that was the only article of human clothing she wore. The rest of her body was that of the bear, and its thick pelt gleamed, glossy as chestnut in the firelight. She lay with her hands crossed over her belly, arms cradling the bear skull.

There were murmurs from around the crowd and people pushed and shoved to be able to see the bear woman. Frigga stood with her torch blazing next to Brigid and announced:

'Here lies Brigid of the Bears. Let all those who respect the bear come up and make your peace. It was a wrongful deed that killed her, and what will follow from it we cannot know. But for now, let all the innocent folk come here and thank her for the good she did us; let the fearful ask her to be gentle when she reaches the spirit world, and let the sad come together and comfort each other.

'I was by her mother's side the night that Brigid came into the world. It was a full moon, the night of spring equinox, nearly thirty years ago.' Frigga began to relate the story of Brigid's life, winding her way from her learning of herbal lore and magic from her mother, the medicine woman, through to her strife over her mother's funeral

173

ceremony, and finally her banishment.

'We did not honour her mother in the traditional way, and perhaps that was a part of the reason for our troubles ever since. Let's not make the same mistake again. Brigid of the Bears, we honour you.'

That was her speech, and when it was done she stepped aside and looked about for somewhere to put her torch. Moran took it from her and someone proffered a bench that she could sit on, which she accepted. It had been a long way to carry a wooden torch and she felt old in her bones tonight. She took the beaker of rowanberry wine that was handed to her and the oatcake that followed, and sat watching, munching and sipping as the villagers stepped forward one by one to touch the bear's fur or Brigid's hair, some murmuring to her, some leaving an offering of some food, a pot of honey, a bowl of berry jam, or pieces of dried fruit, then stepping back into the crowd to let the next come forward.

Til sat opposite Frigga playing his clarsach, sometimes with someone who wanted to sing, sometimes just letting the old tunes flow from the strings. Tess joined him on a whistle for a lament that everyone knew, and the crowd's voice swayed with the flames.

Then all heads turned as a horse-drawn cart rolled down the track from the big house, Iain Kay at the reigns, Bjorn and Margaret behind him. The crowd parted for them to approach the fire, but the cart stopped a little way off.

Iain jumped down and first gave Margaret a hand, then the two of them helped while Bjorn shuffled to the back of the cart and carefully lowered himself to the ground. He leaned heavily on Iain, nodded to Moran and waved him over. Moran kept close by him on one side, and with Margaret on the other, he took his own weight and slowly walked towards Brigid. A murmur of approval bubbled up from the crowd.

Margaret stopped short of touching Brigid, but Bjorn stood gazing at her, stroking her furry arm. Her dead face had lost none of its defiance, her jaw was still strong. She looked as if she was thinking hard. He lifted her arm gently, careful not to disturb the cradled skull, and clasped on a torc of twisted bands of silver, just above the paw. Holding it like a hand he shouted, 'Hail Brigid! Bear Shaman. Medicine Woman. Thank you for my life, for healing me, for protecting me from the anger of the bear spirits when I killed one of their kind. Brigid, if you can, protect us from their greater fury at your murder. Forgive us our foolish ways, our stupid mistakes, our wickedness. We will never forget you, Medicine Woman, Bear Shaman, Brigid.'

The power in his voice was like lightning, and his final words were repeated by the crowd with a shout that echoed back from the loch like thunder.

Bjorn stood for a while longer in a daze, poring over the face of the woman he had loved. He noticed the faint hairs above her mouth, its uneven shape, the tiny scar above the right lip. He wondered what else about her he had not had time to notice. He reached out to her hair, but its softness brought tears to his eyes. Frigga beckoned him, patting the bench next to her.

'Sit down, Bjorn.'

He swayed. Margaret stepped up to him and made a feeble effort to help, but it was Moran that held him up and all she achieved was to get in the way. She looked awkward, dressed in the long gown of a Viking noblewoman, and held her head stiffly as if the thick neckband of beads and silver would choke her. Someone produced a stool for her too, so she sat next to Bjorn, who put one arm around Frigga and accepted a beaker of wine with the other. Margaret refused the cup offered to her, rubbing her pregnant belly as if in explanation.

Bjorn noticed Enya standing behind Frigga, holding Tess's hand. She smiled at him and he winked. 'I've something for you,' he said, beckoning her to him. He gave his beaker to Margaret to hold, and dug gingerly into a pocket in his leather jerkin, which was engraved and laced with designs of otters, lynx and foxes. Enya reached out and touched it admiringly, then whooped as she saw what he had produced from his pocket.

'It's the Lucky Bear!'

'It is indeed, and you must have it back. It's helped save my life. I just wish that Brigid had had it yesterday instead of me. Look after it well, Enya, now that it's back in your safe hands.'

She beamed at him, stepped forward and planted a kiss clumsily on his cheek then, clasping the bear in her hand, she stepped back to the comfort of Frigga, who wrapped an arm around her waist and held her tight.

A drum began at the lochside, and everyone turned to watch

Caphel and the other boys as they bore the coracle above their heads, chanting a song that the villagers would sing when carrying the body of a fisherman drowned at sea. The crowd picked up the mournful tune and stamped, slowly, in time. When they reached the fire, the boys tossed the boat onto the flames, and with a roar it caught. It had been smeared with pine resin to make it burn fiercely, and so it blazed, lighting up the village and the loch and the tears on the mourners' faces.

More drinks did the rounds and more songs were sung, but when the boat had burnt itself out a restlessness grew in the crowd. Husbands hugged wives goodnight, sisters grouped together and the women gradually separated out from the men, gathering towards Brigid and Frigga.

'Will you join us for the burial?' Frigga asked Margaret, but she shook her head.

'I'll go back with Bjorn.'

Frigga shrugged.

'You're doing it the old way, women only?' asked Bjorn.

'Of course. It's what she would have wanted.'

'I'm sure you're right. I'm pleased the village is honouring her. Thank you, Frigga. I'll watch you leave, if I may?'

Frigga nodded. Four of the women, Tess among them, had each seized a handle of the stretcher and were ready to set off. A quiet fell on the crowd and Frigga took the moment to begin to sing 'Mama of the Lark,' a warbling lament about the death of the Lark's mother. The song had a note of joy in the middle of the chorus, a trill of hope like the lark's song itself. Singing this strange uplifting song, she relit her torch from the fire and set off through the village towards the low path into the woods that followed the burn upstream to the bear's cave. Behind her came Brigid, borne on the stretcher, then several more women carrying torches, and all but the tiniest and most feeble of the girls and women of the village thronged at the back.

It was a long walk in, but they took turns carrying Brigid, all the women and older girls keen to help.

At the clearing they set the stretcher down and lit the funeral spirit fires and once again they sang, weary now. Frigga pushed Enya forward with a small basket, and she walked around Brigid sprinkling her with the yellow gorse flowers she had collected. They

176

all sang the final song of the funeral.

The gorse flowers every day of the year,
for the earth our mother is full of cheer,
come rain come shine,
come hail come snow,
the earth our mother is full of cheer.

So, dear one, your memory too
is sweet whenever we think of you,
come rain come shine,
come hail come snow,
the gorse will always remind us of you.

Then Maeve, Tess, Ishbel and Elma carried Brigid up to the entrance of the cave and lifted her off the stretcher. Frigga entered the cave and she and Tess pulled Brigid in beside the leaf-covered bear. They didn't cover her, but Frigga put a pillow of cloth under her head, smoothed out her hair, and then retreated. All the women had found stones, and one by one they came and laid them in the doorway of the cave, piling them up into a great mound that blocked the cave entrance completely except for a small hole.

'Why are we blocking the door, Frigga?' asked Enya.

'Because we have no bear shaman now, little one.'

'Will there not be another one?'

'I don't know. Brigid had no daughter to take her place.'

'Can't I take her place?'

'You're much too little, and you're not her daughter.'

'But she gave me her lucky bear!' Enya held it out.

'Well, if you turn out to be the next shaman of the bear when you grow up, you can come here and open up the cave again.'

'Can I?'

'If your magic is strong enough.'

'Brigid said I'll be good at magic.'

'Did she now?' Frigga ruffled her hair. 'Come along. The fires are burning, the dawn's on its way. Time for home.'

177

ᚢ Ur - Heather

The next day, Bjorn's wounds were much improved though still sore. He called for Frigga but was told that she was still at home. Moran came with a painkilling draught and a clean poultice.

Bjorn was jittery. 'Brigid's murderer is walking around out there and I'm lying here doing nothing. Tell Frigga I need her advice.'

The house was quiet and Bjorn fidgeted in his bed, racked by questions. He asked for Til, but was told he had gone hunting. Eventually, he summoned Iain Kay to his bedside.

'Iain, I'm grateful to you for taking me to Brigid's funeral last night, but I noticed you didn't take part. Why was that?'

'You're my leader: I'll obey your commands. But Brigid was banished as a witch. There's no way I could pay her the honour you did, all due respect to yourself.' Iain glanced at Bjorn as he spoke, then lowered his gaze to the floor.

'So you believe that in the eyes of God she was a witch.' Bjorn kept his voice even.

'I do.'

'And her punishment was just.'

'Yes.'

'But she was to be punished with banishment, not murder, is that not right?'

'That's correct.' Iain looked up at Bjorn.

'So whoever killed her was not acting justly, since she had already received her punishment, and taken it. And moreover, she had saved my life. There was no justice in her paying for it with her own.'

'Put like that, I suppose not.'

'So do you agree with me that there's a crime to be answered?'

'I suppose there must be.' Iain nodded, looking down at his feet again, his dark hair hiding his eyes.

'Do you know who killed her, Iain?' Bjorn's voice was gentle, and Iain looked him straight in the eye.

'No, I don't.'

'She was killed by someone on a horse.'

'So I heard.'

'And that horse had far bigger hoofs than the wee garrons.'

'That can't be.'

'It must be. I've the testimony of Til, Frigga, Coll, Tess – even wee Enya saw the prints of a horse's hoofs. Big prints.' He showed how big with his hand.

'But there's only the one horse here with hoofs that size, and it could never be that one.'

'Go on. Why not?'

'Because it's yours. Thor, the white stallion.'

'The wedding horse. And why could it not have been that one?'

'Why? Because you've been laid up in bed.'

'But that doesn't stop someone else riding it.'

'But it's a simple matter of the law. No-one else has the right to ride your horse.'

'We're not talking rights here, Iain. It's all wrongs.'

Iain walked over to the window and looked out of it for a while, then turned back to Bjorn. 'So your question is, who rode out on Thor two days ago?'

'That's the question. Do you think you can find out?'

'I can try.'

'Do so, and quickly please.' Bjorn smiled encouragement at Iain, who frowned and then headed for the door. 'By the way, when will the boat be ready for sailing? The weather seems to be fairing up. We need to take Bran to his family and I'd like us to set off as soon as we can while the weather's clear, or the next gale'll keep us trapped here.'

Iain frowned. 'Are you well enough?'

'Nothing the sea-air won't put right,' Bjorn replied, sounding more certain than he felt.

'I'll see if I can find Angus for you. I heard he was working on some ropes at the shore. He'll know. I think they're slowed down without Donald to help with the metal work.'

'Do that. And send James to me if you see him.'

When Iain returned he shut the door carefully behind him, stood close to Bjorn's bed, and bent down to whisper. 'I have some information.'

'Good, what is it?'

'Niall denies that anyone took your horse out two days ago. In

179

fact, he says he's been stabled ever since the hunt. But that's not all. He reminded me that yours isn't the only horse here with big hoofs. It could be any of the Dalriadan ponies. James' mare is the same.'

'Of course it is. How could I forget that?'

'So it seems the murderer may have taken either yours or James' horse.'

'Or it casts suspicion on James.'

'But it couldn't possibly be him.'

'Why not? He hated Brigid more than anyone else.'

Iain shook his head and frowned. 'He's a holy man.'

Bjorn scoffed. 'I wouldn't like to know what that man could do in the name of God.' Iain looked uncomfortable, but said nothing. The silence grew awkward until Bjorn switched tack.

'What about the boat?' he asked. 'Is it ready?'

Iain shrugged.

'Well, go and find out. I want to leave tomorrow if we can. It may take us more than one day at this time of year and Bran awaits his funeral. Apart from which, I need someone with more authority than me to judge this murder. I need to bring Sigurd into it.'

'Will you take James to Orkney?'

'Aye, and anyone else we suspect. Your son, for that matter.'

'Diarmid was with Angus all day, and you can ask him if you don't believe me.'

'All right. It was just that he also seemed to have it in for Brigid.'

'He said she humiliated him. He's impetuous, but he's no murderer.'

Bjorn sighed. 'All right.'

After Iain had gone, he lay mulling over the scanty evidence he had, convincing himself that his brother-in-law had done his worst. As if on cue, James was next through the door.

'You wanted to see me again. I'm flattered. Seeking penance for last night?'

'I am not. I'm inviting you to come to Orkney. In fact, I'll put that differently. I'd like you to accompany me to the funeral of Bran. You'll have your opportunity to talk to the Bishop, and I to get to the bottom of this murder.'

'I don't see how my going to Orkney will help that.'

'To be quite frank, James, I consider you to be the most likely culprit. I can think of few people with both a reason to kill her and access to the murder weapon. You have both.'

'The murder weapon? What are you talking about?'

'You tell me. I'm just telling you I'm considering you a suspect. If I'm wrong, perhaps that'll motivate you to help me.'

'This is outrageous. I've been here throughout, anyone will tell you, I've been busy with my chapel plans…'

Bjorn said nothing, and watched James blush and bluster until he stormed out of the room. He lay for a while longer, then he got up and went out to the main hall. There he found Diarmid and Alan with the great main sail of the longboat spread between them.

'How is it? Bjorn asked.

'It looks fine to us, you'd better check it.'

Bjorn looked it over with approval.

'Are we really going tomorrow?' Alan looked excited at the prospect.

'If the boat's fit for it I'm keen to go as soon as we can. There's a good wind just now, but the next gale won't be long away and I don't want Bran to wait much longer.'

'I saw Angus this morning, and he said the boat was ready for sailing, bar the ropes,' Diarmid said.

'That's what I want to hear. I'm expecting him. Let me know when he arrives. I'm going to raid the kitchen while the women are all away with the fairies.'

The young men laughed and began to roll the sail. Bjorn emerged shortly with some bread and cheese which he shared with them.

'Do I have sixteen pairs, do you know?' he asked between mouthfuls.

'Oars or men?' asked Alan.

'Both, of course, though I can't believe it'll be calm enough for us to need the sticks much at this time of year.'

'You'll have more volunteers than you can take,' Alan assured him.

While they were chewing, Angus the Boat arrived with Iain Kay.

'Angus – the very one. Is the boat ready?' Bjorn called.

'Aye.'

'Good man. Can we leave in the morning, first light?'

'I see no reason why not.'

'Then it's on. Get everyone ready. We only need provisions for two days, and if the wind's on our side and we're off early we could do it in one. Iain, is Bran's body ready?'

'He's in the shed down by the boat.'

'Good. Let's meet there this afternoon, all willing men, and choose the crew. Pass the word around to meet at the shore this afternoon, all those who are coming.'

Bjorn strolled down to the shore a couple of hours later, feeling sore but able to walk. He was pleased with his choice of crew: mostly young fit men who had never been to Orkney and relished the opportunity, and a few of the older, more experienced sailors. He included a few women, Tess and Ishbel among them, for he knew how they helped morale and somehow toned down the debauchery that the crew would inevitably indulge in when away from home. And of course they were as strong at the oars as most of the men, and could look after themselves perfectly well.

On the way back up from the shore, he met Til with his dogs. He had killed a roe buck in the woods behind Brigid's camp, and offered it to Bjorn, who invited him to the big house to share it. They fried its heart and liver over the fire in the kitchen. Margaret shunned the food and hunched in a corner of the great hall, embroidering by candlelight. Til and Bjorn talked long and hard about Brigid's death, circling over and back over the possible suspects. Again and again they returned to James: he had both means and reason to have wished the medicine woman dead. Bjorn tired, and Til sent him early to his bed to rest before the sail.

The next morning, most of the village was there to see them off. They were at the shore before dawn by lamplight. The ship had been floated off the beach the night before and stood at anchor. The body of Bran was already on board, wrapped in cloths and blankets and lashed to the stern. The corpse was beginning to smell: they would be glad of the wind.

Bjorn said goodbye to Margaret. She had tried to protest at his going and showed concern for his injury, but looked relieved to see him back in action. He had asked if she would come too, but she was terrified of the sea – as was James, though his protests and excuses had fallen on deaf ears.

Coracles ferried the crew from the shore. Bjorn was one of the first onto the boat, taking it gently. From there he urged the others on board. By first light they were ready, and set off down the uigh that emptied the loch. It was full, rapid and rocky and it took all their nerve to steer down it, bobbing and bouncing. But Angus the Boat was at the tiller, and he had navigated it many times. Bjorn was confident in him. The throat was short and soon they were in the main body of the sea loch, which opened out into a broad expanse of water. The wind was fresh out of the south-west and they raised the big sail and tacked up the loch, heading north-west out to the headland where the bear had lived. They looked for signs of smoke from the spirit fires in the woods. Bjorn convinced himself he could make out a whisp.

The swell at the mouth of the loch heaved the boat about, its bow swooping and diving by turns. Experienced sailors reassured newcomers. Bjorn saw that Tess was clutching at her bench with eyes wide. 'Don't worry Tess. Getting out of the loch is always the worst bit. The loch funnels the motion. It'll not be so bouncy outside.' She swallowed and nodded her head.

Then they turned north, side on to the waves. There were wide eyes and screams as the breakers towered over the shallow boat. It was long and narrow, but low, with only a few feet below water level and no more above. But it was a brilliant design, lifted by the rollers like a cork, and it scudded along them like a cormorant about to take flight. The water sprayed off the bow as if the dragon, whose head reared at the front, was spouting smoke. The big sail captured all the wind it could and they soared, the boat leaning to one side with the fabric billowing. Bjorn sat up front, a smile lighting his face, his heart pounding with exhilaration at being on the sea again. This was where he belonged, shouting commands. He'd been a sailing captain since he was a lad: he'd been reared to be a seaman, to lead a crew, to ride the white horses.

In the stern, perched just in front of Bran's body, James cowered, clammy-skinned, eyes closed, rosary shuffling between his fingers, lips moving.

The wind picked up in strength as they turned north-east up the coast to Cape Wrath, and the ship careered along with it. The sea was powerful under them, and they made tremendous progress, reaching the Cape in just a couple of hours of sailing. Most of the crew were moon-faced with the thrill, though some sat white-knuckled and pale, less trusting of the ship as endless grey walls of water thrust up and threatened to overturn them. There were bangs as the boat, lifted by one wave, fell onto the next, and plenty of sea water splashed over the crew, but otherwise the day was dry and clear. Bjorn's mood was buoyant, his spirits lifted by the song of the sail and the positive thrust of the keel. Invigorated by the drama of the sea cliffs and skerries, he felt as if the spray was encouraging them onwards.

On the north coast they were sheltered from some of the wind and the sea was lighter, but there was still enough breeze to keep them moving. Bjorn marvelled at their luck: he couldn't think of a better day's sailing. By noon they could see Ben Lyon. By mid-afternoon they were approaching the islands, and Bjorn knew, if the wind kept up, that they would reach Birsay by nightfall.

And they did, sailing among the Orkney islands at sunset, the sky a blaze of orange, the mood of the company all high expectation and pride in their boat, in their captain and in their seamanship.

They were met by surprised fishermen in a full harbour, boats lying several deep. They tied their ship to one of the others. After explaining their mission, messages were sent up to the Jarl's hall and the monastery, and Bran's body was carried ashore.

Stiff and wobbly after their sail, they clambered shoreward over the boats, where they were met and welcomed by Bjorn's cousin, Ivar, another nephew of the Jarl. Ivar was a giant of a man: swarthy, bearded and long-haired, with a booming voice and easy laugh. He was dismayed to hear of the death of Bran, an old childhood friend and his companion on many a raiding spree. They had shared the same hard-drinking, brawling, feasting priorities and though they had argued over spoils on more than one occasion, their friendship ran deep. Bjorn and Ivar had never been so close: Bjorn found him too brash and too pugilistic, but his boisterous welcome seemed somehow appropriate to complete the windswept day and they were soon blethering their way to the Jarl's palace with the crew in train, where they were promised enough food and drink and fires and dancing to see them from there to Norway.

So the people of the Braes found themselves in the Great Hall in the Jarl's palace, with a barrel of heather ale broken open, and they settled down to the Orcadian hospitality of the biggest and most powerful man of the North.

EAHADH - ASPEN

'So, nephew, what brings you? We don't get many passing sailors at this time of year,' Sigurd bawled. Bjorn had not seen his uncle for several years, and he was fatter and uglier than ever, with his thin, slimy hair and beetly eyebrows. They sat with full tankards at the top of a lavish table, long enough to seat all the hungry crew and plenty of other excited householders.

'First, tell me how you're keeping,' Bjorn replied.

'My wife tells me I'm even more bad-tempered than usual, and the bloody gout keeps me in bed half the year.' Sigurd's breath rasped between shouts. 'But I still bring in more taxes than any of the other Jarls, so I must be doing something right.'

Bjorn had known Sigurd since childhood, and had always loved him. His gruff behaviour and huge size had earned him the family nickname Sigurd the Bear, though he was known as Sigurd the Stout to most others.

'You set a good example by being generous with your wealth,' Bjorn said, admiring the spread.

'I've heard that you do the same, my boy.' Sigurd put a paw on Bjorn's shoulder. 'I always thought you'd be a good leader, ever since you were a lad. You had the right feeling for what was fair and what wasn't. And you're curious about the locals, that always helps.' He tapped his mug of beer. 'Drink up.'

Bjorn slurped, hoping he looked more cheerful than he felt.

'So was it a good sail?'

'Marvellous. We flew here as straight as a gannet.'

'Rather you than me. I can't abide the water, as you know. I like to back the seafaring of others in the hope they'll do the sailing for me.'

'Well, it looks like it's paying off: your harbour's full.'

'Aye. We might not have many trees here, but we've any number of boat-builders and fitters. They get the timber from somewhere, mostly your part of the world I imagine, and the rope and sail-makers are thriving.' He emptied his tankard and waved over a servant, who filled both his and Bjorn's mugs from a large bronze jug. They toasted, and Sigurd pinned his nephew with his brown watery eyes, his pupils like the points of claws. 'So, what brings you here?'

'We bring no good news, I'm afraid,' Bjorn replied, holding his gaze. 'We bring the body of a dear friend, Bran, to bury him and grieve with his family.'

'I see. He'll be much missed. His family will take it sore. It's noble of you to bring his body.'

'He was too young. He'd not lived his fair share at all, to my mind,' said Bjorn.

'How did he die?'

'As part of what I've no doubt will become a legend,' said Bjorn, 'if I can persuade Til here to put it into song.'

'It's still too early for that.' Til smiled. 'But it will make a good one, one day, I agree.'

'You're the harpist?' Sigurd asked. 'I think we've met before.'

'That's me. Til. Though I hunt more than I play.'

'Aye, he's our man of the hills.'

'Are you a man of God?' Sigurd asked.

'I'm not a Christian, if that's what you mean,' Til answered. 'Nor do I want to be.'

'I see we'll need to get the mission to your place,' Sigurd growled with a smile.

'He's already causing us enough trouble if you want my opinion,' Til said. Sigurd raised his eyebrows and looked pointedly at Bjorn.

'That's the second reason I'm here, Uncle. We've a difficult situation to resolve that needs the thinking of someone with clearer judgement than I have at the moment.'

'Is that part of your legend as well?'

'You could say that.'

'Well you'd better tell me the whole tale. Let's eat and toast to Bran and then we'll have the story. I always appreciate a saga better with a full belly, don't you agree, Til?'

So, with the meal under way, Sigurd enquired about the identity of all those around the table, asking after others he had met but who were not present. By the time dinner was over he knew about Margaret's pregnancy, and had deduced from the news of the deaths

186

of Eachan, Donald and Ro Moine, all of whom had been on earlier Orkney trips, that the story Bjorn was to tell would be serious. He had noticed that the Christians among the crew were seated together in a bunch at the far end of the table from Bjorn, looking grim, and not talking to the Orcadians. He saw a divided community and grief not fully expressed, and he saw that Bjorn was in pain and close to exhaustion.

After their plates had emptied for the last time and their tankards were refilled, Sigurd turned to Til and said, 'If you're the bard, perhaps you can tell me the gist of your tale. I can see your crew need sleep.'

Bjorn was happy to be able to listen rather than tell, and so Til related the events, from the storm when the wolves attacked, through the hunt, to Bjorn's encounter with the bear and its consequences, finishing with the death of Brigid, the unknown perpetrator, and their suspicion of James. Sigurd listened intently, without questions, and when Til finished he simply asked Bjorn, 'Is that right?'

Bjorn nodded.

'Then let's sleep on it. I'm glad you came. We'll find a resolution to this crisis in the light of day, not in a tankard.'

And breaking up the feast, he set the household to finding places where the crew could sleep, and took Bjorn off to his own quarters to give him a comfortable bed.

Next morning, it was raining. The sky was low overhead and grey, and everyone was pleased they had reached land the previous evening. Without the clear sky the dawn was sluggish and the day, when it came, was dark and short.

Bjorn was stiff and sore when he got up, so he was relieved when Sigurd approached him and said that they wanted to wait a day or two for the funeral, to allow Bran's family to gather and prepare his grave. It would also give him time, he said, to consider the story he had heard the previous night, to ask questions and clarify his understanding of what had gone on. Plus it would give the crew from the Braes a chance to rest.

Sigurd was concerned about Bjorn's injuries and called for his doctor, who appeared that afternoon. He was a dark, shriveled mouse of a man, but Sigurd insisted he was the best of his profession and had trained in Rome. He poked at Bjorn's belly and groin with tentative fingers and said he was impressed by the stitching Brigid had done. He reassured Sigurd that the wounds were healing, but confirmed what Bjorn had feared: he would father no more children. Bjorn grimaced and made a silent wish for Margaret's baby to be safe.

It was a reduced, though no less congenial, gathering in Sigurd's hall that night: the men and women of the Braes had dispersed around the Viking farmstead, and at low tide in the afternoon several of them had walked over to the mainland to go to stay with relatives or friends. James and some of the other Christians were offered accommodation at the monastery.

The day of Bran's funeral was brighter, with a cold breeze and beams of sunshine that swept the rolling islands like beacons. King Olof of Norway, the young, charismatic monarch, had succeeded in converting Sigurd to Christianity the last time he had been on Orcadian soil and most of Bran's family had converted with him, so it was a Christian burial ceremony. As Bishop Peter, dressed in purple satin, read a blessing at the graveside, an opening appeared in the clouds overhead and shafts of light shone through. 'Behold,' he beamed, 'the pillars of heaven!' There were titters from some of the people of the Braes, but they were met with stony stares. It was otherwise a solemn affair, the young friends of Bran struck quiet by the realisation of their own mortality, his family mourning their premature loss.

Sigurd invited them all to his hall for a feast of remembrance and as the ale flowed, so did the memories and tales of Bran's adventures and misdemeanours, conquests and accidents. In the end, among the tears there was much laughter too, with old friendships mended and new ones forged.

Later there was a call for music, and Til got out his harp and sang some songs from the Viking Sagas and some tunes in the old language, including one that he said was an ode to the bear and told of its death every winter and rebirth every spring.

There was a hush as everyone listened to his deep voice and the gentle strum of his clarsach. He changed the mood by announcing a song he had just written in honour of Bran. It told the tale of the hunt in the rhyming metrical style the Vikings loved. It had a chorus with a howl at the end, like a wolf, with which everyone was joining in by the end. There was an explosion of clapping and cheers.

When people had calmed down, Sigurd's young wife Edith sang some Irish songs. Her voice was delicate, and suited the haunting airs of mourning and loss that she sang in the Gaelic of Dalriada and Ireland that sounded strange to the northerners. Like her younger cousins Margaret and James, Edith came from the Scottish aristocracy: she was a daughter of King Malcolm of the Scots, and of high birth also through her mother's line. Her marriage to Sigurd was, like Margaret's to Bjorn, a political move to try to bring the northern part of the mainland and northern and western isles within the grasp of the Scots, and under some control of Malcolm's. But Sigurd's allegiance was still firmly with Olof of Norway, and his young son Thorfinn, sitting on his nurse's knee and not yet 'mighty', was being brought up to think of himself as a Norseman. Edith, like her cousins, was a pious woman with strong links to the church. She had brought with her several nuns, monks and a generous endowment for the monastery. Having done her duty providing Sigurd with a son, she spent much of her time there, avoiding both of them.

As the music finished, Sigurd got to his feet and pronounced to the gathering: 'We are thankful for the good music of our guests, and pleased to be able to share the songs from our many different homelands. I am honoured to live and rule over so many people with such richness in their cultures. We Vikings have come to trade and to settle, but not to overthrow the local customs of these beautiful lands with their plentiful seas and admirable people. We, Vikings and Scots, bring new ways to these old lands. Sometimes these ways clash and instead of harmonies like those we have heard tonight, there is discord. At such times we must listen to the notes that jangle together, listen to them separately, one at a time, and find a new way for harmony to be found between them. It has come to my notice that among the people of the Braes there is such discord. Tomorrow, I want to listen and try to help you to retune your community, rediscover the harmony you have lost. Tomorrow, at dawn, we will debate, discourse, and resolve your discord. Until then, my friends, enjoy the music and harmony of Birsay.'

There was a great cheer for this rhetorical flourish. Til was joined by some other harp players, a piper and two drummers; together they struck up music for dancing and the party began in earnest. The drink flowed, the voices grew louder and, perhaps inevitably, by midnight there were fists flying, fights breaking out between the Christian and Pagan factions of the Braes crew, and between people from the Braes and old rivals among their Viking hosts. Ivar, for once not directly involved, spent much of the night separating brawlers, receiving a few direct hits himself as tempers overflowed and the tensions of the past ten days were released in accusations and misunderstandings.

The next day at dawn there were some swollen lips, black eyes and downcast faces. Bjorn had taken himself to bed to avoid the dancing. Of the other Braes men only Til, who had been too busy playing to get drunk, and James, who never drank anyway, were free of a hangover.

Sigurd looked none the worse, despite much drink and little sleep. He was used to such nights and was looking forward to the debate. He took up his seat at the head of the hall with Edith at his side, and called the room to order. He instructed Bjorn and James to sit on either side of a semi-circular arrangement of stools and filled the others with people from the Braes: Iain Kay, Til, Tess, Ishbel, Moran, Alan, Niall and Diarmid among them. There was also a scattering of other people: monks from the monastery, the Bishop of Orkney and some minor aristocrats from the islands. All others were invited to sit behind on benches and instructed to be quiet. The debate began.

Sigurd called first for grievances. He began with Bjorn, who stood and made an impassioned speech describing the murder of Brigid, her healing of his wounds and the evidence they had found of the prints of the horse, which could only be his own or that of James. He related how James had constantly opposed Brigid, going so far as to banish her from the community, and how he had made his hatred for her plain for all to see. The motive and evidence all pointed clearly, he said, to James as the murderer of Brigid.

There was a murmur from the crowd. Sigurd thanked him for his speech and sought a response from James. But to Bjorn's amazement he deferred, and instead the Bishop of Orkney rose to his defence, eloquently and at length. It transpired that the Bishop had known James since childhood, in the court of Malcolm of Scots, and could vouch for his character. It was nonsense, he assured the crowd, to suggest such a man of virtue and godliness could commit such a crime. He suggested Bjorn's evidence was useless and inconclusive, and accused Bjorn of pandering to the heathens.

Sigurd paused, then called for more voices to be heard. He asked Til to give his version of events, questioning him closely about what they had found at the scene of Brigid's death. Then he heard from Niall about the various horses at the big house. He confirmed that only Bjorn's and James' horses had hoofs that matched the prints, but swore that he had seen neither leave the barn on the day of Brigid's death. Tess gave her version of the scene at Brigid's camp. Then Diarmid spoke of Brigid's madness, her curses and her animosity towards the church.

Sigurd then questioned James about his activities at the time. He bowed his head with deference and answered in a soft voice, detailing his times of prayer, his business with his chapel plans and giving nothing away that could implicate him in Brigid's death.

'I'll ask you straight.' Sigurd flexed his fingers. 'Did you ride your horse that day at all?'

'I did not,' James replied, looking him straight in the eye.

Bjorn sat with his hands clenched, and as James returned to his seat he whispered, 'Liar.' James kept his gaze firmly on the Jarl.

Now Sigurd changed his tack, asking questions to find out more about the big storm, about how Margaret's horse, which also had the large hoofs of the Southern breed, had been devoured by wolves, and the nightmarish wolf attack on the hunt that had followed.

'Could it be,' he suggested, 'that this attack by wolves, that seemed to affect even trained dogs, was some kind of curse?'

There were voices of assent. 'And do you think that this woman, Brigid, was a powerful enough shaman to bring off such a curse?' He frowned at Bjorn, who eventually nodded, as did several others.

'It seems to me, from her banishment, that she would have a reason to set such a curse.' More voices of assent. 'But might the casting of such a spell not be the sort of thing that might rebound upon the caster?'

There were murmurs of agreement and several calls to speak, mostly from clerics about witches whose spells had backfired, poisoners who had ended up poisoned, and ill-wishers of sailors who had ended up drowned themselves.

'Now tell me more about this woman's role as shaman of the bear and how you came to be the bear-slayer, Bjorn.'

Bjorn recounted his unfortunate meeting with the bear that fateful

day, and Til, Moran and others told of the traditional lineage of
medicine women whose powers originated with the bears, whose lives
ran parallel and entwined with the totem animal of their tribe.

'So there must be many bears in your forests.'

There was no great certainty among the people of the Braes
about other bears.

'Til, you are the great hunter; do you not know of other bears?'

'I do not. In recent years I have only ever seen the female bear
that Bjorn killed.'

'And so do you think it possible that the death of this bear may
have signalled the end of the tradition of bear worship, that it was
predestined perhaps that this woman, whose life you say paralleled
that of the bear, should die with it. Perhaps she couldn't live on
without the bear?'

Again, no-one could refute such a suggestion.

'It seems to me that there may be no crime to answer here, that
Brigid's passing may have been quite natural given the death of
the bear. Perhaps, and I am only guessing, this was the last bear,
and it signalled the ending of this old pagan tradition now that the
light of God shines across our land. Perhaps, Bjorn, you by chance
have cast the last fatal blow against a dying heathen practice. I
conjecture that Brigid may have speeded her own demise with a
curse that backfired, sending wolves to kill a horse whose spirit
then reappeared to kill her in return.'

At this Bjorn broke in, protesting. 'What spirit horse leaves
hoof prints?'

To his surprise Edith spoke in answer.

'Your own stableman swears no horses left the stable that day,
yet hoofprints were found. It all points to a supernatural cause. A
spirit horse, sent by God, to right the wrong of the pagan woman's
curse and put an end to her wickedness.'

'What right do you have to talk of wickedness?' Bjorn bellowed.
'She was a good woman, a healer, a gentle soul, close to nature and
loved by children. She rescued a drowning boy and brought him
back to life. She didn't curse anyone. Who are you all, conspiring
to protect her murderer?'

But his appeal met few eyes of support. The logic of the supernatural explanation was too strong, answering as it did all their
questions about what had brought the wolves, on that first night

of fury, to the Braes.

Til, too, spoke in Brigid's defence, but the Christians were the stronger force in the room. The crime of her murder was replaced by the presumed crime of her curse. Their arguments prevailed. They were tenacious and soon Sigurd, at least, was beyond doubt. As the debate dragged on, he began to become impatient.

'Friends, it seems clear to me that we have an explanation of the events that is both logical and likely. The old ways are passing everywhere, times are moving on, and the Christian truth is reaching into even the furthest corners of our land and driving the old heathen myths out. I know it is painful to accept, Bjorn, Til and you others of the old gods, that the one true God has come and is sweeping the old mistaken beliefs aside, turning old curses back on their makers, correcting the heathens whether they want to be corrected or not. Believe me, I have had to be corrected myself, and it was not easy for my teachers! There is no point in resisting, Bjorn. I have learned that God will prevail; his anger will be wielded.'

Bjorn bent his head. He recognised defeat, heard the latent threat and remained silent.

'If I may ask for a prayer?' Sigurd signalled to the Bishop, who launched into a long prologue, mostly to do with sheep, miscreant lambs, disobedient flocks and their better herding, then finally led his audience into a prayer that the people of the Braes should be brought out from the darkness of their forested wilderness full of wild and dangerous animals and into the bright light of the Lord's pastures, guided by the shepherd Jesus.

The debate was over, the murder dissolved rather than solved, and the participants drifted away to eat and discuss the outcome. Some, like James, were jubilant; others, like Bjorn and Til, were in deep dismay, but most were satisfied with an explanation that was deep and strange enough to seem completely plausible.

❧ ❧

On the crags high above the loch, an eagle crouched on an aspen that clung to the rockface. Coll watched it as it unfurled itself into the sky and flapped once, twice, soaring upwards into the mist, out of sight. Then he turned and stomped off into the forest.

193

Idhadh - Yew

'Is this the oldest tree in the world, Gran?' Enya stood under the Shield Tree, gazing up into its wizened branches that had been fused by time into wooden plaits.

'No, not by any means,' Frigga called from inside the lean-to. She came out and wrapped a scarf of the softest lambswool around Enya's neck. It was woven from fine, soft threads, the bronze of oak leaves and bracken, a mossy gold, a russet like rowan leaves and the green of heather, ivy or holly. Enya fingered it and rubbed it on her cheek.

'The oldest trees I know,' Frigga went on, 'are the yews in the old graveyard. They say they've been there as long as ever there were people here.'

'Can we go there to see them?'

'Yes, of course. Later, though.' Frigga returned to her task in the lean-to, tidying together Brigid's possessions, taking care of her treasures, meagre though they were.

'Here's that cup she loved so much,' she said, handing the whalebone beaker with the bear engraving out to Enya. 'It must be time for a drink of something and a nibble, don't you think?' She passed the little girl an apple, then crossed the clearing in the direction of the bender.

Halfway across, something glistening on the ground caught her eye. She bent to pick it up: a crucifix, silver, with an intricately carved pattern, two snakes and a rose depicted in knotwork, cleverly done. Her mind raced, thinking about possible owners.

She bent again and picked something else up out of the mud: a bit of leather thong, presumably the cause of the dropped crucifix.

'Who's missing their pendant?' she muttered. 'The priest, I'll wager.'

Beithe, Brigid's cow, gave a low grumbling moo. 'Yes, yes, old cow. I'll feed you by and by.' She pulled back the deer-hide door of Brigid's shelter. 'Come in here and stay warm,' she urged Enya, who was listless, her dark brown eyes thoughtful.

Inside, Frigga lit the fire with birchbark and chose some ash sticks to make a quick blaze to brew up on. She brewed an elder and bramble tea with a generous dollop of honey. Enya stuck a finger in the honey pot and hummed with satisfaction.

'Can you taste the gorse?' Frigga smiled. 'Sweet, sweet.'

She found a bag of hazelnuts and passed some to the little girl who began to crack their shells between her teeth with deep concentration. Then Frigga began folding up the blankets on the bed, getting Enya to help with the big ones. Between folds, Enya stroked the blankets reverentially.

'Yes, she had a talent, that's for sure. No-one wove quite like her. It was the colours she used. I don't know what they all were. She knew every leaf in the forest and every bit of bark and root and who knows what; she could get a dye out of a stone. I remember she had a sky blue once, to make a slip for Beathoc's wedding, that she said she'd made from elderberries, sloes and pine roots. It was beautiful, such a lovely colour, like a summer sky, but she was so worried it would be unlucky.'

'Why unlucky?'

'It was the combination of the different trees together. She said it was a risky combination. She knew so much about those things. Elder for magic, pine for sadness and the sloes for a secret. She said it might be a bad omen. I guess she was right.'

Tears came upon her, as they did often these days. She sat at the edge of the bed. Enya cried too, and they held each other, stroking the beautiful woven blankets as if they were cats, until their softness soothed them, as cats do.

Then Frigga, with a sniff, set to with a broom, sweeping the floor vigorously until she had regained her composure.

'What'll we do now?' Enya asked.

'We'll carry on, little one. Why don't you pack those blankets into that basket? That's right, the nice willow one. Which reminds me: I must begin the cradle for the new baby.'

'Which new baby?'

'Bjorn's. Margaret's getting fat. It's about time we had a birth after all this dying. We need a new beginning, and there's nothing like a new bairn to get the wheels of life rolling again. Just like the aspen trees, when the old trees wither, new young suckers spring up to keep things going.'

❧ ❧

Margaret sat by the window of the outbuilding that had been James' cell. She had taken to coming here since he had gone to Orkney. It reminded her of him and it was quiet, a place to retreat to now that she was too heavily pregnant to walk in the forest alone. She looked out at the wild land. It seemed barren now, with the wreckage of the felled woodland, the black of the charred hillside, the gruesome shapes of the old hawthorns and rowans beyond the wall.

'I saw you,' said Caphel, who was standing beside the closed doorway.

'Go on.'

'I saw you riding out along the lochside that morning on the white stallion.'

That morning, when she had taken Bjorn's horse and stamped Brigid out. 'Who have you told?' she asked.

'No-one.'

'So it will be our secret, won't it, Caphel? After all, no-one will believe you anyway, and I can make it so much more worth your while to stay quiet.'

Caphel looked again at the knife Margaret had given him, with its glittering blade of sharpened bronze, unlike anything he had seen before except in the hands of leaders, and at the quill, that symbol of prestige.

'This is your chance to improve yourself, Caphel. You're a bright boy. You'll go far with a bit of help from the right people.'

'But what if I'm asked?'

'No-one will ask you anything.' Margaret smiled. 'It's all over now. Everyone accepts that the witch's death was caused by the forces of evil she invoked turning back against her. No-one wants to believe anything different. Trust me. It's over.'

'And I get to live at the big house?'

'Of course. Niall will find you a warm place to sleep. You'll have the best of everything. Food, clothes, armour – and education, of course, true education. Consider yourself on track for the honour of a thane. As Bjorn favours your sister, I will favour you.'

Caphel looked up at her. What were his options? An orphan. A life in the cottage with old Frigga and Enya. He nodded slowly. 'All right.'

'So we pledge to silence and honour, in God's name.'

'In God's name,' he repeated, taking the outstretched hand and clasping it, striking his deal.

❧ ❧

Their son was born early one morning, after a night of labour that had left everyone in the big house with nerves on edge. Margaret's screams had seemed as if they would split the very stones of the building.

Bjorn called the boy Bradan, which means salmon, hoping to appease the bear spirits with something they liked without having to invoke them by name. Frigga told him the salmon was a symbol of wisdom in the old tradition, and he took that as a good sign. The baby wanted to suckle but Margaret was suffering profuse bleeding after the birth, so Elma was fetched to act as wet nurse, sharing her milk between her daughter, who was almost weaned, and the headman's son.

As evening drew in Margaret developed a fever, sweating and tossing in delirium. Bjorn sat by the fire, head bent, frowning.

'Can you do nothing more, Frigga?'

'I'll try another compress. Can you see if she'll take a spoonful of the poppy and yarrow? If she'd only hold it down, I'd feel more confident.' Frigga swept her grey hair back from her face and bent again to dip the pad of wool into a bowl of foul-smelling herbs. 'What I'd give to pick Brigid's brains just now.'

Bjorn sighed and stepped up to the head of the bed.

'I'm sorry, Bjorn,' Frigga muttered. 'The herbs for childbirth were always the most closely-guarded secret. I guess that's why we valued the medicine women so much. You never realise it until something's gone.'

'Perhaps it would be better if I weren't here,' Bjorn said, as Margaret swung her head away from his proferred spoon.

'The child's sleeping; shall I try?' Elma suggested. 'The same happened to me when wee Tara was born, and Brigid got me through it.' She smiled at Bjorn. 'Go and rest, sir. Things'll be better by morning.' Bjorn and Frigga exchanged nods and Bjorn headed off to whisky and male company.

But Margaret was not better by morning, and as the next day

197

passed she slipped further and further away, first into delirium, then into a ghostly state where only her breath remained, like rustling leaves, to prove she was alive. Frigga remained by the bed, leaving only when Bjorn came to sit with her. The single candle shrank by her bedside.

From his pocket Bjorn brought out the crucifix that Frigga had given him. He turned it over in his hand, and back again. The rumour had spread fast that the cross had been found, and everyone assumed it had belonged to James. Bjorn had not disabused anyone, but he recognised it. He had kissed the neck it had hung around. She had denied it was hers, and he had let it rest, biding his time.

He was hunched beside the bed on the third morning as she breathed one last shuddering gasp. Silence fell on the big house. It was a calm, grey, drizzly day and hazel catkins hung motionless on the trees. He sat watching the waxy face of his wife, hearing only the sound of his own heart pumping inside his chest. He thought about the crucifix and about what it pointed to. Had this pale being really had the power in her to kill? She had always seemed so fragile, so delicate, so different from Brigid. Could a flower really overpower a tree? He would never understand it, but perhaps, in the end, that was what he must bring himself to believe. He clasped his hands and racked his memory for a prayer, but found only emptiness. Then a blackbird began to sing outside, and he roused himself and went to find Frigga.

⋄ ⋄

As the sun went down Bjorn retreated to the graveyard, seeking solitude. Beyond the seven old rowans, three yew trees stood against the far wall, grotesque with their ancient struggle against the wind, but undefeated. He sat beneath the biggest. Despite the rain, the ground under it was dry. His fingers drifted among the soil, picking it up, letting it go, picking it up, letting it slide between his fingers, over and over, as yew needles let the wind through, as a creel allows the water through, until at last his heart allowed the tears to flow.

⋄ ⋄

Upright as a sapling, Til strode along the beach at dawn, toward

198

the waning blade of moon. As he walked, a song came to him. The wind snatched it from his mouth and tossed it into the breakers but he sang on, note by note, word by word, line by line, as Brigid sang through him her legend of the last bear.

and the wombs of creatures pulse with the moon
and trees run rings with the tide of the sun
and the bear lives on in the soul of the soil
and the bear lives on with spirit and song

do cross or crown destroy by choice?
are they only ever mistaken?
now sleep and dream and then one day
perhaps we'll reawaken.

Fiction from Two Ravens Press

Love Letters from my Death-bed: by Cynthia Rogerson
£8.99. ISBN 978-1-906120-00-9. Published April 2007

Nightingale: by Peter Dorward
£9.99. ISBN 978-1-906120-09-2. Published September 2007

Parties: by Tom Lappin
£9.99. ISBN 978-1-906120-11-5. Published October 2007

Prince Rupert's Teardrop: by Lisa Glass
£9.99. ISBN 978-1-906120-15-3. Published November 2007

The Most Glorified Strip of Bunting: by John McGill
£9.99. ISBN 978-1-906120-12-2. Published November 2007

One True Void: by Dexter Petley
£8.99. ISBN 978-1-906120-13-9. Published January 2008

Auschwitz: by Angela Morgan Cutler
£9.99. ISBN 978-1-906120-18-4. Published February 2008

The Long Delirious Burning Blue: by Sharon Blackie
£8.99. ISBN 978-1-906120-17-7. Published February 2008

Double or Nothing: by Raymond Federman
£9.99. ISBN 978-1-906120-20-7. Published March 2008

The Falconer: by Alice Thompson
£8.99. ISBN 978-1-906120-23-8. Published April 2008

The Credit Draper: by J David Simons
£8.99. ISBN 978-1-906120-25-2. Published May 2008

Vanessa and Virginia: by Susan Sellers
£8.99. ISBN 978-1-906120-27-6. Published June 2008

Cleave: New Writing by Women in Scotland: Sharon Blackie (ed)
£8.99. ISBN 978-1-906120-28-3. Published June 2008.

For more information on these and other titles, and for news, reviews, articles, extracts and author interviews, see our website.
All titles are available direct from the publisher, postage & packing-free, at
www.tworavenspress.com
or from any good bookshop.